ABOUT THE AUTHOR

HELEN MOFFETT is a South African writer, free-lance editor, activist, and award-winning poet. She has a PhD on PreRaphaelite poetry and has authored or co-authored university textbooks, short story antholo-gies, non-fiction books on the environment, two poetry collections, and various academic projects. *Charlotte* is her first novel.

She blogs at helenmoffett.com and can be found on Twitter @heckitty.

Charlotte

Helen Moffett

**MANILLA
PRESS**

First published in Great Britain in 2020 by Manilla Press
This paperback edition first published in 2021 by
MANILLA PRESS
An imprint of Bonnier Books UK
80–81 Wimpole St, London W1G 9RE
Owned by Bonnier Books
Sveavägen 56, Stockholm, Sweden

A CIP catalogue record for this book is
available from the British Library.

ISBN: 978–1–83877–076–1

Also available as an ebook and an audiobook

1 3 5 7 9 10 8 6 4 2

Typeset by Palimpsest Book Production Limited, Falkirk, Stirlingshire
Printed and bound in Great Britain by Clays Ltd, Elcograf S.p.A.

Manilla Press is an imprint of Bonnier Books UK,
www.bonnierbooks.co.uk

For Sarah, Paige, Lauren, Tom. My book children.

PROLOGUE

No prospects – or so the neighbourhood believed. Her own family thought it. Her dearest friend Elizabeth assumed it with the blithe arrogance of someone who could give her own wit and liveliness free rein because she had the gloss of both youth and beauty.

Charlotte was about to prove them all wrong, God willing. That morning, that very minute in fact, she intended to go out and roll the dice with all the bravado of a rake in a London night-haunt. She brushed down the folds of her best poplin day dress, with its pattern of minute sage-green flower fronds against a white background – no chainmail and pennant, but armour of a sort. Peering at herself in the glass, she was satisfied with what she saw, in as much as a tall, plain, and angular woman of twenty-seven and no prospects could reasonably be satisfied.

She took one more look at herself – her hair was at its best in the mornings, freshly released from the curlpapers that tackled a tendency to lankness, and her colour would be higher once she had been walking a little. Then she reached for her new straw bonnet, trimmed with the same fabric as her dress. Gentlemen did not notice such details, in her limited experience, but they responded to a sense of order, of patterns meshing. Anomalies in appearance startled them.

She tiptoed down the stairs, feeling no need to advertise her early rising. In the passage that led to the kitchen, she thought for a moment, then donned an apron that would protect her gown, slid her feet into sensible boots, and took up a trug and cutting knife. She intended to show off not only her physical charms, such as they were, but her more practical attributes; that, while fond of healthful exercise, she was nevertheless attentive to the gifts of the fields and woods. She would collect mushrooms and pick apples. And, if necessary, choose and cut late roses and early chrysanthemums for dressing the house. Her intention was to appear something more than handsome; she wanted to look like a chatelaine. Someone who would run a small household with efficiency, taste, and economy; someone who would bestow comfort and order.

She knew what she needed to do.

1818–1819

CHAPTER I

T HE BOBBING LIGHT AND SHADOW thrown by the candle woke Charlotte. She sat upright, not alarmed, but alert: there was no soft wail or snuffling from the room alongside. Her husband stood by her bedside, looking down at her with speechless compassion. His face shone wet in the sliding glow of the candle-flame; it gave the impression of movement to his face, and she realised that the hand that held the candlestick was shaking.

And then she knew, before he spoke, reaching for her with his other hand: 'Come, my dear.'

They stood beside the cot, still as statues, the only movement in their enmeshed fingers, kneading convulsively at each other's knuckles. Charlotte always imagined that if, when, this moment came, she would snatch up the little form, would shake, cajole, love it back to life. But after that first long look, bending over Tom with the candle held close to his beloved face, she had not moved. Even in the unreliable light, the purple stains under his eyes and the waxen appearance of the pinched nose were unmistakable. No breath disturbed those nostrils, or raised his chest.

Eventually, she tried to speak, but only a hoarse

growl came. Mr Collins nevertheless understood her: 'About half an hour ago, dearest. I came in to see him, and it was immediately apparent. I touched him; he was already quite cool.'

'What were . . . why did you go to him? Was he fretful?' Even as she spoke, she knew she made no sense. If Tom had made the slightest sound, she would have reached him before his father. She had had an extra ear attuned to him since the day of his birth more than three years ago, a sensitivity to any distress he might feel or encounter far more heightened than she had experienced with her daughters.

Her husband's hand clenched in time with the bobbing of his Adam's apple. 'I came in to pray for him. I do so every night. When I . . . when I found him, I could see there was no help. So I prayed, like I always do. I stood by him and prayed.'

And then Charlotte broke, a sheet of salt tearing from her eyes and nose as she scooped up the body, not yet cold, but long since past the warmth of a living child. She clutched him to the breasts that had nurtured him, a process that had given them both such delight, happy animal satisfaction on his part, pangs of more complicated joy on hers. She stroked the long little fingers, with nails like soap bubbles, that would never slide trustingly into her hand again. She kissed his neck, soft and pliant under the weight of his head, palmed his sturdy back, fixing the familiar scent of his skin in the atoms of her body. For one moment, the world slid sideways and righted itself: he still smelled like Tom, he couldn't possibly be dead,

4

they would prove all the surgeons wrong, he would wake and burble 'Mama' and she would kiss him and kiss him, all over his chubby hay-fragrant little body and face, and the globe would resume spinning on its everyday axis.

But the child in her arms did not wake. And looking across at her openly weeping husband, she knew that he never would.

※❦※

A small mercy: it was a mild, soft day, the sky a bowl of curds. Charlotte could not have borne the mockery of sunshine, or the misery of rain and spiteful wind, as they stood, a cluster of crows, in the churchyard. She adjusted Laura's weight on her hip. Her second daughter's warm body was the only thing anchoring her to the earth, to this place. Nothing else made sense, not the sexton, not the grave into which the pitifully tiny coffin was being lowered, not the words being intoned by the parson, not even the grief coming off her husband so thick she could almost taste it catching at the back of her throat.

He stood by her side, allowed on this occasion the role of the bereaved parent. Not even the most stoic clergyman could be expected to bury his own child, and so Lady Catherine had sent for a parson from a neighbouring parish to conduct Tom's funeral.

Charlotte, in that slice of her mind that continued to function rationally, conceded that Lady Catherine had indeed been useful in the past few days. She had written messages and made arrangements, she had offered mourning garments and shades, had even sent her carriage to Meryton to fetch the elder Lucases. She had objected to Charlotte's intention to bring Tom's small sisters to the graveyard, claiming that at almost five and six years of age they were too young – but, for once, she had allowed herself to be overruled without argument.

Charlotte, unable to look down into the grave, stared across it at the other mourners present. Her sister Maria was in tears, and her mother sobbing into a handkerchief, supported by her father, whose usually rubicund face was pale with distress. Lizzy had arrived the night before, escorted by her husband, Mr Darcy, who was standing beside her, all bleak gravity.

On some level, Charlotte was moved – even if slightly surprised – that her old friend, the mistress of Pemberley, should have made the journey down from Derbyshire to Kent for Tom's funeral. She and Mr Darcy were guests of Lady Catherine – an arrangement that might have been desperately awkward if not for the solemn circumstances. With pressing business to attend to, Mr Darcy would be leaving for London the next day, but Elizabeth would be staying at the Parsonage to keep Charlotte company during the first weeks of mourning.

Although, Charlotte noted – in the dispassionate way she kept noticing the crack in the glass of one of the windowpanes in the drawing room, the fungus speckling the leaves of the late roses in the garden – that Lizzy was gazing across at the bereaved family with an expression on her face that could only be described as forlorn.

Laura wriggled in her arms as the first clods of earth fell on the coffin. 'Mama, I don't want Tom to be cold,' she wailed into her mother's ear. 'He doesn't like the dark.' Charlotte murmured the same lies she had been telling both girls since the day that had dawned relentlessly after the night Tom had perished: that their brother had gone to be with the angels, where there was no cold, or dark, or pain. Although how could she possibly know for certain? Was her husband certain?

She glanced over at him and Sarah, her little changeling: thin and whippy like her mother, and with her father's dark hair, her dark brown eyes were nothing like the grey and blue of her parents. She was in as much distress as Laura, flinching as each spadeful thudded onto the coffin, but remained silent, leaning against her father's side, a thumb jammed into her mouth.

Trying to keep herself tethered to the moment, to prevent herself floating outside the scene, as she so often had in the last days and hours, a state in which she looked down on herself with both detachment and such acuity she could see the pink line where she parted her hair, Charlotte turned her head back towards Lady Catherine, who stood on the other side of the grave. Like herself, her ladyship was wearing unrelieved black – although this was not so much a statement of condolence as a matter of habit. Nevertheless, Lady Catherine was gazing at her with a rare expression of sympathy on her craggy face and, as she caught Charlotte's eye, she gave a small, tight nod of something close to approval. She had earlier complimented Charlotte on her fortitude, while seeming to use the words as code for something else.

Laura wailed again, softly, now just a general expression of misery and confusion, and at the same time, Mr Collins began to shudder. One hand still resting on his eldest daughter's shoulder, the other pressed a handkerchief to his face, and a long, low moan emerged from behind it. Something burst and surged through Charlotte's veins: it was as if he was feeling her agony, voicing it, giving her relief via emotional ventriloquism. She held Laura still more fiercely to her and, in a spasm of gratitude so violent it threatened to stop her breath, she stretched her other arm towards her husband, who still clasped Sarah. The hand she covered was cold, but their daughter's hair falling over it was warm and soft. And so it was at the grave of her son, with both her daughters present, that Charlotte Collins, née Lucas, realised that she loved her husband.

Mrs Darcy paced up and down the drawing room, as Charlotte tried in vain to make both herself and her guest comfortable, offering a seat by the fire, to send for refreshments. Since finding her son dead, she had found it impossible to settle – to lie or sit or stand in any one place for more than a few minutes – without wanting to leap to her feet and hasten elsewhere, anywhere. It was a while before she realised she was

8

trying to escape pain the same way a mouse would try to escape a toying cat. This made condolence visits even more than usually difficult – while gratified at the kindness of parishioners and neighbours, every several minutes she found herself battling the impulse to rise and flee the room. But this morning Elizabeth outdid her in restlessness. Her face was wan, and there were shadows under the famously brilliant eyes, now immortalised by one of London's most sought-after portrait artists.

'I cannot comprehend the enormity of your loss, my dearest Charlotte,' she said. 'To lose a beloved child, and a son, not yet four years old! It is too cruel, no matter how much reason – and indeed the teachings of your husband, and the convictions of mine – may attempt to console or soothe.'

She paused and wrung her hands. With the detached part of her brain, Charlotte registered that she had never seen her friend do such a thing before. Elizabeth went on, 'I do not mean to burden you. That would be unfeeling, a piece of unkindness. But I must impose on our friendship, your patience, and good heart, even at such a time. I miscarried a few months ago. The baby was a boy.'

Charlotte raised her head, surprised and yet not surprised, uncertain what to say. Lizzy burst out, 'It is the second child I have lost in these past three years. Charlotte, forgive me – while I cannot pretend to understand what it must be to have a living, breathing child perish, how my own losses gnaw at me!'

Now the brilliance of Elizabeth's eyes owed something

to the tears that trembled in them. 'It has been a shock – a ruinous shock – to realise how ill-prepared I was for marriage. How ill-prepared both Mr Darcy and I were. We believed our regard for each other had been tested, that it had grown to overcome all that stood in our way – the distinctions between us, the differences in our temper, his pride, my hasty prejudice. He had done so much for me, my family. His love was in no doubt, and the strength of my feelings matched his. There was nothing, I thought, that we could not discuss, could not face together. I was a fool.'

She sat down at last on the sofa next to her friend, and said, 'I did not see the truth that stared me in the face: a great man, from a great family, marries for one reason primarily: to beget heirs. Neither of us gave this any thought. We believed that children, a son – or two or three – would present themselves as if by magic. But it has been five and a half years, and there is still no infant in the nursery. I walk through the chambers of that great house, knowing myself to be the envy of many who do not consider me fit for the office of being its mistress. And I pass beneath the eyes of all those portraits, those Darcy ancestors, all witness to my failure, watching me break the chain.'

Charlotte murmured the necessary words of hope and encouragement, or at least she tried to, but Lizzy went on: 'I live in terror of one of the stone-faced doctors who attend me opining that there can be no more children, or attempts to bear one. If that happens, Charlotte, I swear I shall jump off the Pemberley bridge.'

She began to weep in earnest, as her friend sat

dry-eyed beside her. 'Fitzwilliam would have been better off wedded to a brood mare. For that is what is required for these great estates, these honourable names. Succession. And my husband is of course too much the gentleman to reproach me for my failure in this regard. So we do not and cannot speak of it. And we speak less and less.'

Charlotte's mind took a vertiginous leap: she had not yet thought of Tom's death in these terms – of what it might presage for her daughters. And even as she stumbled through the required assurances that Lizzy would surely indeed soon have issue, the thought occurred to her at the same time as her friend put it into words: 'But what if I give birth to a girl?'

Charlotte felt an old rage rise up in her. Tom was beyond her help, but this was a new anxiety. With her beloved and damaged son gone, and with him the security of his inheritance of the Longbourn estate, how could she safeguard her daughters? How was she to assure them a home and the respectability this proffered, beyond the lottery of matrimony? If Lizzy had daughters, they would at least have considerable dowries – in which case, Pemberley could go to Bonaparte for all Charlotte cared.

Her mind scoured clear by grief, the reality of her situation came into sharp focus: she and her daughters were at risk of falling into the same trap that had yawned before Elizabeth's family, the Bennets: their future inheritance entailed away from them because they were mere females.

Why had she never taken Mrs Bennet's anxiety, the

'nerves' they had all mocked, seriously? The business of her life was to find her daughters husbands: what else could it be, given the blind roll of the dice that exposed them all to the kind of poverty perhaps worse than that seen in hovels; that of genteel beggary, of imposing upon distant male relatives who had their own children to set up in life, of being grateful for a roof, no matter how reluctantly or resentfully it was offered.

Elizabeth's marriage had changed all that; indeed, her sister Jane's alliance with Mr Bingley alone had offered the remaining unmarried Bennet sisters, Mary and Kitty, a substantial degree of protection. While they might one day lack a home to call their own, they need never fear want as long as they could reside with one or the other of their elder sisters. But on the other hand, Charlotte could see there was no way out for the Darcy line; only males could inherit an estate as profitable, as *visible* as Pemberley.

Charlotte set her lips. Silently, she vowed to spend the rest of her days circumventing the law of the land so that her daughters need fear neither penury nor charity, as had been the case for herself and her sisters, and indeed many of the daughters of the families she knew. She had no idea how to proceed in this regard, and little understanding of what instruments could be useful, but she knew better than most what dogged determination might do.

Besides, she had an unexpected example of success in this regard, perhaps even an ally, right next door: Lady Catherine had inherited Rosings upon becoming a widow. Even more impressive, she had secured the inheritance for her daughter, Anne de Bourgh. And if Lady Catherine, with her strictures on rank and society, could manage such a thing, surely it was within the bounds of possibility?

CHAPTER II

S OME DAYS WERE BETTER THAN others. Somehow,
the hours were endured. Letters addressed to the
bereaved parents continued to arrive, and responding
to these provided some object to each monstrous day.
Lady Lucas wrote to her daughter almost daily, not
even awaiting any reply, and although each note
repeated the substance of the last, Charlotte valued
these tokens of her mother's affection. Lizzy was not
the only member of the Bennet family to try to comfort
her; she was touched to receive from Mrs Bingley,
Elizabeth's elder sister, a letter of condolence all the
more sweet for its evident sincerity. As the mother of
two young boys and a by-word for kindness, Jane was
deeply affected by Charlotte's loss and, while she had
no remedy to offer for grief, the indication of her care
was itself soothing.

The weeks trudged by. Charlotte found that watching
how differently her daughters experienced time to
adults was enlightening: there were hours when they
ran, played, and whooped as joyously as if nothing
more grievous than a grazed knee had ever marred
their days. It was their knack for forgetting she
marvelled at. There were moments when she envied

them this gift; at others, she understood that they might never remember their younger brother, and the very idea made her feel as if her skin had been removed with a paring knife.

Her memories of Tom were at that stage not yet memories, but as much part of her daily life as rising, dressing, breakfasting, feeding the chickens, and all the routines to which she now clung as a means of passaging through days as thick as treacle and grey as ash. He was with her everywhere, sometimes receding momentarily, but mostly at the edge of her vision, her hearing.

Katie, the maid, her florid face swollen with tears, and Mrs Brown, the housekeeper, had each offered to pack away his clothing and toys, but Charlotte had refused to allow this. Lady Catherine had, on one of her visits, indicated that she would send over one of her maids to undertake the sad task, but Charlotte, accustomed to acquiescence, along with biting her tongue a hundred times in the presence of her ladyship, had uttered a flat refusal, excused herself, and left the room.

Normally, such rebellion would have been punished with a withdrawal of attention from Rosings, with no cucumbers from the hothouses or invitations to drink tea after church until Charlotte and her husband had made an adequately fulsome display of regret, but this time, no umbrage was taken. Lady Catherine continued to call on Charlotte in the mornings, on which occasions they spoke of the weather, the health of their respective surviving children, and the prowess of Charlotte's hens, while acknowledging the superiority of the Rosings poultry. The matter of Tom's few possessions was not alluded to again.

So the days were bearable, most of the time, if only just, leavened as they were by the presence and playfulness of her daughters, as well as the attentions of her husband. Charlotte sometimes wondered if he too had felt that shift in the tone of her emotions as they had stood by Tom's grave. She dreaded his uttering platitudes that might drive away her unexpected new warmth for him, but he was quieter than usual, his customary torrent of wordage muted by real grief.

Theirs was not a union in which marital candour or intimate communication had ever featured; Charlotte had always considered that part of the bargain she had struck was to withhold, even hide, her true feelings and thoughts. Marriage had required her to become an even more than ordinarily contained person, and she assumed the same held for her spouse. So they had no way in which to find their way towards one another through words; but now Mr Collins would hover over her chair after meals, come and find her at intervals in the day to enquire after her health; he would press her hand, pat her shoulder, or kiss her forehead, gestures she received gratefully.

The nights were the problem. Charlotte went to her bed the way a witch or heretic went to the pile of faggots: knowing that certain torture lay ahead, but with no avenue of escape. She could have summoned a doctor or apothecary – Lady Catherine would have been delighted to be consulted for advice on such a matter – and asked for a sleeping draught. But she was afraid that after years of sleeping with one ear open, she might, if insensible, somehow miss a sound indicating that Sarah or Laura were in distress or afflicted, that her inability to wake might prove fatal.

And what she could barely articulate to herself was the hope that if she remained alert, she might hear the familiar chirruping indicating that Tom needed her. That she would take a candle into his nursery to see him light up with smiles at the sight of her, chubby arms windmilling over the edge of the cot, eager to wrap themselves around her neck. That she would scoop him up into her arms, slot him onto her hip and tuck his head into the crook of her neck, the nightmare of the present dissolving, the flow of life reverting to its normal channels, no longer jarringly out of step.

This meant that she dared not take wine with dinner, not even when Lady Catherine sent over a half-dozen bottles of Constantia wine from her late husband's cellar, a magnanimous gesture that had required both a full-page letter of thanks and a visit for the sole purpose of expressing gratitude.

So Charlotte would lie in sheets that would grow rumpled as the hours crawled by, rehearsing that last day of Tom's life endlessly, wondering if there was a sign she had missed, something she could have done to change the events of the night. Had he been unduly subdued? Had she missed his catching a cold? She should have supervised his supper instead of leaving it to Katie, fed him special treats. Why had she not played with him longer that day? Held him tighter? How could she have kissed him goodnight so lightly, unconcerned, with no sense of the savage beast waiting to snatch him away, to tear her world to pieces? How could she not have known nemesis was waiting, hidden and leering in the shadows, for her to lower him into his cot and walk away, leaving him unguarded?

Her mind would roam further into thornier fields: should they have consulted more doctors? Heaven knows, Lady Catherine had recommended enough, as well as having so much to say that one might be forgiven for thinking her an expert on water on the brain. Had they accepted too easily the claim that his condition was untreatable, apart from the regular draining of fluid from his poor swollen head? He had always seemed so content, with none of the fretfulness one might expect of a child with such an impairment: he loved his food, the games they played, music . . . Oh God, she had promised him and his sisters a visit to the piano in the housekeeper's room at Rosings, for one of their occasional sing-along sorties – why had she postponed an outing he would have enjoyed so much? Why had she trusted that another day would come, another tomorrow, and another? *Wait, not yet, not yet*, her heart cried. *I am not ready*. And then, as the clock downstairs chimed away the plodding hours: *I shall never be ready*.

She would at last wrench her mind away from such self-flagellation, only to have the fate of her daughters rise like a spectre. Within ten years, Sarah would be sixteen, Laura close to fifteen; precious little time to find a means of securing their futures, if that security was to be provided in the form of a sum sufficient for independence. How could she possibly set by enough? She ran their household with such efficiency, she made a small annual profit; not for nothing was she the child of William Lucas, a merchant before his elevation in society. But she had no illusions of being able to provide substantially for both girls. She would have to find a legal way around the Longbourn entail, and how was she to succeed where Mr Bennet had failed? Lady Catherine might be cultivated as an ally: she who had managed to preserve Rosings for her daughter. But how was she to approach her ladyship on such a matter, and in such a way that Mr Collins – who would most likely be appalled to discover his own wife intended tampering with his inheritance – did not find out?

She drew up numerous plans, friends who might be prevailed upon to assist, avenues to pursue; but in those bleak midnight hours, she quailed at the enormity of the task and her own ignorance of the law.

CHAPTER III

CHARLOTTE FOUND HERSELF AFFLICTED BY a more private matter of bodily health as well. A few days after the funeral, she had begun her monthly courses earlier than usual. Charlotte was physically robust, and this was not usually a matter that troubled her, but after more than a week passed with the flow as heavy as ever, she grew alarmed. Visions of a canker or wastage that would render her daughters motherless haunted her already hideous nights. She was tempted to mention the matter to Elizabeth, who, after the early impulse that had led her to share her own sorrows, had shown her old friend nothing but kindness and many attempts at solicitous distraction during the fortnight of her visit. But something held Charlotte back from discussing the vagaries of the female body with a friend who had recently suffered a miscarriage.

When another week had passed, with no lessening of her problem, she paid a discreet visit to Mrs Talbot, the village midwife, under the guise of dropping off napkins for a parishioner's laying-in. Mrs Talbot had delivered all three of Charlotte's children, and the two women were close without the expectations or rituals of friendship. She uttered condolences all the more sincere for being terse, and did not allude to Tom's condition or suggest that his death had been in any way some sort of merciful release, commenting only on the sweetness of his temper.

The conversation turned to Charlotte's weeping body, and the midwife was able to reassure her that such a physical reaction was, if not normal, certainly not unusual in the wake of grief: 'It is a bodily expression of mourning. I have seen it before in women who are sorrowing. It may persist for a while. In the meantime, take plenty of beef broth, and eat liver if you can.' She also recommended drinking a tea of raspberry leaves in the mornings, and chamomile before retiring. 'And you may indeed find wine helpful, but no more than a glass at a time,' she cautioned.

Greatly relieved, and with the sense of pleasant exhaustion that often follows relief, Charlotte took Mrs Talbot's advice and a package of herbs. Whether it was the raspberry-leaf tea or nature taking its course, after a few more weeks, Charlotte's body settled back into its usual schedule.

But still she could not sleep. She stumbled through the days red-eyed and frantic for rest, dozing off in her sewing chair or at her household accounts and jerking awake, sweating in panic. To her shame, she found herself snapping at Katie, knocking over her water-glass, breaking crockery, crying out in near-hysteria when Laura slipped while trying to climb a stile into the cow-pasture. She was either weak with fatigue or as restless as a caged animal, desperate to walk for miles, swinging her arms, seeing and speaking to no one. But the deepening winter thwarted her, both with the darkness that settled earlier each day, and with rain and fog that did not invite strolling. Besides, the wife of a clergyman – much less one who had the Hunsford living and the patronage of Rosings – could not roam the lanes and fields at will. She required an object for any journeys she made, and there were only so many parish visits she could make.

Her husband at least had the usual business of his office, and the winter pruning to attend to – the walnut and mulberry trees had to be cut back while their sap was dormant, to prevent weeping – and he would sally forth with leather gloves, knives and a bullhook, returning hours later with a face red-chapped by cold, exertion, and the private expression of grief. At those moments, his wife almost envied him his labours, even when the east wind nagged with the sting of sleet.

One evening, Charlotte found herself almost feverish with agitation and exhaustion. Mr Collins, concerned and perplexed as to how best to provide comfort, had finally broached one of Lady Catherine's bottles at dinner, and the silky red liquor had provided his wife with welcome warmth, colouring her cheeks and easing some of the knots from her neck and shoulders, which, these days, felt permanently crimped.

But after retiring to bed, she found herself as tense as always. She thrashed for what felt like hours, conscious of a semi-familiar pressure in her lower body she associated with the middle months of pregnancy. The heat of the wine had slid from her throat, chest and fingers to pool in her pelvis, thudding along with her pulse.

Charlotte did not have the vocabulary to give a name to sexual hunger, but she did know that the sense of urgency and loneliness she felt could no longer be endured. Sitting up in bed and flinging back the quilt, she called, 'Mr Collins!' Then, more loudly, 'William!' She was about to scramble out of bed to go and wake her husband when she heard footsteps and fumbling at the dressing-room door.

He stumbled into her bedchamber dishevelled in the dim light, and extremely anxious: 'My dearest Charlotte, whatever is the matter? Are you taken ill? Must we send to Rosings? Should I wake the servants?'

By now, she had managed to light her bedside candle, hands shaking, and saw that he had come to her with such alacrity, he had not even put a shawl or gown on over his nightclothes. Unable to speak, but hoping he could see that nothing physical ailed her, she simply stretched out her arms. He bustled to her side and bent to embrace her. She snared him around the waist and lay back, tugging him towards her. At his slight resistance, born of confusion, she urged, 'Get into bed, William. You'll freeze to death otherwise.'

He scrambled under the covers with her, still hugging her awkwardly, still murmuring queries: 'Are you in distress, my dear? Are you sure you are not ill, or in any pain?'

'I am quite well. But I cannot sleep!' It came out as a wail that caused Mr Collins to cluck with great tenderness. 'Here,' Charlotte added, with a fine disregard for logical sequence, 'your feet are blocks of ice. Warm them on mine.'

24

They lay wordless for a minute, tangling their legs together, panting slightly. Then, with blind instinct, she pushed up the tail of his nightgown and ran her hands up his back, digging her nails into his flesh. He began to kiss her all over her face, and she was overtaken by animal hunger that had her dragging up her own gown, and lunging upwards with her hips.

He all but fell into her, burying himself in the warmest part of her, and they both groaned. It was usual during their congress for Charlotte to lie still, but this time she bucked under him, unable to stifle her cries. Within seconds, she began to spasm in an agony of relief. He gasped and shuddered in response, and tears welled from Charlotte's eyes. It was a while before she realised that he too had shed the tears wetting her face.

Eventually, her grip on her husband slackened. She wriggled in his arms until he rolled alongside her, and then she hugged him again, less forcefully. He cradled her head against his chest, and she began to weep, but quietly. She cried for a long time before detaching herself and sitting up to search for a handkerchief. Stretching brought new awareness of how the wires in her body had uncoiled and loosened, and she took and kissed Mr Collins's hand gratefully.

He in turn sat up preparatory to leaving, and began to thank her, as was their usual pattern. Again, she tugged him back down. 'Stay.' And at his perplexity, she recited, 'Ordained for the mutual society, help, and comfort, that the one ought to have of the other, both in prosperity and adversity.'

She sensed him smiling at that, as he should, the

words coming from the vows in the Book of Common Prayer he read whenever joining in matrimony members of his congregation.

'Perhaps we may be blessed with another child. I had hoped – I did not want to intrude on your grief – is it too soon to speak of such matters, my dear?' But Charlotte, on the verge of voluptuous sleep, did not answer.

After that, things were a little better. Whenever she was having an especially bad night, Charlotte would call her husband, and he would hasten into her chamber, making ritual enquiries as to her health. She would reach out to him, they would couple both frantically and slightly furtively, then lie heaving in each other's arms. Sometimes one or the other would shed tears. Occasionally Mr Collins would express the tentative hope that their nocturnal activities would result in another child. Charlotte understood that this arose from his slight discomfort at the shamelessness of their marital incontinence. Their conjugal relations had indeed become first sporadic, and then rare following Tom's birth, something Charlotte had not particularly regretted. She did not know if this had arisen from reticence on the part of her husband – perhaps in response to her deep preoccupation with her youngest child – or the fact that regardless of his frailty, Tom, as the future heir of Longbourn, provided them all with the semblance of a secure future.

Neither had she cared to enquire. Having had three children in under five years, while not in the first flush of youth, she had welcomed the respite from pregnancy and child-bearing, the weariness that bit deep to the bone, the combination of hunger and nausea in the early months of carrying a child, the indigestion of the later months, the softening and swelling and leaking of her body. She did not begrudge the physical tax of bringing her beloved children into the world, and had refused the services of a wet nurse for each one, preferring to nourish her infants herself, even as Lady Catherine tutted and scolded; but she had enjoyed having her body to herself once Tom had been weaned. All the satisfaction she needed, she found in the affection of her three children, the physicality of their small bodies, the unselfconsciousness of their caresses.

While she welcomed the re-entry of Mr Collins to her boudoir, and the embraces that undid the knots in her body, she also knew that Tom could not be replaced, no matter how beloved a new infant would no doubt be. She was not yet ready for there to be another occupant of the cot in the nursery. So after another discreet visit to Mrs Talbot, Charlotte made certain to drink pennyroyal tea for a week each month, an ancient remedy against conception, according to the midwife. Meanwhile, ever-practical, she learned to lay out cloths to protect the bedsheets from undue amounts of laundering. And after these marital encounters, she would sleep.

She still startled awake with a cry of alarm from dreams of a child calling her, she still woke before dawn, fretting over her daughters, but those few hours of deep physical relaxation and slumber made it possible to taste the toasted bread and bramble jam served at breakfast, to calculate her accounts with her usual accuracy, to adjust the amount of corn fed to the hens to encourage better laying, to smile more widely and curtsey more deeply when Lady Catherine came to call.

CHAPTER IV

ONE DAY CHARLOTTE HAD A package, which had been misdirected to the Parsonage, to deliver to Rosings. She took no pleasurable anticipation in the task the way her husband would have done, and might have left it to his return from parish business to ask him to carry it over the lane and through the park. But it was a clear day with a sharp edge to the distant blue sky, frost still holding bare trees and plant stalks in its crystalline grip, and she relished the chance to escape her routine for half an hour.

Upon arrival, she was surprised to be ushered into the presence of Miss de Bourgh only. Lady Catherine was at the same parish meeting as Mr Collins, no doubt advising men of the cloth on how best to write sermons and administer relief to the poor, and Mrs Jenkinson, Miss de Bourgh's regular companion and chaperone, was laid low with a megrim.

After handing over the parcel, which contained embroidery threads from London, Charlotte folded herself onto a chair and made the necessary conversational gambits. Miss de Bourgh drove her phaeton and ponies past their gate whenever the weather allowed, and she regularly stopped to exchange a few civil words with Mr or Mrs Collins, but she usually declined invitations to come indoors. In fact, Charlotte could count on the fingers of one hand the occasions on which the Rosings heiress had entered the Parsonage, and did not believe she had ever been tête-à-tête with her before. As she cast about for topics beyond the weather, her hostess asked: 'Do you ride, Mrs Collins?'

'Not since I married, Miss de Bourgh. But as a girl growing up, I had my share of stumbling around on a faithful dappled mare.'

'Do you miss it?'

Charlotte stared at her interlocutor, surprised by the turn the conversation was taking. 'I miss the exercise it afforded, and the opportunity to travel further abroad than my own two feet might carry me,' she replied.

'We have in our stable at present a very quiet gelding no longer fit for carriage work. If you wish, I shall instruct Walter that you should have the use of him when your time permits you to ride.'

Charlotte did not know how to respond. Her shoulders loosened at the thought of an innocent avenue of temporary – not escape, exactly, but reprieve – as winter tightened its hold on the countryside and made walking less and less pleasant. But how was this to be managed? And what would Lady Catherine make of this unprecedented offer?

As if reading her thoughts, Miss de Bourgh followed with, 'Do not concern yourself with my mother, Mrs Collins. I shall settle it with her, and she shall settle it in turn with your husband, if need be. You would be doing Dobbin a kindness; I am sure the fellow grows bored standing around idle. I know I do.'

This indeed was a surprise. Charlotte looked more closely at Anne, always a pale, thin creature, small for her age. Her features suggested eggshell delicacy, but were not without appeal; and the curls that escaped from her cap were the colour of moleskin. With surprise, she realised that the heiress must be at least thirty by now; and if it were possible to feel pity for someone who stood to inherit an estate as grand as Rosings, she felt a pang for the younger woman, with no prospects of matrimony or a family. She wondered why no suitors presented themselves, but imagined that Lady Catherine would suspect and see off fortune-hunters at every turn.

There was, of course, the matter of Anne's frailty, which Lady Catherine kept trumpeting as the only reason the world was denied the privilege of witnessing her daughter's hypothetical triumphs – from a glittering appearance at court to dazzling displays of musical and artistic talent. And yet Anne's thin arms were like whipcords – Charlotte had seen her steer and temper the ponies pulling her phaeton with a mere flick of her wrists and set of her narrow shoulders. She had also glimpsed her bowling along the lanes in her fragile conveyance at a pace that would have made the boldest of rakes blanch.

Miss de Bourgh coloured slightly under Charlotte's scrutiny, or perhaps at the unguardedness of her own remark, and added, 'And of course you are always welcome to walk the grounds and the parkland, as you know. In inclement weather, remember that you can at least take a turn in the conservatory or the greenhouses. Many of the plants will be dormant until spring, but at least there will be both shelter and an illusion of outdoor life. I imagine you will be glad of the distraction.'

This was interesting, given that Anne had not attended Tom's funeral, on grounds of poor health, and while accompanying the Rosings party on the official condolence visit, had spoken not a word. Charlotte was grateful both for this evidence of concern, and for the cough with which their conversation turned to more general matters.

Back home, she was not sure how to proceed, or how much weight to give Miss de Bourgh's invitation, but three days later, a note came from the great house, signed by Anne herself, stating that Walter expected Mrs Collins at the Rosings stables later that day. When presented with the note, Mr Collins knotted his hands in confusion rather than any real dismay, but made no objections, and Charlotte duly walked over to the stableyard once she had finished her morning tasks.

Here waited a brown horse whose size might have been daunting were it not that his barrel sides and scooped spine suggested a beast of considerable age. His height was a boon, given Charlotte's tall frame, and his placid temperament was still more welcome. To her embarrassment, Walter mounted another horse, evidently intent on accompanying her.

'The mistress says to lead you out at first and show you the lie of the land,' he explained. 'After that, if you feel able, you are free to ride unaccompanied. You need only send a note in the morning should you wish the use of Dobbin here, and you will find him saddled and ready for you.'

Charlotte could not speak, immersed as she was in the long-forgotten sensations of seeing the world from a different height, the rich scent of the animal beneath her, the coarseness of the mane into which she twisted her fingers, the stretch and pull of muscles and sinews grown rusty from lack of use.

The world from her new vantage point seemed to spring into greater clarity; a chaffinch on a branch ahead appeared to be cut from glass, the sweep of bare willows at the water's edge suggested an Oriental etching. The lines of the surrounding lands, soft when swathed in summer foliage, seemed stronger now, as if the bones underlying the gentle Kentish hills were visible. For an hour, Charlotte was able to exist only in the present moment, fixed as she was on holding her seat and enjoying this new exertion, swaying in the saddle as her steed set down his bucket-sized hooves.

Upon finally returning to the stables, she felt all the effects of gravity as her shaky legs once again stood on solid ground, but the sensation was far from unpleasant. She was aware of physical and mental relief, almost as sharp as the scent of horseflesh now clinging to her. Effusive in her thanks to the groom, she was uncertain as to whether she was expected to visit the great house to offer further gratitude in person. But as it was growing late, she went home, where her husband complimented her on her high colour, remarking approvingly that the outing seemed to have done her a power of good.

Attending to her daughters, who clamoured for an account of their mother's adventures on horseback, Charlotte silently agreed with Mr Collins, at that moment writing Lady Catherine a note of thanks for her gracious kindness in allowing his wife the use of an old and idle animal. The excursion had indeed done her good; by granting her the chance to escape, for a brief time, the burden of grief added to her daily round.

In the weeks that followed, although diffident about imposing herself at first, Charlotte became accustomed to walking over to the Rosings stables, and the replenishment she found in following the local rides on Dobbin's broad back. He was the perfect companion: mild in temper, needing only a press on the flank or a gentle tug on the reins to suggest direction, his presence nevertheless offered comfort. The loss of her child was not something this large beast could ever comprehend, and his perfect indifference steadied her more than human concern could do at this time.

A few times, Anne was waiting in the stableyard when she arrived to ride Dobbin, and accompanied her on her rides, mounted on a grey mare with a gawky-limbed foal at foot. At first Charlotte was somewhat dismayed at the prospect of giving up the solitude these excursions afforded, but found that Miss de Bourgh did not consider them opportunities for conversation. Apart from the necessary consultations as to which routes to follow, their rides took place mostly in silence, broken only by the cawing of rooks, the faint jingle of bridle and bit, and the differing percussions of hoofbeats at walk or trot.

On one of these rides, they came into a field sufficiently sheltered to offer patches of grass, and reined in their mounts to offer them a minute or two of grazing. The foal, which had been circling its dam as assiduously as a bee in a clover bed, bounced towards them as if on springs and thrust its head under the mare's belly to suckle. Something about its awkward eagerness, its wide-spaced eyes and long lashes, reminded Charlotte so piercingly of Tom that she bent at the waist, almost hissing with pain. She was not conscious of weeping, only of wetness coursing down her cheeks, and small splashes on Dobbin's withers.

Miss de Bourgh looked back over her shoulder: 'You are not taken ill, I hope, Mrs Collins?'

By now Charlotte's face was stinging in the raw air, and she was obliged to fumble for a handkerchief. She tried to speak, but found herself unable to offer her companion any reasonable reassurance or explanation. Eventually, all she could say was, 'The foal. It is the foal. Miss de Bourgh, I miss him so much. So much!'

Anne's frown deepened. 'Of course, you are speaking of your son. I, who have never desired children, and am almost certainly unlikely to bear them, will not claim to understand your grief at the loss of your child, Mrs Collins. Such presumption would be disrespectful. But with my family history, I can contemplate and grasp the implications of the loss of an heir. You might not know that before me, my mother gave birth to three sons – none of whom lived more than a few hours – and thus was the shape of all our lives determined.

'I have had my mother's lawyer in to explain the details of my inheritance until the man is hoarse. As long as my mother lives, or I live, I am safe. But I confess the question of what happens to my home and fortune once I am dead plagues me more and more. I love Rosings: every hare in its fields, each tree in its spinneys. It is the child I will never have. So, detached as I might be from the feelings involved, I can comprehend the enormity of the loss of your son and heir in this regard. You are now none of you safe.'

Even as she struggled to master her own runaway feelings, Charlotte found herself gaping. She did not think she had ever heard Miss de Bourgh speak at such length before. She was once again rendered silent, not only by the bluntness of Anne's words, but also by the sense that someone understood her worst anxieties, the implacable and inescapable laws of inheritance that stalked them all, her gnawing worry for her daughters.

Her companion took up her reins and suggested they trot on in single file, which precluded any further pursuit of this line of conversation, but Charlotte felt fractionally less alone, and took comfort from that.

On the homeward stretch of their journey, Miss de Bourgh spoke again, equally bluntly: 'Do you speak to Mr Collins of your grief? Do you share memories of your son?'

'I cannot. Such reminiscing would rake him raw. If I am truthful, it rakes *me* raw. But it is like picking at a scarred wound; it pains, but there is also relief in it.'

'I see. Your loss has had unforeseen consequences for me, Mrs Collins. I am a profoundly solitary creature – some might indeed say selfish. Yet one would have to be an insensate brute to remain indifferent to your recent loss, and your fortitude in bearing the unbearable. It has impressed upon me that life is a cruel business, but that perhaps there might be comfort to be found in connecting with our fellows.'

Without pausing for a response from her companion, she continued, 'Shall we canter this last stretch?' And the galvanising movement of their horses, and the crunch and clatter of hooves as they came first to gravel and then cobblestones where stablehands waited to take and tend to their mounts, momentarily cleared Charlotte's head.

Several days later, the establishment at Rosings received a visitor in the form of Anne's cousin, Colonel Fitzwilliam, who was also the cousin and confidant of Mr Darcy. The unexpectedness of the visit caused a small flutter in their immediate circle. Charlotte remembered the Colonel very well, especially from the early days of her marriage, when he and Mr Darcy had visited Rosings to pay their respects to their aunt. She had liked him for his wit, gallantry, and easy way with Lady Catherine, while not inclined to consider him wholly trustworthy. She recalled the avidity with which he had sometimes regarded Miss de Bourgh, and the different kind of avidity with which she had occasionally caught him watching Elizabeth, on the occasion of her friend's first visit to the Parsonage.

She wondered at his travelling at such an inclement

time of year, but assumed that Kent made a convenient stop en route to the winter pleasures that London afforded. The Collinses were invited to dine at Rosings on the evening of his arrival, but Laura was fretful with a cold that day, and Charlotte refused to stir from her side. One slippery aspect of grief, she had found, was the unreasonable but no less real anxiety that any lack of attention or vigilance might lead to disaster. So Mr Collins argued in vain that Katie could tend to their daughter and send for them in case of need; Charlotte would not be moved, and her husband was obliged to walk over to the great house by himself.

On his return, he was able to list the dishes served, the sad matter of Lady Catherine's vexation upon discovering that the fish was perhaps not quite fresh, along with the extreme obligingness of his noble hosts and their guest. The latter had offered to accompany him the following morning on a visit to a parishioner, a wounded soldier, with an eye to providing advice as to what aid could best be offered the crippled man. However, Mr Collins could shed no light on the reason for the Colonel's visit, which he ascribed to the irresistible joys of Rosings, and the delight of Lady Catherine's company.

The next day, the Colonel did indeed pay the Parsonage a short visit, during which he was as habitually civil and charming as always, offering Charlotte his condolences on the loss of her son with real and gratifying kindness, before heading out with Mr Collins on their errand of mercy.

About a week later, after a spell of biting wind and

freezing rain had kept Charlotte from her rides, a note arrived from Miss de Bourgh: would she care for a ramble round the hothouses the following afternoon? Charlotte handed the communication to her husband, whose response, once he had recovered from his surprise, was predictable: 'My dear, what a mark of honour and affability! Could any couple be happier in the notice of noble patrons? This emanates from Lady Catherine, I am sure of it. This is testament to her good opinion of you, that she suggests or encourages such a visit. And indeed, she is not wrong to value your amiability and steady temper. Miss de Bourgh is gracious indeed in marking you out for attention this way. I would offer to accompany you in this most happy enterprise, but I am not unaware that ladies sometimes feel the need for exclusively feminine companionship, and my presence, while surely not unwelcome, might indeed be unwanted.'

Charlotte forbore from pointing out that for months on end, barring the presence of menservants, Rosings could pass as a nunnery, with only Lady Catherine, Miss de Bourgh, and Mrs Jenkinson in residence, and settled to writing a note of thanks and acceptance. Mr Collins hovered over her, suggesting a word here and there, and although the servant who had brought the note was waiting for the reply, he even offered to carry her letter across the park in case the opportunity for expressing personal thanks to members of the household arose.

CHAPTER V

THE NEXT DAY, CHARLOTTE PRESENTED herself at the Rosings hothouses, magnificent structures of glass and iron that branched off from the main conservatory. She had not explored them since the early days of her marriage, when Mr Collins was determined to wring from her praise of every aspect of Rosings. Now she was instantly struck by the softness and wetness of the air, the faint sound of running water, the near-tropical warmth, and the all-pervading sweet odours. One of the hothouses was reserved for salad leaves and vegetables too tender to withstand frost, but the one in which Miss de Bourgh awaited was given to plants from far-flung balmy corners of the globe, as well as those table flowers that required respite from more punishing cold during the winter months.

Anne did not waste time on pleasantries. 'Mrs Collins, as you know, Colonel Fitzwilliam, Mr Darcy's cousin, visited my mother and I last week. I believe he called on you as well. His purpose in coming here was to make me an offer of marriage. Again. The man grows desperate. His purse does not match his tastes.'

Whatever Charlotte was expecting, it was not this,

but she masked her expression of astonishment and waited for her companion to continue.

'He has proposed before. You are aware, Mrs Collins, of my unusual situation. My mother managed to settle the estate on me as her heir, but if I die a childless spinster, all our property and fortune reverts to the next surviving male – who is Mr Darcy. The one man in England who does not need a single extra penny. This while so many impecunious young men have fast horses, gambling debts, and other necessities to pay for.'

Charlotte stared at the younger woman – she did not think she had ever heard Anne speak with such asperity in their several years of acquaintance.

'Forgive me,' she said, trying to think of a delicate way of asking why Miss de Bourgh had presumably and repeatedly declined the Colonel's proposals. 'But it sounds like an unobjectional offer. Is it sincerely made?'

But even as she spoke, she thought she understood. Anne lived in comfort, even splendour. For as long as she lived, her home, the vast and handsome roof over her head, was secure. She need never fear deprivation, or possibly worse – all the uncertainties of relocation, starting out in an unknown neighbourhood, with a new household to run, new servants to manage. She breathed familiar air, saw only familiar faces and sights. In as much as anyone who lived under Lady Catherine's sway was able, she had only herself to please. Why would any woman fortunate enough to find herself in these circumstances expose herself to the risks, the haphazard lottery of marriage?

'The Colonel is sincere enough. It is not me he

42

wishes to marry; it is Rosings. It pleases me that he does not dissemble. The first time he proposed, it was with all the flutter of flattery. I confess I laughed out loud at his protestations of esteem. The man is no fool – he soon retracted his claim to have lost his heart. I had knowledge that it was in fact his chaise and pair he had just lost, and I charged him with this. Oh, his face!' Anne snorted, a surprisingly robust sound coming from her tiny form.

She reached down towards a green shrub with a spreading aspect and pale pink blooms cross-hatched with darker pink, and picked a star-shaped leaf. She passed it to Charlotte: 'Here, crumble this between your fingers and then hold it to your nose.'

The leaf was tough, almost leathery, and covered with a down of fine hairs. Charlotte did as she was told, and was overwhelmed by the bright smell of citrus, with a powdery undertone of rose. She exclaimed, and Anne answered her unspoken query: 'It is a pelargonium, from the Cape of Good Hope down at the tip of Africa, family to the geraniums found in our northern gardens. A transplant, like you. If you wish, I shall send over cuttings, but you will need to keep them in a warm spot indoors. They will not withstand frost.'

They strolled on, and this time Miss de Bourgh picked a forced peony and began to shred its petals. 'Mrs Collins, you might have been fortunate enough to marry for affection, but matrimony for the rich is a matter of cold, hard business. Of contracts and lawyers' agreements, of land and estates, pounds and shillings. The Colonel keeps making what is essentially a business proposal. A merging of assets, an exchange of goods. But the assets, and hence the power, are all on my side. He has only status, a certain position in society as his wife, to offer me. And such things carry no weight with me.'

Charlotte winced. Her marriage might not have been a matter of papers and seals in a dusty lawyer's room, but it had been as brazen a trade as in any marketplace: her husband's intact pride in exchange for her security. She had known this from the start, even if he could not acknowledge it. And yet their union had made them both content. She gained true pleasure from knowing that she was a good wife and helpmeet, and real affection flowed through their family. Their children were happy. Tom – oh, Tom! – she could swear he had enjoyed every minute of his short life; and for this and all her other blessings, she counted herself fortunate.

She wondered how to respond to these unexpected intimacies. Every question she wanted to ask was indelicate, but her companion seemed to have lost all reserve: 'I see you wonder why I should not accept an offer that means I will stay in my home, but under the protection of a charming and universally liked man, educated and a brave officer, enjoying all the standing and congratulations due to a married woman. But I have never longed for union with any man; the truth is that I shudder at the idea. And my health will not stand the bearing of children. My line will end with my own flesh. There will be no issue from any marriage I might undertake.'

Charlotte stood still. The trickling of water through the pipes that warmed the hothouse seemed loud as she tried to compute what she had just heard.

Miss de Bourgh turned to her. 'I see you are shocked. Well now, imagine the Colonel's surprise when I was equally candid with him. He would indeed be safe, respectable and comfortable, married to me. But men assume that marriage means heirs, and the means of making heirs. I can offer no such thing.'

She wrinkled her nose. 'I have read too many Gothick romances, Mrs Collins. Why would I enter such a marriage, and pay for my husband's pleasures – which will no doubt include a mistress and her establishment in town? I would not mind the mistress, but I would baulk at footing the bill. And men who fancy themselves in love are not to be trusted: what if he began to see me as an impediment, and I had an unfortunate tumble down the stairs and broke my neck?'

Charlotte must have allowed her amazement to flicker across her face, because her companion added wryly, 'I see you think that I grow wild and rave – blame my habit of indulging in novels at a tender age, if you wish.' She sighed as she picked a spray of rosemary and began to strip its leaves. 'Ah, this reminds me of Provence, and the scent of the maquis there!'

For Charlotte, the fragrance suggested only her own herb garden and the savoury aroma of roasting chicken, but she remembered that Miss de Bourgh and Mrs Jenkinson had indeed spent a winter abroad a few years back, for the sake of the former's health. She had returned a little browner and with some much-needed flesh on her bones, but had soon reverted to her usual wraith-like appearance.

'You see, Mrs Collins, the Colonel is at a crossroads. He *must* marry, and he must marry well. And I am not the only wealthy single woman of his acquaintance. Miss Georgiana Darcy – I believe you met her three years ago, when she visited here on her way to London – is now twenty-two. She is beautiful, accomplished, a charming young woman now that she has overcome her natural tendency to shyness. And she has a fortune of thirty thousand pounds. The Colonel is her cousin, and her brother's close friend. He is, along with Mr Darcy, her legal guardian – there are no family secrets or matters of business that can be kept from him. He has access to her. All seems set fair, should he cast his eyes in that direction. But women are not items in a shop window to be chosen, picked up, set down again. It is Miss Darcy's very beauty and youth, allied with her wealth, that gives her room to choose, too. She was the toast of London society when she was presented at court. So you see the Colonel's dilemma.'

Charlotte frowned. 'I beg your pardon, Miss de Bourgh, but I do not understand.'

'I am small, feeble, and advancing in age. I have no special talents or beauty to attract admiration or even envy. Miss Darcy is every impecunious young aristocrat's dream: rich, exquisite, from one of the first families of the land. Her brother is a byword for diligent guardianship and excellent management. All bodes well for her future. But while she has a dowry – and one that is magnificent by any standards – I have Rosings: the buildings, land, grounds, woods, cottages, rents, crops, livestock. Every acre I see—' here she gestured at the wavering aspect of the land seen through the rippled glass of the hothouse windows '—will be mine when my mother dies. There is almost not a woman in England, no matter how rich or high-born, who can say the same. And yet the moment I sign the marriage register in Hunsford Church – or St James in London, or wherever the ton stage their weddings – every particle that is Rosings, every stick, plant, and pheasant on the property, every sod of soil, becomes the property of my husband, to do with as he pleases.

'So the Colonel is in difficulties. He is enough of a gentleman not to court two women simultaneously. He cannot be suspected of any double-dealing; Mr Darcy, and indeed his own conscience, would not countenance it. And he cannot be sure of Miss Darcy, should he turn in that direction. Who is to say that his attentions will inspire her affection? They are indeed close, but he has been in the position of an elder brother to her all her life; and some young women require the novelty of a fresh admirer. Miss Darcy might harbour dreams of romance. Her wealth and position allow her that luxury.

'And so Colonel Fitzwilliam presses me hard for a favourable reply. He offers new terms: should I accept his hand, we will live as brother and sister. He will accept that there will never be issue from our union, no heir to inherit. He speaks of fostering instead, perhaps a boy from a family close to ours. And I confess, I am tempted even as I feel harried. It would be something to be settled, to know what the future will hold.'

She looked into Charlotte's face again: 'Forgive me. I did not wish to burden you. I have said far too much. I understand that without even asking your permission, I have treated you as a confidante, and enjoyed all the ease of speaking freely while placing you under constraint. But I have had no peace since receiving the Colonel's offer several days ago, an offer he repeats in a letter I received this morning. I must reply; at the very least, I must not torment the man. He is no villain who deserves to be played with. Hence my need to speak my mind to someone of sense.'

Charlotte murmured something about Lady Catherine's advice being always helpful, and was answered with another snort: 'Mrs Collins, this is not a matter to canvass with my mother. Believe me, beneath her officiousness lies real shrewdness, and genuine awareness of and compunction for the lot of women in our society, both high- and low-born. After the death of her sons and my birth, she moved heaven, earth, a tribe of lawyers, and my father in her attempts to safeguard Rosings for herself and me. She spent the first two decades of my life not so much determined – as decided – that I would marry my cousin Darcy, deliberately, almost wilfully blind to the lack of any mutual interest or affection beyond familial connection between us.

'Yet she is no fool. Disappointed in her first goal, she is well aware of Colonel Fitzwilliam's ambitions in my direction. The very fact that she has never spoken of the matter to me – she who never ceases to advise and browbeat all and sundry – means that she is prepared to leave this decision to my judgement. And I must use that poor judgement as best I can, and take the consequences.

'One last thing; might I depend on your discretion in this matter? I have not had you as neighbour these years without observing that you are a close-mouthed woman, not given to gossip or tattle, or even idle rattling on. Having already abused your kind nature, I must now ask you to betray the rule of marital candour; please discuss none of this with Mr Collins. He is a well-meaning sort of man, but I cannot believe he would have any advice of value to vouchsafe, and indeed, I do not seek advice. I must make my own decisions here. I have spoken to you for entirely selfish reasons: I wished the relief of speaking aloud.'

Charlotte gave her companion all the assurances she could wish for; in any case, she could not imagine explaining any part of the strange tale to her husband in a form that would not baffle or alarm him.

Back home, she was nevertheless absorbed by the account she had heard, so much so that her husband had to rebuke her for inattention as she sat stitching by the fire. Who would have thought that Miss de Bourgh faced a dilemma both so different and yet similar to the one that had faced Charlotte in her spinster days? One thing was clear: it was poverty only that made celibacy contemptible in the eyes of the public; with her wealth, Anne would always be respectable.

CHAPTER VI

CHRISTMAS CAME AND WENT, AND Charlotte made an effort at cheer for the sake of her daughters. She knew now how every date that was marked on the calendar and in the Christian year carried a tax: 'this time last year', the days mocked or murmured, tugging at her, tormenting her with her own blindness, her unreadiness. Had she not been told often enough that they would lose Tom, that he would never grow to be a man? And yet each day that passed when he was so very present in her life, so solid and vividly himself, had lulled her. The human heart imperilled itself with its inability to live in the future, and hers was no different.

The anxious first year of his infancy, where every sniffle, every spot on his skin, had had her guts knotting, had passed without crisis; and he had seemed to thrive, growing stronger each day, passing through the same stages of growth as his sisters; producing a set of teeth as beautiful as seed pearls and as sharp as fishbones on her nipples, pulling himself up on the fender, putting handfuls of earth in his mouth, staggering across the lawns, thrilled at his own locomotory cleverness, bawling heartily when he tripped on his own petticoats. She had accepted the salve of each day that passed without incident or alarm; she knew that disaster stalked, but at a distance. She had given in to the lure of security. But how could she regret this? Was she to have set her heart aside, barricaded it because of impending loss? No parent possessed of normal feeling could have done so.

And so the season of goodwill passed in a blur of carols and new candles for the church, holly branches laid out on the window-ledges, all the tiring work of extra parish business, visits to Rosings to drink mulled wine and eat fruitcake studded with cherries and cloves. On these occasions, Anne de Bourgh sat close to the fire, huddling into her chair as if wishing to recede into its frame and fabric, not letting any word or glance suggest even a hint of their recent intimacies. Charlotte took her lead, and supplied only slightly warmer smiles upon greeting, giving no other indication of any private communication between them. She assumed, in the absence of any happy announcement, that Miss de Bourgh had once again declined Colonel Fitzwilliam's proposal – a decision that raised her esteem for the other woman.

In January, the countryside shuddered in the grip of a cold snap, and the ground rang like metal under hard frosts. The days were short and sunlight meagre; spring had never seemed so far off. Charlotte still viewed the nights as battles to be survived, with whatever weapons she could muster. She had the upper hand some of the time but, at regular intervals, sleep and wholesome rest found new ways to elude her.

One night she woke only an hour after retiring, with a new torment; her hands and feet possessed by a sense of heat and ferocious itching. She lay unquiet, trying to stave off the desire to scratch, and failing. As soon as she had attacked one spot with her nails, another began to itch. Then it was the turn of her scalp and the V of skin just beneath her throat.

In desperation, she threw back the bedclothes, and found a little relief in the chill air on her inflamed skin. Mr Collins was away overnight on a visit to his bishop, and Charlotte felt suddenly trapped, stifling, a bird caught in lime. She had to get out. Surely she could leave her sleeping children for an hour, with Katie slumbering in the attic room above?

She did not dress, but wrapped a heavy mantle and shawls over her nightgown, and went downstairs as quietly as possible, pushing her feet into boots kept in the mudroom, finding mittens in an apron pocket. She slipped out the back door, leaving it unlatched. No thieves would be abroad in this weather; the cold was intense, bracing, overwhelming – as she needed it to be. It bit at her skin, wrenched tears from her eyes, insisted that she keep moving.

She found the ruts in the lane difficult to navigate by faint starlight and a half-moon only, and turned into Rosings park; she would follow the paths there for a while, until the restlessness and burning left her limbs. She soon struck out across the frosted grass, the crunch under her boots as satisfying as the lungfuls of icy air she sucked in.

The silence was intense; no sleepy chirrup of bird

or chime of church bell broke the spell of deep night. Only the sound of her own steps, the blood rushing in her ears, echoing her heartbeat.

And then her heartbeat took on a life outside her body, thudding into a distant gallop. It took a few minutes before Charlotte realised she was indeed hearing the drum of hooves, approaching fast. She had no time for more than a moment's panic – what would highwaymen be doing on the Rosings estate? – when the shape of a horse and rider loomed, silver and black in the black and silver night, tangible more through scent and sound than vision. There was a long harrumphing snort, the equine form convulsed as it shied, a figure tumbled from its back with a thin cry, and the rhythm of hooves broke apart in panic.

Charlotte ran for the broken-bird figure on the ground, only to be sent back by the voice, which, to her amazement, belonged to a woman: 'Catch him! Catch the damned horse, for God's sake!'

Such was the voice's urgency that Charlotte whirled round, trying to make out a denser patch of dark in the darkness. Fortunately, she did not have to go far; loud snorts and the jangle of bridle and tack led her to the trembling bulk of a horse. Several frustrating minutes followed, during which it evaded her every attempt to approach it, but just as she was beginning to wonder if she would ever catch the animal, it paused to nibble at a hedge, and made no objection when Charlotte felt for and took charge of the reins.

She led the beast back to the shape on the ground;

she already knew its identity, although she could not believe or fathom the evidence of her own eyes and ears. But it was unmistakably Anne de Bourgh's voice that greeted her: 'For the love of God, Mrs Collins, what are you doing out here in the middle of a winter's night? Bruno almost ran you down. You startled us both, and now look at the poke we find ourselves in. My ankle is hurt, and I shall need your assistance.' This last was resentfully said, and Charlotte found herself apologising for her trespass as she hunkered down beside Anne, stretching out tentative hands.

The Rosings heiress was recognisable by her voice only; the person before Charlotte was a young man, in breeches and riding coat of antique cut, cursing as fluently as any sailor. Charlotte set her shock aside for the moment; she could deal with only one crisis at a time, and questions could come later. How badly was the midnight rider injured?

In response to her queries, she received only tart replies: 'Just my ankle is amiss, no thanks to you. Bruno is usually as sound as a rock. What d'ye think you're doing, roaming about our park at night?'

Charlotte, wondering why she should be the defensive one – given that her interrogator was a lady dressed in man's clothing, out alone on horseback in the middle of the night – stammered something about sleeplessness, her compulsion to be outside, to feel only the roof of the sky.

This seemed to mollify her interlocutor. 'Ah Mrs Collins, it seems we both needed an escape. Well, now you see: this is my means of making that escape. But

I require your help. Let me see if I can stand – if my foot will bear my weight.'

The two women fumbled in an uneven parody of an embrace, Charlotte hanging onto the horse's reins with one hand, and trying to raise Anne with her other arm. The velvet coat worn by the younger woman smelled musty, and very slightly of cigars. More startling curses ensued as the two women hopped and staggered. Anne sucked in air. 'It is no good. I doubt anything is broken, but I cannot yet walk. Mrs Collins, do you think you can boost me back onto Bruno? And then I fear I must ask you to come back to the stables with me and help me dismount.'

It took them a quarter of an hour, and some moments of pure despair, before Anne was on horseback again, sitting astride. The horse was spooked and skittish, and would not stand still to be mounted; and although it was fortunate that one of them was so slight and one tall – they would not have managed otherwise – it was still only by supreme effort that Charlotte managed at last to heave Anne back into the saddle. In spite of the iron chill of the night, she was sweating like Bruno himself by the time it was done.

Then came the journey back to the stables, Charlotte's hand on the reins, Anne occasionally speaking from above to navigate. There was something bizarre about her conversational tone, given the shocking nature of their situation. Neither mentioned Lady Catherine, but both knew that discovery – of either of their transgressions – by her ladyship was not to be contemplated.

As they approached the stables, Charlotte realised a

fresh bout of difficulties was about to begin. They had to get the horse unsaddled, currycombed, and stabled without discovery. 'Walter is a very reliable fellow, but porter keeps him sleeping soundly at nights – plus he is partly deaf, which aids my cause,' Anne explained. Charlotte realised, with a jolt, that this midnight ride was not Miss de Bourgh's first such excursion and, as if reading her thoughts, the younger woman said: 'At night, galloping across the Weald – Mrs Collins, it feels as if I can fly – am flying. I cannot live as a caged bird every hour of every day. It cannot be borne.'

Charlotte shook herself back to their current dilemma. She had to help Anne slide from the horse, then attend to the animal. Everything took longer because of the need for quiet and darkness; they dared not light a lantern, and every clatter of Bruno's hooves brought fresh fright of stirring from the groom's cottage nearby. But if Walter did wake, he had the sense to lie quiet; and agonisingly slowly, task after task was completed.

At last the animal and his accoutrements were safely stowed; the next challenge was to get Anne back to the house. But first it was time for some nursemaiding. The eldest of six children, Charlotte was an old hand at sprains and bruises. She forced Miss de Bourgh to remove one boot, itself a production, as the ankle had swelled, and could be released only by strenuous efforts that left tears freezing like diamonds on Anne's cheeks. Then Charlotte made her sit with her injured foot in the water trough – where first they had to break a crackling skin of ice. She hunted around in the dark for a handful of dock leaves spared by the frost – she was lucky to find a rosette of them close to the muck-heap – and something she could use as a bandage. It was only in story-books that heroines ripped strips from their clothing, she thought, contemplating the unassailable thick cotton of her nightdress under her outer layers. She was perishingly cold, and could only imagine what Anne, one bare leg in ice-water, must be feeling, but there was no help for it.

Her treatment, though brutal, did the trick, and her patient, leaning heavily on Charlotte's shoulder, was able to shuffle back towards the house. After an interminable journey, they slid into the kitchen quarters, the comparative warmth of the house offering relief as solid as any embrace. Here, too, they dared not light a candle, but the fires, though banked, gave off a faint coral and gold glow, as well as blessed, glorious heat. At last Charlotte could treat Miss de Bourgh's injured ankle by wrapping it first in the leaves she had picked, and then in a cloth girth purloined from the tack room.

The dim light meant that Charlotte could take in Anne's appearance more thoroughly, and the younger woman saw herself scrutinised; once again, with her uncanny knack of answering Charlotte's unasked questions, she said, 'These are my father's hunting clothes, made at least thirty years ago. I took them from his quarters after his death, and stored them in a trunk in my dressing room. Thank heavens he was a small man! I am very like him in appearance, you know.'

Charlotte thought it wisest not to comment on the matter. 'Can you get upstairs undetected, do you think?'

Anne grinned, something Charlotte had never before seen, and it transformed her narrow face: 'My co-conspirator! Yes, I am sure I can return to my chambers now. I thank you for your assistance, Mrs Collins. I spoke harshly when first I took my tumble, but you understand how necessary it is to evade discovery, especially in what sometimes feels like a court of Jacobean spies. How lucky it was you I encountered; *you* I know I can rely upon.'

Charlotte nodded at the unspoken pact: they would keep each other's secrets. She said only, 'I shall send over some comfrey for the bruising tomorrow. I have some dried leaves in stock, and you can ask your maidservant to prepare a tea.'

It felt like a blow to step back out into the bitter cold of the night, and she hurried home as fast as she could, driven by both the lateness of the hour and the need to keep moving against the blood-slowing chill. Safely back indoors at the Parsonage, no sound in the house, itself an innocently slumbering creature, she heated milk on the range, grated a little sugar into it and, as a special treat, broke off the end of a rare vanilla pod and stirred it in. The hot drink ran through her veins like brandy without the burn, and she was aware that sleep was no longer refusing its gifts, but beckoning seductively. She barely made it back to bed before slipping under its sway.

CHAPTER VII

THE WINTER DRAGGED ON, ONE day after another which Charlotte endured by the simple expedient of putting one foot in front of the other. Not once did Miss de Bourgh allude to their extraordinary midnight encounter, although considerable fuss was made over the ankle injury she had sustained in a night-time 'slip on the stairs', with a surgeon summoned from London to pronounce what was already known – that nothing more than time was required for healing. Charlotte knew it was the only cure for what ailed her too, but the hours passed so slowly. There were still nights that lasted centuries, although sometimes, as she lay in bed listening to the drumming of her own pulses, she wondered if she was indeed hearing hooves again.

The next painful milestone came in early February, on what would have been Tom's fourth birthday. It was that time of year when all patience with winter was at an end; lanes full of slush, perpetually lowered iron-grey skies, chilblained fingers and dripping noses – these were no longer endurable, and yet spring still seemed dispiritingly distant. At family prayers that morning, Mr Collins spoke words expected of a clergyman, of a beloved son and brother gone to a better place among the heavenly choir of angels, precepts of love and gratitude, faith and fortitude, along with exhortations to accept the will of the Almighty and look to the day of reunion. But then his voice faltered.

Charlotte opened her eyes to see her husband's head sunk in his hands and his shoulders shaking. When he finally revealed his face, it was wet. Sarah and Laura, their small fingers still steepled, began to cry as well, more from confusion and distress at seeing their parent stricken than with real grief. Charlotte, herself deeply affected, realised they were but moments away from communal collapse into sorrow, and called out, 'Let us sing! We shall sing Tom's favourite hymn to remember him by!' She raised her voice before it could be overtaken by tears, and Mr Collins's thin baritone soon quavered along beside:

> *Praise God, from whom all blessings flow;*
> *Praise Him, all creatures here below;*
> *Praise Him above, ye heav'nly host;*
> *Praise Father, Son, and Holy Ghost.*

The children joined in with gusto and their parents split their voices on the second verse to sing it in the form of a round. This was what Tom, too young to appreciate the finer theological points, had so loved; it had had him waving his arms enthusiastically whenever they sang it in church, no matter how beadily Lady Catherine might peer at him from her raised pew.

A few days later, Charlotte found the first snowdrops trembling in the woods, proof that the year was tilting timidly back towards the sun at last. Time, both her friend and enemy, was indeed passing.

March marked the 'hungry gap', that period of the year when the poor were winter-gaunt, but the first spring crops were still seeded or sprouting in the soil. The old and the infirm were easily carried off, and Mr Collins buried more than the usual numbers of his flock at this time. Charlotte was, as usual during Lent, rationing the bacon, using chunks of smoked and salted fat to season the leeks and kales that formed a staple at table for rich and poor alike at this time.

And yet the hedgerows and gardens were burgeoning with buds and glimpses of green. The lanes, fields, and farms saw not only the return of growth both fresh and familiar, but faces as well: the first showing of the gypsies and other workers on whom the hop-growers and other farmers depended.

One blustery morning soon after the arrival of gypsies in the neighbourhood, Miss de Bourgh drew her phaeton to a halt outside the Parsonage in a spray of mud, Mrs Jenkinson clutching her side of the conveyance for dear life. Charlotte slipped on her pattens and ran down to the gate to discover the purpose of this stop.

Miss de Bourgh, holding the reins taut as her ponies fretted, leaned towards her and spoke without preamble: 'Mrs Collins, would you be prepared to ride out tomorrow morning with Walter and myself to visit the tinkers in the pasture up by Dingle Wood? There is a matter to be taken care of there that will benefit from your understanding and advice.' She barely waited for Charlotte's nod before giving her ponies their heads with a snap of the reins, and speeding off.

Charlotte was quite willing to accompany Anne on her errand, but was perplexed by the novelty of the request, especially considering its source. As the resident clergyman's wife, she had infrequent but regular dealings with the itinerant gypsies who flooded into Kent twice a year, in straggles in spring, then in much greater numbers when the time came to harvest the hops in September.

They brought with them a swelling in the problems of indigence, as well as other small upheavals; petty theft, poaching, the occasional chicken disappearing in the night, quarrels when liquor had been taken, but they were a mostly welcome and accepted part of country life in that corner of England; they made, mended, and sold trinkets and household goods, and Charlotte was able to set aside a good sum each autumn through selling them cider and perry. She did not romanticise their colourful kerchiefs and beads, or their musicality and dancing, but neither was she dismayed by the dirt and dismal ignorance of their children, who, although treasured and petted, mostly remained unlettered; and when called upon to offer what relief or comfort was in her power, she did so without fuss.

Charlotte explained the morrow's errand to her husband, who fortunately ascribed it to the bountifulness of the ladies of Rosings, and who was in any case accustomed to the local women sometimes preferring to approach his wife for aid rather than deal with him directly, especially where feminine mishaps and misfortunes were involved. Ever-practical, she packed up a pot with a handle that needed mending and checked her purse in case the visit was productive of something useful to purchase.

The next day, their party met at the stableyard, Anne dressed in a sober black riding habit. Walter did not lead out Bruno; instead he saddled the quiet grey mare, foal still circling its dam, for his mistress to mount. Charlotte had her trusty Dobbin, who whickered a welcome at the sight of her. They set off across the park, the foal cantering in wide circles around their little cavalcade, its ears like furred lilies pricked and broom-brush tail straight up in the air. Once they reached a fairly broad track, Anne held her horse back, letting Walter go ahead and opening up a small distance between them. Once she was sure she could not be overheard, she said quietly to Charlotte: 'They know about my riding. At night, that is.'

She swiftly related the facts of the case: a few years ago, she was returning home late one night under a bright moon, her reins and body loose after a refreshing gallop, when she met a gypsy woman coming stealthily along the path in her direction, two fat hares flopping limp from her hand. Both froze, their minds instantly flying in terror to the consequences of this mutual discovery: Anne seized by the possibility of being unmasked; the woman by the thought of gaol, a transport ship, or worse.

At first, the gypsy's terror was the greater, confronted as she was by a young gentleman on horseback; but as luck or misfortune would have it, she had presented her rushwork to the ladies of Rosings only the week before, and her eyes fastened onto her interlocutor's face with shock, then comprehension, exclaiming in recognition as she identified Anne by name.

Words then flew, made harsh by mutual misunderstanding and fear, culminating in Miss de Bourgh demanding that the woman say nothing of their meeting, or face the most dire consequences. The gypsy, with remarkable quickness of mind, seized the opportunity for mutual negotiation. She gave her promise of silence with alacrity, but then announced her intention to beg a boon in return. Would her ladyship return with her to their encampment?

It took some time for the two to come to terms; Anne dreaded further exposure, but in the end she reasoned that the contraband hares condemned not just the gypsy but all her fellows, who would require a cloak of secrecy even more urgently than she did. Suspicious but curious, she followed the woman back to the site where a small cluster of wagons and tents stood, a cheerless spot in the middle of a muddy strip of land squeezed between a track and a still-bare wood. A fire smouldered, and a child could be heard coughing.

A half-circle of faces pale in the moonlight turned towards them, and there was a quick and low ripple of Romany; then two men approached with offers to care for Bruno while his rider rested and took some refreshment. Their soft words and pats to her horse's neck reassured her almost as much as they soothed her mount, inspiring her to leave the height and safety of his back. There was relief in finding that no one seemed scandalised by her dress or unorthodox midnight appearance; if anything, they were relieved to be dealing with a woman, however she might be attired.

Over mugs of strong black tea, she established what the tinkers' needs were, and these were indeed simple: a dry bit of pasture where they could make camp unharassed, with a good source of clean water and firewood nearby. She promised to make the necessary arrangements and, while their reciprocal agreement of utmost secrecy remained unspoken, it was clearly understood by all.

It took several days, meetings with the estate managers, and a steady refusal to engage with her mother's expostulations and objections, but in the end, no one could dispute the charity of her wishes, however much it might baffle them. Anne was thus able to arrange that this particular troupe should, on all their visits to the district, be given the use of a field on Rosings land, with access to a stream and copses holding plentiful dead wood.

'Since then, I have visited them during their sojourns here – not often, as my mother will not hear of my going unaccompanied, and Mrs Jenkinson deplores the very idea, anticipating squalor and smells,' she told Charlotte. 'But Walter sometimes rides over with me, when he can be spared. I think he quite enjoys it – he slopes off to look at the ponies and talk horseflesh with the men, assuming that I am there because I wish my palm read or my fortune told.'

She nodded at Walter's stolid back ahead of them. 'I do not correct this misapprehension; if the district thinks I am in search of some sort of scrying, no doubt a matter

67

of beaus and balls, that is to my advantage.' She shot Charlotte a sidelong glance: 'And sometimes at night, the camp makes an object to my rides. It is no bad thing to pause for something to drink, to have company by firelight or starlight, to hear singing or stories. We are part-outlaws together, held equal in a strange comradeship of mutual blackmail; I ignore the contents of their stewpots, and they do not remark on my breeches.'

Charlotte could not help smiling at this, and said: 'I understand what you relate, unorthodox as it may be, but I am curious as to why I have been invited to join you today.'

'Mrs Collins, I do not offer myself as a benefactor or advisor to these people. It is mere chance and circumstance that has brought about our current relationship. As I have told you before, I am in truth a selfish creature: both parties in this case benefit from our understanding, but I have little interest in providing further forms of aid. However, I am not unfeeling, and there are circumstances of sorrow and suffering I would like to see alleviated. More recently, the women have told me of a specific situation that requires *your* advice and intervention. I will allow them to explain to you in person.'

They picked their way up the sloping and freshening fields until a shrill whinny from the foal, scenting potential friends, alerted them that they were arriving at the encampment: a small circle of wagons, with a midden set a sensible distance from the stream, and smoke rising into the sky. They were not the only visitors: Mrs Talbot, who had come to purchase wild herbs and examine one of the women who was expecting, was already seated by the fire. The new arrivals handed their horses over to Walter, who led them down to graze by the stream with the gypsy ponies, and joined the midwife, settling on rough stools around the fire. Mutual greetings and enquiries were made, and Miss de Bourgh handed over a screw of tea supplied by the Rosings housekeeper, which was promptly set to brew.

An older woman, with a rusty-red scarf bound around her tresses, leaned towards Charlotte and offered to read her palm. When Charlotte demurred, the gypsy said, 'No palm is required, ma'am. You have the face and form of one who has recently suffered grievous loss.'

'What makes you say such a thing?' said Charlotte.

'Ma'am, it is common knowledge that you lost your little boy but a few months past. Besides, I saw the stone in the graveyard last week. I was visiting the grave of my granddaughter. We buried her there three autumns ago; she took ill and died when we were here to pick the hops. Your husband agreed to our burying her in the churchyard, and read the service himself. It's better to think of her here, lying under fair winds and stars, than if she were in a city cemetery in all the press of crowds and smoke.'

'But does it not grieve your family that you cannot visit or tend her grave?' Charlotte asked.

'We come by twice a year, for the hops-twiddling, then the picking. And sometimes we stay on to pick up potatoes. I visit her resting-place then. It's not a bad place to lie, out in the country, with all the birds and blooms around. Besides, I help the sexton with draughts for his gout each time we come, and he keeps an eye on our Annie's grave for us. Yes, m'lady,' nodding at Anne, 'she was also Anne. Ma'am, I would take it very kindly if, when you visit your son's grave, you would say a prayer for my granddaughter too. It helps if we can think of her lying among friends.'

Charlotte agreed without hesitation, and threw Miss de Bourgh a glance: was this why she had been brought here? It seemed not; the gypsy woman called over her shoulder, and a slighter, shyer woman emerged from the mouth of one of the caravans. Her tale, while similar, was an even sadder one, and it took the coaxing of the older gypsy, along with Mrs Talbot's comforting ministrations, to extract the entire sorrowful story, with no small amount of tears shed.

Her little girl, killed in a fall from a wagon, had lain in unconsecrated ground for seven years because Mr Collins's predecessor had refused to accept that the child had been correctly baptised.

'Ma'am, I baptised her myself, when I was first delivered.' The woman hung her head. 'I knew it might not be proper, but I wanted her little soul to be safe. And then when we were up Northumbria-way for the eel-picking, we had her christened again in the parish church. But we had no way of proving it. We didn't ask for a paper. My man went all the way back there to see if the vicar might write a note or some such, but he had died, and the church was all shut up. Can you help us? We have no education, we can write no letters. We are properly heartscalded, ma'am.'

Charlotte was first horrified, then incensed, to hear of such unnecessarily protracted misery. She gave every assurance of assistance she could, taking careful note of all the particulars. The grateful women in turn pressed a new-woven rush-basket on her, and refused to take any coin for it. At last the thick, smoky tea was drunk, Mrs Talbot disappeared into a caravan with her patient, and the others took their leave. As they proceeded home, Charlotte felt her rage growing, mounting to fury at the pettiness of such cruelty.

She rarely gave her husband direct instructions, preferring to hint and persuade until he fell in line with her suggestions, but as soon as she gained her front door, she went in search of him, and did not mince her words: 'Mr Collins, I require you to write at once to whoever is in charge of —diocese, the Bishop himself if need be. There is a child who lies outside the boundaries of our Christian graveyard, denied the dignity and sanctity of decent burial because at the time of her unfortunate passing, there was no proof that she had been baptised. That proof *must* exist, and I *must* insist that you find it. There is a family grieving because no proper prayers were ever said over the body of their baby. I should also like you to conduct a Christian ceremony over the grave at your earliest convenience.'

Mr Collins was immensely surprised, even alarmed, especially when he found out that the family of which his wife spoke were tinkers, although he was somewhat mollified by the fact that they were encamped at the distant edges of the Rosings property and could therefore be considered to be under the protection of Lady

Catherine. However, he looked at Charlotte's set jaw and, with uncharacteristic perspicacity, knew better than to demur or argue.

The necessary letters were written, responses sent, and permissions gained; and within less than a fortnight, a small party gathered to consecrate the little patch of earth that held the remains of the gypsy child. All the women and children of the camp attended, as well as those men whose employers allowed them time away from the pressing demands of the agricultural season. They formed a ring, hats in hand, weatherbitten faces softened. A hymn was sung, to the accompaniment of a fiddle, in spontaneous harmonies that wrung tears from Charlotte. Dry-eyed at her own son's funeral, she now wept copiously for a child she had never known, in company with most of the women present, who made no effort to mute their expressions of grief. Mr Collins, as the presiding officer of the Church, remained solemn and composed throughout, although his voice shook once or twice.

That night as husband and wife sat by the fire, respectively reading and stitching, they did not speak of Charlotte's unusual display of emotion earlier that day; but she took Mr Collins's hand and squeezed it with more than usual fervour, before kissing the knuckles.

CHAPTER VIII

Later that spring, a letter for Mr Collins arrived from Pemberley, from Mr Darcy. He did not wish to inconvenience the Collins family, but his wife was low in spirits after illness, and he believed she would benefit from feminine company, especially as matters of business required him to travel away from home a great deal during the coming summer. Mrs Darcy had no appetite for London at present, and had expressed a wish that either Mrs Bingley or Mrs Collins might visit her, but Jane was approaching a confinement. Could Mr Collins spare his wife for some weeks or longer, if convenient? The girls would of course also be welcomed, nursemaids provided for them, and Mr Darcy would send a carriage and horses to make the journey as comfortable as possible.

There was little chance of Mr Collins refusing the master of Pemberley anything, and a reply was soon dispatched agreeing to the plan. This was in turn met by a letter from Elizabeth to Charlotte closer in tone to her old playfulness, anticipating her visit with great pleasure, and planning sorties and games for her friend and her children.

Charlotte welcomed the invitation. She was finding

the burgeoning march of spring surprisingly painful. The sombreness of winter had matched and kept pace with her mourning. While the lengthening days had at first brought a measure of relief, watching lambs waggling their snowy tails under their mother's stomachs, and the daffodils nodding along in concert, it seemed that all she saw conspired to suggest new life and growth. From ducklings in the pond to the sugar-sprinkle of blossom on tender grass, she kept noticing things that would have given Tom innocent joy. Easter and Mr Collins's sermons on the hope of the Resurrection, spiked with the bright light falling through the chancel windows, had stabbed at her. She knew that Derbyshire was not immune to the seasons, but it would present new scenes, a change of pace, and the journey would provide an object to weeks that trudged past, offering no respite from loss. She would regret leaving her potager so soon after setting out the lettuces and sowing lovage and fennel seeds, but Mr Collins promised not to let it become overwhelmed by weeds, and to guard it from rabbits. They were to leave after Whitsun.

A few days before their departure, Miss de Bourgh once again stopped her phaeton outside the Parsonage gate, and a servant came running to inform Charlotte that she was wanted. Anne was alone at the reins: 'Mrs Collins, may I once again discommode you by begging you to climb into my conveyance? I wish to take you for a spin around the lanes. The trip will be brief; I have sent my maid back to Rosings, and must return home before it is discovered that I am unaccompanied.'

Charlotte hastened into her house to let its occupants know she would be unavailable for a short while, and sped back down the driveway before her husband could speak too long on such mysterious graciousness. She scrambled into the phaeton as he waved and bowed from the front door and, with a clicking of Miss de Bourgh's tongue, they bowled away.

Charlotte had never been in such a sleek and small carriage before, and was alarmed at how vulnerable it felt, like perching in a very large eggshell. She clung to the sides as Anne's ponies whipped round the corner of the lane without any loss of pace.

'I am sorry to carry you away without ceremony, Mrs Collins,' said her driver. 'But I wished to tell you that you will be missed while you are in Derbyshire. I am not one for performances of gratitude; I have witnessed too many to trust their sincerity. But I want you to know that I appreciate the rectitude and discretion you have shown this past winter – and at a time that has been one of deep grief and difficulty for you.

'I have not yet decided whether to write to you while you are at Pemberley. As you know by now, I do not dissemble. I am either frank in my speech and recounting, or silent – mostly the latter. If I do write, I will be as straightforward as in our other dealings, even in the discussion of intimate matters. But I am well aware that to write things down for others is to put ourselves in their power. I also know that letters from Rosings will be a matter of interest – even if that interest is slight – at the Pemberley breakfast table. I have no wish for my communications to be circulated, other than in the form of spoken summaries in the broadest and mildest of terms.' She raised her voice above the sound of trotting hooves and whirring wheels. 'Do you understand, Mrs Collins?'

Charlotte made noises of assent as she held white-knuckled to the edge of the fragile, bouncing carriage, hoping that they would circumnavigate without incident the cart pulled by plodding Clydesdales ahead.

'The same applies to any letters you may send in return. Their arrival will be a topic of conversation, and there will be open curiosity as to their contents. My mother will demand such a full accounting of any news you impart that letters to myself will constitute letters to her as well. You will bear this in mind, should you write. Which you are under no obligation to do. I shall leave it up to your judgement. Which, I might add, I trust.' She shot her companion a look.

Charlotte was both mindful of, and touched by, the compliment, but said nothing beyond a murmured 'Thank you.' She knew that her ability to curb her curiosity made her valuable to Miss de Bourgh, but she could not restrain herself: 'Might I ask—? Colonel Fitzwilliam?'

Anne laughed. 'I am delighted, for his sake, as well as my own, to report that he seems to be on the verge of making an excellent match. And no, not to Miss Darcy, who remains free to wait and look around and take her pick, marry for affection, should she so choose. The Colonel has long been friends with a widowed French aristocrat, a Madame Fauré, who lost her husband in the Terrors abroad. With the cessation of the wars in Europe, and by dint of diligent legal pursuit, her family lands have been restored to her, and she is once more a woman of fortune. They are at last able to marry. I wish him happy, and wish him well. I am sure he will bring his bride to visit Rosings in due course.'

They were trotting briskly around the edge of the park, and a long straight stretch of road had the ponies frisking, then breaking into a gallop. The wind whistled through Charlotte's hair, and any further words were torn from their mouths.

A few minutes later, they were back at the Parsonage, and Charlotte climbed down, grateful to be in one piece, but also exhilarated. The burst of speed they had shared confirmed her new insights into the character of her neighbour, and she could not help mulling over the strangeness of the fact that the loss of her son had delivered to her a new friend – or rather, drawn friendship from the thin soil of distant acquaintance. For surely she could now count Miss de Bourgh a friend.

CHAPTER IX

AFTER THE OBLIGATORY AND OFFICIAL fare-well visit to Rosings, on which occasion they were lectured on every aspect of their impending travels, from the packing of their trunks to the perils of hostelry salads, the journey was at last underway. Mr Darcy sent an excellent coachman and a sensible nursemaid, arranged for inns known for their whole-someness, and the journey proceeded smoothly. Charlotte's daughters were in high spirits throughout and fortunately, neither were sickened by the motion of the carriage. Charlotte herself had never before travelled so far, and was as much caught up in the novelty of all that they saw as her children. All three of them enjoyed observing and even counting the different buildings and properties they passed, from the oast houses of their native Kent, to ancient crooked and timbered alehouses, to handsome modern houses of stone set in parkland adorned with herds of deer. Charlotte was caught by the sense of time rolling backwards as they headed northwards, the signs of lush spring constantly freshening around them and the hawthorn hedges frothing more lavishly the further they travelled.

After three days of travel, excitement mounted as they entered Derbyshire, with the girls demanding to know if each moderately sized property was their destination. At last they were on the Pemberley estate – first climbing a slow incline, passing a handsome church, then winding their way down and across a shallow valley until the carriage rumbled across the bridge spanning the river in which the reflection of the house hung golden in the afternoon light.

It was indeed a sight to behold: a building of great size and elegance, constructed from stone the colour of glazed scones, it hid its history from the onlooker behind a modern façade, windows and pediments, but sculptural ornamentation from past centuries attested to its antiquity. The ground behind it rose steeply to a hanging wood, and to the east lay a lake that anticipated the curving river below. All was verdant and serene.

The Darcys met their small party with every evidence of pleasure, and Charlotte was relieved to see that her friend, although perhaps a little thin and pale, did not seem unwell. A private interview between the two women revealed that Elizabeth had suffered another miscarriage, although an early one. While her physical recovery had been swift, her spirits had plummeted, and her husband was loath to leave her without company for any part of the summer. His sister Georgiana would be returning from a visit to an old school friend in Switzerland in the latter part of the summer, but Mr Darcy felt that a married woman – and perhaps one who had herself recently lost a child

– might be a companion in whom his wife might more comfortably confide her feelings.

Mr Darcy departed on his travels, and those who remained soon settled into a routine. Charlotte discovered that the absence of their menfolk lent an informality to daily life that was refreshing. Meals were much less elaborate, and sometimes replaced entirely by a tray in the nursery, or a picnic outdoors. On rare rainy days, the girls had the contents of the Pemberley nursery to entertain them, including a most superior rocking-horse that soon became a favourite friend. But the early summer weather was mostly fine, and the girls ran about the grounds and gardens whooping like wild creatures, growing rosy and brown.

Lizzy tactfully had her housekeeper unearth clothing from Georgiana's girlhood trunks to supplement their wardrobes, for which Charlotte was grateful: romping round the grounds of Pemberley, and especially the tree-climbing to which Laura was partial, proved hard on the children's garments, even if there was an army of servants to launder them and sew up the rents and tears.

At first, Charlotte had many anxieties on account of the grottos, wildernesses, underground structures, river, lakes, ponds, and other bodies of water for which Pemberley was known – there was even a maze in which to get lost – but her daughters were old enough to exhibit sense, and invariably guarded by reliable servants. Here they were indulged and protected, and there was always someone to watch them as they climbed and clambered, set up camp in the various stone structures, or sailed boats constructed from leaves and twigs on the pond where the mallards had their nests.

Soon she herself was able to relax and enjoy an unfamiliar sense of freedom, a respite from her usual responsibilities – even though she missed her hens and ducks, and had some doubts as to whether Katie would remember not to feed them apple peelings.

She also found growing pleasure in exploring the grounds and gardens of Pemberley, with its grand avenues, woods, and grounds set with mature oaks, beeches, and Spanish chestnuts. Although their garden at Hunsford was a source of pride, occupation, and healthy exertion for Mr Collins in particular, Charlotte herself did not give its beauties too much thought, especially as her husband was more fond of enumerating its contents and excavations than contemplating it in any aesthetic sense. For her, the kitchen garden, herb beds, and orchards were what mattered, and it was these which she was determined to bend to her will. If that took manure in spring and sacking in autumn, hers was always a pragmatic response.

So it was a gradual revelation to stroll around the estate of Pemberley and find that her eye was drawn in certain directions, her perspective and focus coaxed by sightlines and horizons, sweeping lawns, copses, and streams that first looked as if nature alone had sited them, but which blended harmony and proportion in pleasing fashion, sometimes soothing, sometimes stimulating. A climb up the slope behind the house to the top of the stone cascade down which water tumbled soon became a favourite goal of most rambles. With long, fine days, the sunshine persisting long after dinner, she grew into the habit of walking further and further into the long golden evenings, the air heavy with fine dust and the scent of warm grass.

Charlotte's visit also yielded the pleasure of companionable chat with her old friend, whose wit required an audience. At times, Lizzy's tendency to jest bordered on impropriety, but there was no doubting the liveliness of such conversations, something Charlotte missed sorely as a clergyman's wife, who had to consider the possible interpretations and misinterpretations of every word she uttered in company. Moreover, she considered it an excellent thing that they could reminisce about the events of their past – the 'follies of youth', as Elizabeth put it – with only the gentle tax of amusement to pay.

'Oh my dear Charlotte! Can we ever forget that ball at Netherfield all those years ago, when we were still unmarried women? How Mr Darcy grew stiffer and colder, stalking about as if his boots were pinching him? My sister Mary would not stop singing, my mother would not stop boasting to all who would hear about Jane's conquest of Mr Bingley—'

'And you declared you detested Mr Darcy, and I had to scold you into behaving when you stood up to dance with him,' said Charlotte, laughing a great deal. 'Never did a couple seem less intended for union, he so haughty and you so indignant; and yet within less than a twelve-month, I was throwing rice at your wedding and wishing you joy.'

'How you upbraided me, and rightly so, for my conduct that night. I was so blind, so stubborn! And Mr Collins! How he talked and talked that evening!' Lizzy glanced sideways at her friend, to see if she was perhaps stretching the bounds of marital loyalty too far, but Charlotte was still smiling. 'Such a flood of words, and almost all of them "Lady Catherine this" and "Rosings that". Truly, Charlotte,' she said more earnestly, 'you were kinder to us both – to us all that night – than we deserved. So young and foolish we were. And I the most foolish of all.'

'Nonsense, Eliza! Everyone was foolish that night. Never before in the history of balls did so many conspire to act as simpletons. Anyone would have thought we were competing with one another for a grand prize in foolishness. It is as your father always says: "We live to make sport for our neighbours."'

This led to the exchange of news concerning their Meryton fellows, in whom Mrs Darcy maintained a lively interest. The Bennets' Aunt Phillips had recently put Mrs Bennet's nose out of joint by accidentally annexing a young clergyman who had taken up a living nearby, and sending him in the direction of Charlotte's sister Maria. The mistress of Longbourn had considered that he would do very well for her daughter Mary, but Aunt Phillips had by mischance sent her husband to invite the newcomer to a supper party at her home the same night Mary was kept from attending by a sore throat; she had compounded this error by carelessly inviting Maria to be present and, in a trice, the damage was done. Both Charlotte and Lizzy were able to laugh heartily at this tale, of which each had heard sufficient partial accounts to piece together a whole. Time, loss, and, in Elizabeth's case, elevation, had softened their awkwardness on the topic of clerical courtships as they pertained to the Bennet and Lucas families.

'Mary cares not a jot, however,' Lizzy explained. 'She is in raptures because she is at last an Author; she wrote an improving book, of mottoes and strictures and deep thoughts, and she would have no peace, nor give anyone in her family peace, unless it were published. My father sent it to Mr Cadell, a publisher in London, but he declined by return of post. I must confess I used my influence with my husband, and he sent the manuscript to another publisher with a note he signed himself. This time, it was accepted. Mary was paid eighty-five pounds for it! And has been beside herself with joy and pride ever since. I am surprised she has not yet sent you a copy. Her friends and family have all been importuned to buy the work.'

Charlotte murmured an enquiry about Lizzy's two youngest sisters.

'Oh, Lydia!' Mrs Darcy laughed, then sighed. 'I swear, she is incorrigible.'

Charlotte was familiar with the events that had transpired a few years earlier: Napoleon Bonaparte's penchant for escaping from imprisonment in exile and belligerently dragging the Continent into repeated wars had produced consequences that extended as far as the Bennet family. Lydia's husband, a Mr Wickham who had once served in the —regiment, had gone off to fight in the final outbreak of hostilities in France, declaring a calling to honour and patriotic duty not that easily discerned in his character, and likely to stem from disenchantment with his marital state. Here he had disappeared – either killed or deserted, it was impossible to tell – at some point during the Battle of Waterloo. There was no certainty about his fate because his commanding officer, himself mortally injured, had penned a hasty note to say that he feared Mr Wickham was slain in battle, but no reliable reports had yet reached him. No body was ever found, nor any person who could give testimony, and not all the combined powers of Mr Darcy, Mr Bennet, nor even Colonel Fitzwilliam, had been enough to establish the facts of the matter. It had seemed kindest to assume that Mrs Wickham had been rendered a widow, and the doors of Longbourn, Hartscrane (the Bingleys' establishment near the Derbyshire town of Ashbourne), and Pemberley were all immediately thrown open to her.

Lydia, while piteously declaring that she would never survive without the affection and support of her family, refused to quit the lodging-house where she had taken up residence while her husband was fighting abroad. Her elder sisters assumed, from past experience, that this reluctance to move most likely arose from debts the couple had incurred, which would no doubt have to be discharged before Lydia could change quarters; they prepared their purses accordingly.

Mrs Bennet flew to her bereft daughter's side, and the pair spent a fortnight indulging in noisy and extensive expressions of grief before the mother reluctantly returned home, where she continued to write letters pressing her youngest daughter to return to the comforting bosom of her family. However, not six weeks passed before the news arrived that Lydia had remarried – the very innkeeper of the hostelry at which she was fixed. She declared herself the luckiest woman alive to have secured such another fine husband and, with her usual lack of tact, boasted of having achieved two husbands, all before the age of twenty-one, while her sisters Kitty and Mary were yet old maids. It did seem a good match, though, with Lydia's habitual good humour and perennial liveliness in company proving an asset in her unexpected new path in life.

'It does not seem fair, does it?' said Lizzy. 'To think that Mr Darcy once paid such a sum to rescue her reputation! And here she is, twice-married, entertaining strangers and pouring port at The Craven Heifer, flourishing like the green bay tree – and because of *her* history, my father will still barely allow poor Kitty to leave the house, unless it is to visit me or Jane.'

Charlotte could not contain another burst of mirth. 'Never before was a blameless party so thoroughly punished for the sins of another, but only if you consider visits here, or to the Bingleys, a punishment. Lucky Kitty, I would say. Truly, Eliza, it is a great pleasure to be here. And not because of the grand apartments and grounds, but because of the sense of welcome I feel, the peace, the time to reflect. I cannot think when I last enjoyed such repose.'

Her friend squeezed her hand affectionately: 'I am glad you find it peaceful here, my dear Charlotte, and

hope that it provides balm for your heart. It is restful
– is it not? – being here together, like our maiden
days. I am grateful for your company, and I feel better
for your presence, and that of the girls. It was kind of
you to come.'

CHAPTER X

WITH THEIR DAYS AT PEMBERLEY settling into a routine, Charlotte, for the first time in her life, found herself at leisure – a novel sensation. One morning Mrs Darcy was closeted with the house-keeper, Mrs Reynolds, checking the month's accounts, and a nursemaid whose brother was a shepherd on the estate had taken the girls to visit his flock, and witness the antics of the lambs.

Charlotte had already taken her customary walk around the grounds, and now she sat by an unnecessary fire in one of the grand parlours, all ruddy wood panel-ling and chinoiserie. She yawned and stretched. She had written all her letters – Pemberley had a supply of paper and ink superior in both quantity and quality to anything she had ever seen – prompting her to write to her mother and Maria rather more frequently than she did when at home. Now she found herself with nothing to do. Idleness was anathema to her, and it occurred to her that she had the opportunity to prac-tise her music for the first time in years. She considered which instrument should be subjected to her stumbling fingers. Pemberley had at least four: an imposing ebony six-octave grand piano in the Great Hall, a slightly smaller Broadway in the saloon, a beautifully painted harpsichord considered the property of Georgiana, and an older and inferior pianoforte in the schoolroom that had once been the domain of governesses.

Settling on the most humble piano as her goal, and not wanting her rusty notes to be heard by others, Charlotte climbed the stairs to the schoolroom and let herself in. As she closed the door behind her, she heard a muffled string of words she could not understand and a slight thump. To her astonishment, a pair of legs were to be seen sticking out from under the erstwhile governesses' instrument. Too dumbfounded to give voice to her surprise, she watched as the legs – which were male – wriggled out from under the piano, proving to be attached to a complete stranger.

She and the man stared at each other as he scrambled to his feet, both of them momentarily robbed of the power of speech. His clothing was that of a gentleman, she thought, but he was underdressed, wearing only a white linen blouson shirt with no cravat or waistcoat, and breeches of an unfamiliar cut that were attached to tooled leather straps that ran up and over his shoulders. He was dark and slender, with a nose that beaked from his face, and a close-cropped beard, itself something that made him seem otherworldly, a character from a play of past centuries.

They both spoke at once, her to excuse her intrusion, him to apologise for startling her, and as soon as he spoke, the strangeness of his appearance was explained; he was clearly a foreigner. This in itself made him an object of interest, and Charlotte longed to know more.

The man bowed, introducing himself as Herr Rosenstein, a musician from Salzburg in Austria. His father had built the harpsichord Mr Darcy had purchased for Georgiana, an instrument of great value and delicacy, and the dampness of the English weather had caused the strings to go out of tune. To remedy this fault, it had then been stood too close to the fire, and this had cracked the wood of the belly underneath. The senior Rosenstein now being too advanced in age to travel to assess the damage and make the repairs, the son had been summoned to attempt the restoration; also to tune the other pianos in the house, as well as Georgiana's harp. These painstaking operations promised to take some time. Mr Darcy's plan was that Georgiana would find her instruments in perfect working, or rather playing, order upon her return from her sojourn abroad.

Charlotte now understood why she had not yet met the stranger; he was in the nebulous position of being neither a servant nor a guest. His role in the household was akin to that of a tutor, or an artist employed to paint a portrait.

He was clearly a man of education and some refinement; his English was excellent, with only a slight roughness on the 'r's and a crispness at the end of his words to indicate that it was not his mother tongue. She wondered idly where he was quartered – surely not with the servants? – and where he ate his meals. She was surprised not to have at least seen him at morning prayers, the one occasion when the family and all the staff gathered in the chapel, the family in the balcony seats and the staff standing in respectful rows on the chequered floor below.

'You had a purpose in coming here, madam. I hope I have not disrupted your plans. And might I know your name?'

Charlotte stumbled through her own introductions, explaining that she was a friend of Mrs Darcy's, and that she had come in search of an instrument with the notion of playing a little.

'But why not address one of the pianos in the main part of the house?' he enquired. 'I am sure the family will have no objections.' This obliged Charlotte to explain that she had played little other than nursery rhymes in years, and was reluctant to entertain any audience.

'Ah! You wish to play in solitude, not perform,' he said. 'If you like, I can retire and leave you to test your fingers in peace.'

Charlotte hesitated. Now that she looked around, the tools of his trade were present in an open leather box, and a coat of a foreign cut hung over a chair. She did not wish to disrupt the man's work, and began to demur.

'Or perhaps I should play something for you?' said Herr Rosenstein. Without waiting for a reply, he drew up a stool, laid his hands on the keys and began to play without sheet music, a gentle piece that was quite unlike anything Charlotte had ever heard before. The principal melodic line soon exploded into a blizzard of notes, but she could hear the tune emanating from within the rapidly circling embellishments, still gentle, still yearning, even as the brighter, swifter notes clamoured around them. She drew closer, and was struck by the musician's hands – long and delicate-fingered, yet flecked with small scars that suggested work with lathe and saw.

He played on, and Charlotte shut her eyes against the sun slowly stirring the dust motes, the man's swift and sure ivory-coloured fingers, giving herself over entirely to the bright flurries of sound, as clear and satisfying as running water.

When at last there was silence, she was reluctant to break it, but had to ask: 'What music was that?'

'A sonata by Herr Wolfgang Amadeus Mozart in the key of A: variations on a theme. He was Austria's greatest composer, I believe. Possibly the greatest the world will ever see. He was a friend of my father's, and he would sometimes perform in our home. One of my earliest and fondest memories is of sitting under a piano as he sat down to play. How astonished and delighted I was as the notes came pouring down around me like a shower of gold! It made a strong impression on my tender mind. Sadly, it was but months before he died, at the age of only thirty-five – far too young, especially for one of such genius.'

Charlotte, struck by the sound of the foreign words in his mouth, offered him her condolences on the loss of his colleague. But she could not stay any longer; the man had work to do. But before she could withdraw, he spoke her thoughts: 'Frau Collins, forgive me, but I have tasks I must complete this afternoon. I hope we shall meet again soon. You now owe me a recital.'

Intrigued by her unorthodox encounter, Charlotte went in search of Elizabeth to recount her meeting with Herr Rosenstein, and pressed her friend for details.

'Oh!' said Lizzy, upon hearing of the impromptu concert. 'I should have thought of asking him to play for us earlier. The children will enjoy listening to him. He is quite the musician. He plays the violin too, and the English flute also, although perhaps not as well as he does the pianoforte. If you would like to hear more, I shall ask him to join us after dinner tomorrow. Or let us not stand upon ceremony: we can have a cold collation in the saloon – we have a good instrument there – and see if he will attend. He has been taking his meals in his quarters, but he seems very obliging. I am sure he will have no objection to joining us. He can entertain us all, and we can teach your daughters some country dances.'

It transpired that the elder Rosenstein and Mr Darcy's father had formed a significant attachment to one another, the differences in language, rank, and nationality notwithstanding. A shared appreciation of the arts of music and interest in the construction and care of fine instruments had led the two men to take pleasure in each other's company.

The younger Rosenstein had accompanied his father on his last two trips to England, but while no similar friendship sprang up between the two sons, who had little in common, a mutual goodwill and esteem for the abilities of the other persisted, and had established a foundation for cordial relations, if not actual closeness. This made a visit to Pemberley no hardship for the younger musician, whose pleasure in accepting the commission was no doubt influenced by agreeable memories of his previous stays and treatment there.

He had the freedom of the library and public rooms, and seemed happy to join in such society as was on offer; but was apparently equally content to closet himself away with his instruments and apply himself to his work.

The following day, he joined the women and children at an informal early supper in the red saloon, as suggested by Mrs Darcy. The little girls, already full of the importance of dining in adult company, were squeaking with excitement at the prospect of music and dancing to follow, and Herr Rosenstein showed a good-natured patience in responding to their many questions. He brought a small tambour to show the children, and this was promptly commandeered by Laura, while Sarah essayed a scrape on his fiddle, a performance that had the resident tabby fleeing the room in outrage.

After a simple repast of soup, buns, cheese, and fruit, accompanied by wine for the adults and milk for the children, Sarah was especially delighted when her new friend lay down on the floor and slid under the pianoforte to show her how the guts of the instrument operated. She wriggled underneath to join him while her sister undertook the daintier end of the operation by kneeling on the piano stool and plinking away at the keyboard with gusto. Charlotte opened her mouth to issue a caution for her elder daughter's clothing, then held her peace. What did a little dust matter?

Besides, there was something both comical and touching in the picture presented of the two sets of legs, both narrow and lanky, but otherwise dramatically different in size and dress, emerging from under the piano. The thought came that Tom would have loved an occasion like this, the noise and the jollity, the sense of unexpected festivity. She batted it away as firmly as she could, and called encouragement to Laura, who was demanding that her mama admire her prowess on the keys.

It was with reluctance that the children gave up their respective stations, and allowed the musician to resume control of the instrument, but Elizabeth's sly bribe of grapes did the trick. Charlotte found herself longing to hear the piece Herr Rosenstein had played for her the day before, at the same time as being reluctant to request it. Part of her wanted to keep it locked in her head along with the memory of the dust motes that had wheeled as golden as the notes to which she had been in thrall.

As it happened, Herr Rosenstein confined himself to playing music suited to children: gay tunes and marches, short pieces and songs they could all enjoy. Some tunes she recognised, but he sang the words, in a mild and pleasant tenor voice, in German, while her daughters sang along in English. Lizzy was also prevailed upon to sing for the company, laughingly claiming that she might as well take advantage of a skilled accompanist.

After Lizzy had performed several airs, to the enjoyment of all, each woman commandeered a child and led them through the steps of some basic country dances. They discovered that even if Herr Rosenstein did not know the necessary music, if they hummed or sang the tunes, he could generate a passable replica once he had mastered the required rhythm. And rhythm was mostly what the little girls needed, as their attempts to learn the steps were punctuated by outbursts of mirth at the sight of the older women undertaking the role of male dancers. Charlotte's attempts at bowing in particular were met with gleeful requests for repetition.

Eventually, the delighted but overtired children were dispatched to bed with a nursemaid whose poise and gravitas curbed any propensity on their part to grizzle, and Lizzy rang for more wine and sweet cake. The musician stretched his arms until the muscles in his back cracked, got up from the pianoforte, and ambled over to join the ladies.

'We'll sleep well tonight, shan't we, Charlotte?' remarked Lizzy. 'I feel better than in months. What a tonic this evening has been! We must repeat this entertainment every night while we are grass widows. That is, of course, if Herr Rosenstein will be kind enough to oblige us. He is here to mend Pemberley's instruments, not to amuse a gaggle of women and children.'

'I assure you the pleasure has been shared, Mrs Darcy,' said Herr Rosenstein. 'I miss the company of children when away from home.'

'Forgive me – I have been remiss in my enquiries,' said Lizzy. 'Have you and your wife children of your own? In fact, I am presuming too much, advancing too fast; I do not even know whether you are married.'

Charlotte felt a rustle along her nerve-endings as she listened for his answer: 'I am not married, and I have no children. I have lodgings in the ancient town of Salzburg, but they are bachelor quarters, and I go whenever I can to the home of my elder sister and her husband outside town, in a very pretty part of the country. They have five children, the eldest a boy of twelve. Spending time there is a relief given that so much of my work is – is the word cerebral? It demands devotion to the unseen. Certainly, it is invisible to the eye, if not the ear.'

'But surely your work is far from invisible, Herr Rosenstein,' said Charlotte, attributing her fresh sense of ease to the excellent Rhenisch the Pemberley wine steward had produced. 'Did your father not build Miss Darcy's harpsichord? Where would we be without those who produce the instruments with which we make music?'

'Indeed, Frau Collins. But I wrestle not only with horsehair and wood: I am also a composer. And are you, one who plays the pianoforte, not yourself struck by the transitory nature of music? That the air or song you play or sing exists only as long as you perform it, and there are ears to hear it?'

'But surely the melody lingers in the mind, in the same way as the words of a favourite verse. Memory is the friend, the keeper if you will, of music here.'

'Then you are arguing my case. What we do is akin to creating invisible furnishings for the mind and soul.'

'This is too deep for me,' cried Lizzy. 'Pray tell us of the new musical works coming out of Europe. And explain why our Teutonic friends seem to dominate the world of music. Mr Darcy says the Germans outshine us all.'

Conversation turned to opera and the theatre, subjects

to which Charlotte could contribute little. She listened ruefully as Herr Rosenstein described his travels in Europe, the great concert halls and opera houses he had visited, the performances he had witnessed, musicians he had met. She was quite ashamed of her own narrow education, as he named cities that for her were no more than places on schoolroom maps blurred by time, and spoke of oratorios, symphonies, and concertos she had neither heard, nor heard of.

Listening to her friend's responses and questions, she reflected, not without some pain, that marriage had broadened Elizabeth's horizons; Mr Darcy had been generous in throwing his resources open to expand a mind eager to stretch. Her education had been supplemented in numerous ways, and she had drunk it all in thirstily.

Charlotte's thoughts drifted to her own spouse, and how little a few years at Oxford had been able to do for a young man raised by a father who had revelled in his own ignorance and rigidity. Habits of diffidence had made it impossible for Mr Collins to furnish an inferior mind with new ideas and principles, much less bold ones, and her heart squeezed for her husband, so eternally dependent on the approval of those he considered his superiors.

How very different was this young musician. Herr Rosenstein's standing, in English society at least, might be close to that of a servant or a tradesman, but his education, in life, as well as at the hands of tutors and universities, outstripped that of most gentlemen Charlotte had met. He spoke with an ease and verve that reflected confidence in his own abilities to form impressions and rely on his opinions, while retaining the ability to communicate these impressions and opinions to listeners without appearing to lecture.

The fire had almost gone out, the wine and tea had all been drunk, and the three of them were yawning luxuriantly by the time they retired to their respective quarters. But not before Mrs Darcy, pressing his success with the children, asked their new companion to join them for meals in the future, an invitation Charlotte found herself hoping would be productive of more such pleasant encounters.

CHAPTER XI

CHARLOTTE SLEPT DEEPLY AND DREAMLESSLY, but woke early and restless long before the rest of the household was stirring. She threw open the shutters of her room to a morning of thin gold sunshine, with mist rising like smoke from the lake and river. The early light made the wet grasses sparkle brilliantly, and she found she could not bear to be indoors. She dressed without summoning the maid allotted her, then snatched up a Kashmir shawl Lizzy had passed on to her: soft and sumptuous, it was altogether too fine a garment for a clergyman's wife, but the colour – a light sky-blue – had sat uneasily with Mrs Darcy's dark eyes, whereas it suited Charlotte's to perfection, bringing out a hint of pink in her complexion.

She wrapped it around her shoulders and pattered down the grand staircase, helping herself to a piece of fruit from one of the elaborate dishes that ornamented the imposing entrance hall. The front doors were still forbiddingly closed, and she did not want to summon someone to unlock them, so she headed towards the more utilitarian quarters of the house, finding an escape via the simple expedient of unlatching a tradesmen's entrance close to the vast sculleries.

Once outside, she was drawn to the lake, the fountains not yet playing on a watery surface that exactly mimicked the sky, only heavier in its stillness. The mist was still rising up in twists from the water, dissolving into the air. Charlotte stood for a long time, not quite certain what it was she was watching; but she knew the ease with which she breathed was not entirely due to the freshness of the air, or the vistas along the slopes of the long valley in which the estate stood, or the resounding shouting of birds.

And then she became aware that one of the birds' songs was too melodious to be entirely natural, its notes speaking of human breath; it was a musical instrument, some sort of pipe, that she could hear. She walked in the direction of the sound, but it was deceptive; sometimes it sank beneath the chatter of nature, sometimes it called from the left, then the right. At moments, it sounded so close she would turn in a circle, puzzled not to be able to see the source; at other times, it faded into the distance.

Her pursuit led her towards the upper and wilder part of the garden, through arboretums and along hedged paths, and eventually up rock steps shaded by mature chestnut trees. A gloomy grotto did not tempt, but as she crested the ridge on which it stood, she saw spread before her a vast maze. The sound of the piping was now tantalisingly close.

Charlotte advanced down the slope towards the entrance to the maze. The trimmed edges of box rose high above her head, but the sun glittered on the leaves, and the overall impression was enticing rather than daunting. Wondering if she should be leaving a trail of breadcrumbs or pebbles, she stepped inside, and began to work her way towards the centre, encouraged by the continuing cascade of notes.

She took a few wrong turns, finding herself trapped in blind ends that made her impatient and slightly anxious. It became imperative to find the source of the music, but she did not consider why, other than as an object to her journey. As she turned back from one dead end to seek another route, the angle of the early rays revealed footprints in the dewy path. By following these, as well as the music, the sound of which was growing stronger and more compelling by the minute, Charlotte navigated herself closer to the heart of the maze.

One more turn, then a slide through a narrow opening in the hedge – and there, on a bench in a small chamber like that in the epicentre of a snail shell, sat Herr Rosenstein. He had his recorder at his lips, fingers marching up and down its wooden stem.

He did not cease playing, or make any concession to greeting other than to slide sideways, a wordless invitation to Charlotte to sit. She did so, the narrowness of the bench obliging her to seat herself close enough to him that she could hear the breaths he snatched between notes, feel the emanation of effort coming from his body as he swayed slightly to the music. The muscles of his arms worked under the fine muslin of his shirt, and his fingers, although moving faster than the eye could see, did not blur, but rained down like fine ivory hammers.

Charlotte found that watching his hands obliged her to stare sideways at the man himself, so she closed her eyes once again and immersed herself in the sounds he was drawing from his recorder, in the rose-gold glow of the sun filtering through her eyelids, in the fainter accompaniment of birdsong. And still the notes flowed, busy, swift, almost too much so, their pressing impulsion making Charlotte's ribs ache slightly, as if she had climbed a hill too fast.

She had no idea how much time had passed before silence fell. And stretched. Several times, she opened her mouth to speak, to launch into courtesies and commonplaces, remark on the beauty of the music or the surroundings, and each time she remained quiet. The birds went on chanting dizzily.

Herr Rosenstein felt no urge to commence conversation either. He took a handkerchief from his pocket, and polished the mouthpiece of the pipe. Charlotte felt a flush rising from her bosom to her neck, and unfurled her shawl. Still they did not speak.

Then he put the recorder back to his lips, and began to play again, and it was the melody from the Mozart sonata he had played for her on the piano in the schoolroom. This time, unadorned, its purity was paramount. Charlotte found herself welling with a sensation so strange, piercing, and unfamiliar, it was not until hours later that she identified it as joy. It was certainly not something she had ever expected or anticipated in her life; since Tom's death, she had not even courted the notion of happiness, content simply to endure.

And now speech became impossible. Words could

supply no sequel to the music, the sun on her face, the gold and green of the fresh garden, the softness of the shawl sliding down her shoulders. In the distance, a plume of water burst into vision between the trees, scattering silver-blue against blue: the lake fountains had been set in motion.

Still without having said one word, they took this as their cue to rise and leave the small enclosure that cupped them both. The paths of the maze were too narrow to allow them to walk side by side, and Charlotte had in any case no sense of how to find her way out. Herr Rosenstein went first, making turns with an ease that suggested long familiarity, and led them to the exit without hesitation. Here he offered her his arm, and they made their way back towards the house, still in silence.

Yet there was nothing uncomfortable between them: they both paused at the same moment to watch the force of the fountains throw mercury beads into the air, the breeze blowing the spray so that they both felt a faint wetness on their faces; after a few minutes, they resumed their strolling at the same moment. Their steps matched as they gained on the vast house, with its elegant proportions. Coneys nibbled at the turf, their white scuts bouncing as they hopped away, leaving the guarding of the house to watchful stone lions. They stopped one last time to watch a blackbird alight on the head of the statue of a nymph, survey the lawn for breakfast, then supply them with a dazzling coda of song.

They entered the house, which was now beginning

to stir as fires were lit and pitchers carried, via the same tradesmen's door Charlotte had used to make her earlier escape. The clatter of feet and basins, the scents of porridge and bacon emanating from the kitchen, broke the spell of a morning in which only music – bird, fountain, flute – could speak. Charlotte suddenly felt the urgent need to say something, especially as they were about to part ways in a dwelling so large she was uncertain as to when she would next see her companion. He turned to her at the foot of the stairs, and bowed. And all she could manage was a reciprocal curtsey. It had to suffice.

A little later, in the chapel, with only herself and Mrs Darcy in the balcony above the servants, she looked for him to no avail.

'Does Herr Rosenstein never attend household prayers?' she asked Lizzy as they repaired to the dining room for breakfast afterwards.

'My dear Charlotte, the man is a Jew, like the rest of his family,' answered her friend. 'Did you not realise? He cannot attend any Christian ritual.'

Charlotte was confounded. If she tried to remember what she knew about the tribe of Israel, she could think only of the patriarchs and prophets of the Old Testament, and fleeting impressions of cartoons of swarthy, bearded men in the news-sheets. A vague memory stirred of a play by Mr Shakespeare.

'I do not believe I have ever met a Jew before. I am not entirely sure what that means,' she told Lizzy.

'They do not believe in the triune God, but in the deity of the Old Testament,' said Lizzy. 'They are a clannish lot, I understand, and use the Hebrew tongue for their prayers, no matter where they hail from. Mr Darcy has visited some of their homes on his travels abroad, and he says they eat no pork.'

Charlotte was to receive proof of this with her own eyes when Herr Rosenstein joined them by invitation at breakfast shortly thereafter. He greeted the ladies with courtesy and kind enquiries as to their health, received coffee gratefully, and eschewed bacon and sausage, confining himself to smoked herring and boiled eggs. He also refrained from any mention of his morning performance in the heart of the maze, or Charlotte's finding him there. She, meanwhile, was too taken with contemplation of the new mystery of his religion to find this omission in any way strange. She had a dozen questions to ask about what it meant to be a Jew by blood and faith, but did not know how to broach the topic.

Lizzy, however, had no such qualms: 'Herr Rosenstein, Mrs Collins did not understand that you are a Jew,' she announced. 'We impose still more upon your good nature with our impertinence; we may now ask questions of both a musical and theological nature.'

The musician fixed his eyes on Charlotte, and she coloured. 'I have little understanding of the topic. A confession indeed for the wife of a Christian clergyman! I know our doctrines, of course; but when it comes to the other religions of our fellow men, especially those from foreign lands, I am at a loss. Does this mean you are heathen, Herr Rosenstein?'

As her words emerged, she blushed still deeper at

their clumsiness, but he laughed so heartily that she too began to smile, relieved that she had not given offence. 'It depends on what you mean by heathen, Frau Collins. The Jews share a holy book with their Christian fellows, and in our own homes and temples, we utter prayers and carry out rituals you might indeed find familiar. We are not godless barbarians, far from it. In truth, I doubt whether any tribe, no matter how remote from civilisation, is heathen in the true sense of the word. The most primitive community will have some one-eyed idol, some altar, that represents to them a moral code shared with, and enforced by, their fellows. While you might indeed fear for our souls, we Jews are nonetheless a pious people.'

Elizabeth declared that she needed more coffee if she was to listen to further disquisitions of a spiritual nature, and talk turned to fresh topics, but not before Herr Rosenstein had smiled at Charlotte and said, 'Did you really not know I was a Jew? I should have told you my name: Jacob.'

CHAPTER XII

THE NEXT DAY, LAURA ASKED her mother if they could visit the 'piano man' and watch him as he worked. Sarah was occupied with a book of martyrs she had ferreted from the housekeeper's parlour (and which would no doubt be productive of nightmares), but Laura hung about Charlotte, presenting her request with a combination of sweetness and steeliness her parent knew only too well.

Eventually, after extracting promises that they would visit briefly only if Herr Rosenstein permitted it, Charlotte took her daughter up to the schoolroom, and knocked with diffidence. Upon receiving the instruction to enter, she led Laura in, and presented her daughter's request – to witness him at work – with many apologies.

'We understand that we may not disturb you, that your labour takes all your powers of concentration and focus,' she explained. 'But Laura would not rest until she could see you at work, I fear.'

Herr Rosenstein smiled at her daughter and explained that their timing was perfect: he was almost finished with the schoolroom piano, and was about to embark on the infinitely more painstaking and time-consuming task of repairing Georgiana Darcy's harpsichord.

'But surely you will not want to be disturbed while undertaking such delicate work,' Charlotte said.

'Ah, this task involves long periods of waiting,' Herr Rosenstein replied. 'I have to glue the wood where it has cracked, in very small sections. Only once it is dry, can I risk first sanding the belly of the instrument with the finest of papers, then sealing with varnish, repainting, and then at last correcting the pitch of the strings. It will take great patience, and company will be much appreciated. I fear, though, that it will be too tedious for you and your daughter.'

Charlotte demurred, as did Laura, who was overcome with excitement at the prospect of exploring new quarters of Pemberley.

The trio repaired from the modest upper reaches of the house to the grander corridors that led to the family's private apartments. The damaged harpsichord stood in Georgiana's personal parlour, a sunny room with pale, fresh colours and modern furnishings, the emphasis on lightness and comfort. The vista from the windows stretched up the slope to the hanging woods above the house, the greenery outside echoed in the Chinese wallpaper with its repeating pattern of birds and foliage.

Charlotte took her daughter firmly by the hand, and began listing the strictures under which she would be allowed to remain in a room so pristine and populated by fragile ornaments. Laura was temporarily subdued until Herr Rosenstein began to unpack his box of tools, releasing the scents of linseed oil and cedar. Soon, she was assisting him in this important task, receiving an explanation for each piece she helped lift from the box. The materials of his trade released, he played a short piece by a Mr Bach – to test the keys, he explained – and Charlotte could hear that some of the lower notes were indeed sadly out of tune.

Next, he shuffled through an assortment of wood fragments and shavings as if dealing a pack of cards, repeatedly disappearing under the instrument to hold up samples to compare them with the fabric of the original. When he was satisfied, he lit a spirit lamp, and began concocting a glue mixture, the room now filling with more pungent and less pleasant smells. Once it was the consistency he desired, he began applying it in tiny amounts to leaves of wood he then inserted into the cracks in the damaged harpsichord.

Laura was fascinated at first, but she had an attention span consistent with her age and, after twenty minutes or so, she arranged herself on a divan in the corner. After earnestly explaining that she was *not* sleepy, she was just closing her eyes, she fell into the sudden boneless slumber available only to small children and kittens.

Once again, silence fell between the two adults and, once again, it was an easy one.

'Frau Collins,' said Herr Rosenstein, 'I could require that you entertain me as we wait for the glue to dry. I did warn you that this would be a tedious business. But you are equally welcome to choose a book from Fräulein Georgiana's personal collection, or simply to rest your eyes, as your daughter assures us she is doing.'

111

'I would happily entertain you, Herr Rosenstein,' said Charlotte. 'But truly, I know not how I could accomplish such a task. Last night, listening to you speak of your travels and experiences, I felt – not foolish exactly, but so narrow. My life has been such a limited one by your standards. Until my marriage I never left my parents' home in the small town of Meryton, except for one trip to London with my family – the occasion on which my father was knighted for his services to the Mayor. And this visit to Pemberley is the furthest I have ever been from my home in Kent. I have seen and done very little, you know.'

'But you run a household, you are a wife and help-meet to a clergyman, and a mother to two daughters,' he said. 'Surely this must expose you to all that is most rich in human experience?'

'I have never thought of my domestic life in those terms, I confess. Each day is similar to a skein of wool; I pick up one end and follow it through to the other, trying to wind it as neatly as possible, smoothing out burrs and knots.'

'You must remember, Frau Collins, that your life is as foreign, exotic even, to me as my life in Salzburg and Vienna would be to you. If you are so inclined, I would be grateful if you would recite the story of that life to me.'

Charlotte was both nonplussed and flattered. 'But where should I start? You surely cannot wish to hear of my childhood. I assure you that nothing of any import happened in those years.'

'Why not tell me about life in this village you speak

of? Is this where you met your husband? Was he part of your circle, a neighbour, perhaps? Someone you knew in childhood?'

Charlotte was silent for a moment, recalling her courtship – if one could call it that – by Mr Collins. Could she tell this new friend the entire truth – the very ordinary, but by no means edifying circumstances in which an English gentlewoman of straitened means had managed to attain a husband?

'My husband is cousin to Mrs Darcy, you know. Our families were neighbours in Hertfordshire, and she and I were intimate friends. I met him when he first visited her family.' She paused, remembering the voluble young man she had first met seven winters ago. She had not had the slightest inkling of what the future might hold then, not even the faintest specu- lation: she had assumed that as putative heir of the Bennet estate, he was present to establish some concil- iatory bond with his cousins.

But did the tale even begin there? Had it not started when Mr Bingley and his party had taken possession of Netherfield Park, a few miles distant from the town of Meryton, that same fateful winter? No dramatic event, and yet a tossed pebble that was to create ever-widening ripples throughout their small society, changing the course of the lives of the Misses Jane and Elizabeth Bennet, and spreading to lap at the edges of her own life.

Could she admit that her oldest and dearest friend, the lively and lovely Elizabeth Bennet, had been her husband's first matrimonial object? That in a different life, instead of presiding over Pemberley, Lizzy might have been a clergyman's wife, taking soup to the poor and mending clerical garb? For a moment, a sense of vertigo gripped her, as she imagined Lizzy in her place at Hunsford Parsonage, gliding through the rooms, ordering the pantry, instructing the servants. *In her place.* And where might she, Charlotte, be then? She would never have given birth to her children, to Tom. It did not bear contemplation.

It could even be considered that the beginning of her story, and the root of her troubles, lay in the fact that she, Charlotte, had been born a woman – a gentle-woman of impecunious means. This had never been a productive route for contemplation, and yet, if she was honest, perhaps her current situation stemmed from that one significant day back in Meryton, that moment she had stood in the lane between Netherfield Park and Lucas Lodge, experiencing all the helplessness of her situation as a single woman with no prospects. Perhaps the spark of her present history had been set at that moment of frustration.

She looked over at her sleeping daughter, her hair the colour of ripe barley in the light streaming through the window, then glanced at Herr Rosenstein, trying to discern any trace of mockery in his face. But his expression remained open and sincere. She could not of course tell him all – but perhaps she could tell him some of her story.

She took a deep breath and cast her mind back seven years. It was as good a place as any to begin.

CHAPTER XIII

CHARLOTTE WAS TIRED TO THE bone. Tired of the universally acknowledged truism: that a single woman of no great fortune must be in want of a life, at the beck and call of all who might find her momentarily useful, a blank template waiting for the impress of others. Standing in a lane she had walked since childhood, a shuttlecock batted between the lives of others, she struggled to master sensations of both entrapment and aimlessness.

And the day had started out so promisingly. Mrs Bennet and her younger daughters were to visit Netherfield Park, where Miss Bennet and Lizzy were in residence until such time as the former had recovered from a cold caught after riding over in inclement weather, and the latter was satisfied that her nursing was no longer necessary. Charlotte had been invited to join their party, and her father and brothers, who were keen to see the horses and dogs of the Netherfield gentlemen, had walked over with her to Longbourn shortly after breakfast. Charlotte and her father, Sir William, had squeezed into the Bennets' carriage along with Mrs Bennet and her two youngest daughters, Kitty and Lydia, while the Lucas boys set off down the lane on foot with whoops of encouragement, and were soon left behind.

Netherfield Park was only a few miles distant, and they arrived at the handsome modern house in no time. Charlotte had never been inside before, and was happy to look around at new sights and objects of interest, and admire the furnishings and paintings. The Netherfield party welcomed them with varying degrees of cordiality, and initial bows, curtseys, and compliments were dispensed with graciously enough. Mrs Bennet was soon taken upstairs to see her elder daughters, while the gentlemen exchanged remarks concerning the rotation of crops and the hunting season. These were hardly enlivening topics, especially for the young ladies present, but their turn came soon enough. Sir William asked for a tour of the library, and Mr Darcy was obliged to lead him from the room. Charlotte's brothers, still panting from their walk, took this as their chance to escape to the stables, and more socially interesting conversation could begin, especially once the younger Bennet sisters began a planned attack on Mr Bingley, clamouring for a ball. To this he made courteous noises of agreement, while stipulating that they should wait until their eldest sister had fully regained her health.

The party was a large one, which increased once Mrs Bennet and Lizzy had descended from Jane's quarters, and Mr Darcy returned to join the company, though without seeming to take any pleasure in it, which intrigued Charlotte. She took it upon herself to engage him with a query as to whether he had much leisure for reading, and although he replied unsmilingly, there was no disdain in his tone: 'I do not read as much as I might wish. I feel I must remain informed of developments at home and abroad, and rely on newspapers, especially when in the country.'

Encouraged, Charlotte responded, 'I seldom read the papers, as my father provides us with a daily digest. I never know whether print is his friend or foe, as reading the news seems to aggravate as much as enlighten him.'

Mr Darcy had no opportunity to respond. There was a slight commotion as the parlourmaid bobbed in the doorway. 'Excuse me, madam,' she addressed the lady of the house, 'but Lady Lucas's Jenny is here with a message, madam, to say that Miss Lucas is required at home right away.'

Mrs Bennet shot Charlotte, who was clenching her hands in her lap, a look that combined shrewdness with malice. 'A shame you have to leave us. I hope your mother is quite well?'

Charlotte wanted to scream, stamp her feet, and throw china across the room. Mrs Bennet knew perfectly well that she was being called home to deal with some housekeeping emergency, and not the sudden frailty of a mother generally as strong as a carthorse. 'She was in good health this morning,' she murmured, rising to her feet with as much dignity as she could muster.

And now she was storming homewards, muttering bitter words under her breath. Her brothers, who had no interest or stake in these matters, were free to stay and eat nuncheon and play with the puppies in the stableyard, but she had to hurry home because of some crisis with the day's baking or brewing. Not for the first time, Charlotte cursed the swingeing unfairness of the lot that made her a woman.

She was too angry to pay attention to the condition of the road, until a puddle that stretched the width of the thoroughfare confronted her with a new problem: in her flight, and in the servant's confusion, she had left her pattens behind, and was well on the way to ruining her shoes. What had possessed her to wear them instead of her more serviceable boots? And now she would have to go back to Netherfield. She swung round, irritation compounding anger and hastening her steps.

As she passed back down the driveway and slipped past the house, hoping to collect her pattens from the servants via a back entrance, she caught Mrs Bennet's nasal voice through an open window: 'I fancy she was wanted about the mince-pies.' Charlotte experienced that frisson of exposure felt when realising that one is the topic of overheard conversation, and her dismay grew at the words that followed: 'For my part, Mr Bingley, *I* always keep servants that can do their own work; *my* daughters are brought up differently. But the Lucases are very good sorts of girls, I assure you.'

Mr Bingley endeared himself to Charlotte forever with the words, 'Miss Lucas seems a very pleasant young woman,' and she relaxed momentarily. But Mrs Bennet was far from done: 'It is a pity she is not handsome! You must own that she is very plain. Her own mother has often said so, and envied me Jane's beauty.'

Charlotte's mouth went dry as Mrs Bennet continued to canvass the topic of her, Charlotte's, plainness, in the hearing of all the company present. Given that she had no hope of attracting either the admiration of the gentlemen or the friendship of Mr Bingley's sisters, she found Mrs Bennet's insistence on her lack of physical charms doubly unkind. The beauty of her own daughters surely made such a stratagem unnecessary.

Her skin crawled with shame as she stood powerless beneath the open window. Still worse, Jenny came bustling round from the back of the house at that moment, clutching Charlotte's pattens, and found her listening to others speaking of her, always a moment of awkwardness. It was hard to tell which of them was more uncomfortable, and, as they set off on the three-mile walk towards Lucas Lodge, Jenny's expostulations of 'Oh, Miss!' did not help.

It was not just the exertion of swift walking that had sweat trickling down Charlotte's sides: sheer mortification and mounting anger contributed. She had no delusions and harboured no false hopes: years of watching the Bennet sisters grow and bloom alongside her, of seeing the way people's eyes slid past her to alight on Jane and Lizzy, had cured her of any propensity to vanity, any idle hopes of enchanting others with the expedient of a pretty face. But to have the contrast rubbed in by an idle, mean-spirited woman of little intelligence, to be spoken of in such terms before a gathering of near-strangers who represented the first new company she had met in a long while, was truly galling. The presence of the maidservant meant Charlotte did not even have the luxury of breaking sticks or shouting her rage in the privacy of the lane.

She had never before felt so helpless in her humiliation. And as Mrs Bennet's words replayed in her mind, Charlotte's rage grew. Somewhere, somehow, she swore to herself, she would have her turn. She would make something of herself. Her success would also be her vengeance. Better still, she would take something precious from a woman towards whom she had only ever shown courtesy and affability, who, as her mother's dearest friend, stood in the place of an aunt to her.

She came to a halt as the careless words revealing her own parent's disloyalty repeated in her head. That stung the most: the vision of her mother bewailing her lack of beauty to others. She had somehow hoped that the maternal eye would at least be partial, if not downright blind, in her case. She clenched her lids to halt tears, and muttered something about a stone in her shoe to the anxious Jenny.

In that ordinary country lane, as familiar as the back of her own hand, Charlotte stood in despair – and then another thought came to give relief. Somehow she would escape. She would go somewhere – she knew not where or how – where she was not plain Miss Lucas, a spinster of the parish of Meryton, an object of speculation and pity to her neighbours, a source of anxiety to her family. How this was to be achieved, she had no conception; but she refused to allow the practical difficulties of such a plan to interfere with the momentary respite the thought of it granted.

CHAPTER XIV

FOR SEVERAL DAYS AFTER THE excursion to Netherfield Park, there was little intercourse between the Lucas and the Bennet families, with gusting rain keeping them housebound. This suited Charlotte, who was not yet sure she could face Mrs Bennet and keep a firm rein on her temper. But Lizzy soon sent her friend a note advising of a new addition to the family party: the mysterious future master of Longbourn, the unknown but heartily detested Mr Collins, had taken it upon himself to pay his relatives a visit. This young man had recently taken orders and been granted a handsome living in Kent, life events that had prompted him to pacific thoughts of his distant family. There was much speculation about his motives, which, in a letter to Mr Bennet, he had hinted involved making some conciliatory gesture towards his 'fair cousins'. All in all, the visit provided some interest, and Elizabeth was eager for Charlotte to join them in a walk to Meryton.

The party from Longbourn fetched Charlotte, greeting her all at once in a fashion to which she was accustomed, so that she filtered out Lydia and Kitty's halloos and impatient demands that she hurry along, reserving her attention for Lizzy, Jane, and their escort. A stately and self-important young man, he seemed unable to stop speaking. Words on every possible commonplace flowed in a steady stream, so there were none of the awkward silences that might otherwise attend a group of distant relatives making each other's acquaintance for the first time – especially in circumstances as delicate as these: the interloper and the cousins he would disinherit. Lizzy and Charlotte were able to catch up with their news under the cover of Mr Collins's enumerative praise of all his surroundings; by the time they reached Meryton, they expected to hear him congratulate them on the dirt in the main street.

Charlotte was intrigued as to whether the rumours that he had come to pay court to one of his cousins were true, and it was with some amusement that she thought she discerned a particular interest in Lizzy on the part of the young man. He would have been better off setting his sights on Mary, the most studious of the five Bennet sisters, but it seemed that Lizzy was his object, although she was as yet apparently unaware of her prolix cousin's intentions.

This surfeit of fresh society, both the clergyman cousin and the grander party at Netherfield Park, led to an unusual number of social engagements in and around Meryton. The next fortnight was marked by supper parties, card games, and dinners, culminating in a ball at Netherfield Park. Over this period, Mr Collins's pursuit of Lizzy became more and more apparent, including to the somewhat harassed object of his attentions. At the same time, his habit of lecturing all and sundry on moral matters, his constant deferential references to his patroness, Lady Catherine de Bourgh of Rosings, and the endless volume of speech that emerged from his lips, endeared him to no one except Mrs Bennet, who anticipated soon claiming him as a son-in-law.

Matters came to a head the morning after the ball at Netherfield. With her sister Maria taking her turn to prepare the household's loaves and carry them to the bakehouse, Charlotte was to spend the morning with the Bennets, something of a tradition for her and Lizzy; they considered no ball complete until they had sufficiently talked it over the following day. Hardly had she handed her wrap to the servant who admitted her to the house when Lydia flew into the vestibule and seized upon her with a whoop: 'Oh Charlotte, I am so glad you are come – what sport we have here today! Mr Collins has made Lizzy an offer, and she will not have him, and we are all at sixes and sevens.'

Charlotte was not even able to respond before it was the turn of Mrs Bennet, in an operatic state of distress and dishevelment, to fall upon her, begging her to persuade her stubborn friend to see sense and comply with the wishes of her family. The next minute, an agitated Lizzy hurried in to greet her friend, followed by Jane, ever desirous of keeping the peace between her mother and sister.

Mrs Bennet was not to be comforted: 'Aye, there she comes, caring nothing for the rest of us,' she cried. 'Mr Collins may turn us all out onto the streets when your father dies, but this does not concern you. I tell you, Miss Lizzy, if you take it into your head to keep rejecting every offer of marriage like this, you will never get a husband at all – and I am sure I do not know who is to keep you when your father is dead. I know I shall not be able to.'

These charges against her delinquent daughter were followed by further lamentations on the state of her poor nerves. Jane, with soothing clucks, offered to bathe her distraught parent's temples with lavender water, which took Mrs and Miss Bennet from the room, leaving Charlotte free at last to attend to her friend. It was a moment of some import; she had no more faith than Lizzy in the sincerity of Mr Collins's new-found attachment, but it was the first time her friend had received an offer of matrimony and, as such, it was a mark of some distinction, however unwished-for.

Lizzy now gave her friend a more detailed account of the morning's events. Mr Collins had requested the honour of a private interview with Elizabeth immediately after breakfast, and had launched into a proposal almost as lengthy as it was unwanted. He had canvassed the strong likelihood of Lady Catherine's approval, the honour he did Lizzy in throwing open to her the connection with Rosings, and promised never to reproach her for the smallness of her portion – 'that one thousand pounds in the four per cents that is all you will inherit from your mother.' It was only towards the end of this speech that he remembered to assure his intended of the violence of his affections. Even in the awkwardness of this unexpected crisis, neither woman could restrain herself from smiling as they contemplated the 'violence' of Mr Collins's imaginary attachment.

What had followed owed more to theatrical farce than the pains of thwarted love: Mrs Bennet, upon congratulating Mr Collins, was horrified to hear that Lizzy had not yet accepted his hand, and a family hullabaloo broke out that culminated in a scene in Mr Bennet's library. Here Lizzy's father, once the ins and outs of the matter had been explained to him, declared to his recalcitrant daughter that a painful choice lay before her: if she refused Mr Collins's offer, her mother would have no more to do with her; but if she accepted, she would henceforth be no daughter of his.

It was at this delicate domestic point that Charlotte had arrived, and now she was to witness the final act: as soon as Mrs Bennet reappeared, the rebuffed suitor stalked in to withdraw his application for the hand of her daughter. Lizzy slid out the room, but Charlotte was detained by Mr Collins, who enquired after every member of her family with great determination and minute particularity. Once he resorted back to the matter at hand, curiosity impelled her to linger as the clergyman first announced his intention to be silent on the subject forevermore, then launched into a speech defending his honour and intentions, and resentfully describing his resignation to a disappointment that was receding as he contemplated Lizzy's headstrong and wilful qualities.

The rest of the day passed uncomfortably enough; Mrs Bennet could not refrain from peevish remarks on the ingratitude of her second daughter, and Mr Collins, lacking the finer feelings that might have led an unsuccessful suitor to absent himself from the family circle, hung about pointedly speaking to Lizzy barely at all, while assiduously engaging Charlotte in conversation at every turn. It was not the first time that Charlotte, one of life's natural peacekeepers, found herself acting as a necessary buffer between hostile factions, and her civil and mild responses were welcomed not only by Mr Collins, but the rest of the family as well, most notably Lizzy.

When she left for home, her friend pressed her hand with more than usual fervour: 'Thank goodness you were here, Charlotte. I do not know what we would have done without your cool head and warm heart. And it is a mercy we are dining with your family the day after tomorrow, as Mr Collins shows no sign of cutting short his visit. I know I will be able to rely on you to entertain him as best you can.'

At first, the dinner for which the two families assembled at Lucas Lodge several days later did not seem to be a propitious event. In the circumstances, the awkwardness between members of the Bennet party was only to be expected. Jane made sure she was close to Lizzy at all times, while Mrs Bennet subjected the latter to a continuous fusillade of bitter looks, sighs, head-shaking, and chest-clutching. Lydia and Kitty were no help; they were practically exploding with glee at the expense of their cousin and sister. Mary spoke only to utter platitudes borrowed from moral tomes, and Lizzy's usual ebullience was muted.

Charlotte exchanged a few words with her friend, enough to ascertain that Lizzy was undaunted by the decision she had made. Charlotte marvelled again at the blithe confidence the combination of youth and beauty bestowed. Lizzy showed no regret whatsoever at having rejected Mr Collins's admittedly precipitate and crass proposal; and while it seemed unlikely that he had formed any real attachment to her in the few days he had known her, there was her family to consider. It surprised Charlotte that the prospect of securing their future at Longbourn had not tempted her friend, but it was clear that Lizzy accepted as her due that her future would hold further – and more attractive – offers of matrimony.

She had already arranged the table settings so that Lizzy and Mr Collins were seated as far apart as possible, but it was almost as necessary to keep him away from Mrs Bennet, who kept gazing at him dolefully and dabbing her eyes. So she had placed him by her own side and, as the fish followed the soup, she made an effort to engage him in conversation, finding him unusually subdued. Occasionally, he burst out into feverish commentary on topics such as the weather and the state of the roads, but would then lapse into silence mid-sentence as he remembered that there was no longer any need to praise his environs.

She studied him more closely. He was not unpleasing to look at – in repose, and unmarred by his habitual expression of fawning, his face was unobjectionable. He was one of the few men she had met who was taller than herself. Even Mr Bingley and Mr Wickham, the newly commissioned officer with whom the younger Bennet girls were infatuated, had to raise their eyes to greet her.

His dress was neat, and there was no suggestion of slovenliness. In circumstances in which he might have been tempted to dull his senses with wine, he was drinking temperately. His was a respectable profession, and he already held a living. Everyone in Meryton knew that he had the backing of a powerful and wealthy benefactor in the form of Lady Catherine de Bourgh.

A bubble of possibility rose in Charlotte's brain. Up until now, on their previous encounters, she had drawn his attentions away from Lizzy out of habitual good-naturedness and a gift for managing the more turbulent eddies of social intercourse. The man had come to their neighbourhood openly in search of a wife. His pride was wounded and in need of a salve. Perhaps. Just perhaps . . .

But she was no flirt, having had neither the opportunity nor the inclination to practise her wiles on the opposite sex, or to develop habits of playful chatter. She listened a little more closely to Mr Collins's habitual babble, the recitation of the wonders of Rosings, the graciousness of Lady Catherine, the superiority of the pigeon pie now being served: 'I erred on my first evening at Longbourn, when I asked which of my fair cousins had prepared the dinner I ate there.

I believe Mrs Bennet was very offended at my blunder, although I had only the best of intentions. Miss Lucas, will I give offence if I ask if your hand played any part in the making of this most excellent dish?'

Charlotte reassured him that as the creator of the pie, she appreciated his compliment. Something about his demeanour suggested that while only his pride was injured by Lizzy's frank and final rejection of his proposal – he might be mortified, but he was by no means heartbroken – there was a strain of real sadness or moral bewilderment in his makeup. His understanding was not sharp, but malice did not seem to constitute any part of it. Nor did he appear to have an ungovernable temper – his current relations with the Bennets would have been untenable otherwise.

She made a decision. If this man was likely to respond to anything, it would be simple kindness. She set to asking questions about his education and parish with as much warmth as she could muster. Soon she found that for all his incessant speaking, he was unused to the balm of attentive listening. Little was required of her beyond the occasional gentle prompt, encouraging smiles, and nods.

The effect was marked: he blossomed, sitting more upright, returning her smiles, paying her the occasional clumsy compliment, his embarrassment at sitting at table with a woman who had spurned his advances only a few days earlier all but forgotten.

Charlotte was surprised at the success of her strategy, which had arisen out of a vague impulse rather than any sense of calculation. And although she was not a vindictive woman, and was by no means sure of her prize, she could not help thinking, with angry pleasure, of Mrs Bennet's reaction should Mr Collins turn his matrimonial ambitions in her direction.

It had not yet occurred to her – although it soon would – that such a turn of events would lead to her one day replacing Mrs Bennet as mistress of Longbourn. She, Charlotte, who was so very plain.

CHAPTER XV

AFTER DINNER, ONCE THE GENTLEMEN had rejoined the ladies, Charlotte realised that with Mr Collins's visit to Hertfordshire rapidly coming to an end, she had scant opportunities to fix herself in his remembrance – she could not hope for more at this stage. Thus, when the goodnights were said, she hinted that her father might enjoy Mr Collins's company at breakfast the next morning, should he be able to spare the time; and while he made no firm promises – he was still at the disposal of the Bennets – his face lit up at the prospect.

The next morning, Charlotte dressed for battle and waited at her window. To her relief, she saw the tall figure of the clergyman approaching in the distance. And so it was that by the time he reached the lane that led to Lucas Lodge, she was waiting to be discovered, in her best sprigged poplin day dress and bonnet with matching trim, her basket filled with late russets, mushrooms, and the last of the autumn blooms, a pleasing picture of wholesome English country bountifulness. Mr Collins fortunately did not question the coincidence that led her there; he was too relieved to find an opportunity to speak privately to Miss Lucas had fallen so easily his way.

To Charlotte's astonishment, almost before she could finish greeting him and commenting on the fairness of the morning, he had embarked on praises of her person and nature that lent themselves to one interpretation only. She was all that was amiable and delightful; she had the qualities of a most desirable helpmeet in life; her domestic talents and good sense were remarked upon and admired throughout the neighbourhood; and in short (although it was clear he knew not the meaning of this word), he begged the honour of offering those talents an opportunity to be cherished and to shine as the chief ornament of his home.

Charlotte listened to what was the first and would surely be the last proposal she would ever receive with no small degree of emotional tumult. Mostly, she felt relief: she had nursed modest hopes after the promising interest and warmth which Mr Collins had shown her at dinner the previous day. But she had not dared imagine that he would propose to two women – close friends at that – within almost as many days.

Having heard the substance of his offer to Lizzy, she was also relieved that her friend's rejection of him had somewhat altered his line of attack: his speech was less fluent than usual, and real anxiety about another 'nay' gave his words a sorely needed gloss of humility. While he went on to lay out the benefits of his association with Rosings and Lady Catherine de Bourgh as an inducement no right-thinking woman could resist, he refrained from alluding to the size (and he had to know it was pitifully small) of Miss Lucas's portion, and remembered to make repeated claims to ardent admiration. She did not begrudge his praises, which included at least three references to her preserves, and several more to her light hand with pastry; after all, what more did he know of her? Mr Collins was not a sensible man, but he showed sense in recognising that marriage to a woman with good housekeeping skills promised future domestic tranquillity, if not actual harmony. Charlotte had little doubt that in this respect, she could boast, at least to herself, that the advantages offered by the match did not lie all on his side.

As soon as her suitor paused, which admittedly he did not do for some time, she accepted his offer with as much speed as was consistent with modesty. Fortunately, he was looking neither for declarations of devotion from her side, nor speeches about her good fortune in receiving such a propitious offer. For him, it was enough that she accepted his proposal without hesitation, and in terms that left no room for doubt.

The newly engaged couple took several turns up and down the lane, a little unsure about how to proceed, until Charlotte invited the man with whom she was to spend the rest of her natural life to join her family at breakfast. This reminded the successful suitor that his next step was to gain parental approval for the impending match. However, on this score, he told her that he had no anxiety, and as they approached the house, he pressed Charlotte to name the day that would secure his perennial happiness. She demurred for the moment, while making it clear that she had no intention of delaying the happiness to which he laid claim. She had little interest in a prolonged court-ship or further declarations of imaginary ardour; her aim was to secure a future free of anxiety and material want, and, short of some disaster befalling her new fiancé, that future now seemed assured.

Mr Collins lost no time in applying to Sir William and Lady Lucas for their consent, and the habitual length of his speeches enabled them to make the transition from astonishment to delight by the time he paused for breath. While innocent of Mr Collins's interest in their daughter, and somewhat unflatteringly surprised that she should have attracted his addresses, their surprise only enlarged their pleasure at the news of the engagement. They had no intention of raising any objections or asking any difficult questions, and bestowed their blessings upon the union with almost indecent haste. The house filled with cries of congrat-ulation, joy, and no small amount of relief: Sir William could give his eldest daughter little fortune, and her advancing age had been a source of growing anxiety for them all.

Charlotte suspected that her mother was calcu-lating how much longer Mr Bennet might yet live with more interest than ever before. Her father mean-while had visions of himself and his good lady making their appearance at court, something he announced his intentions of doing as soon as Mr Collins took possession of the Longbourn estate. Maria was entranced at the thought of what opportunities might now fall to her, and her younger sisters anticipated being able to come out and take their share of the pleasures of social intercourse sooner than they had dared hope. Her brothers were relieved of their fears of their sister dying an old maid, which they celebrated with boisterous halloo-ing throughout the house. Charlotte did not think she had ever before united her family in this much happiness, and there was comfort to be taken in this.

Having achieved her object, she had time to reflect. She was tolerably composed, although there was a recurring tightness across her ribs. She felt as if she had flung herself across a river in spate, scrambling to the dubious safety of an unknown shore, with no way back across. She had no illusions concerning her future husband's declarations of love and devotion: while she did not suspect him of outright hypocrisy, she had already established that he felt, in almost all matters of the human heart, what he thought he ought to feel – or had been told to feel. He was predisposed to be in love because the patron to whom he was in thrall had advised him to marry. Lizzy's refusal had wounded his pride and spurred him on to achieve success elsewhere, and the glow of emotion he now felt stemmed no doubt from triumph rather than affection.

But she had calculated the risks as best she could. While thinking highly of neither men nor matrimony, she would be married, an avenue she had always considered her pleasantest preservative from want. There was no doubting that it was the only honourable provision for well-educated young women of small fortune, and that provision she had now gained, with neither the blush of first youth nor a fair face to act as inducements. She would have an establishment to call home, and to run according to her taste and her husband's purse – which was certainly, in this case, ample for her needs.

A new problem now arose: Mr Collins, both relieved and jubilant at the success of his proposal, was expected back at Longbourn for his last dinner with the family before his return to his duties at Hunsford. He was eager to burst the news upon his relatives, while Charlotte quailed at the thought of the consternation that would reign as a result, and most especially at the thought of Lizzy's response.

She valued her friend's good opinion, although not enough to sacrifice a matrimonial opportunity to maintain it – such high-minded delicacy was too fine a luxury – yet it gave her pain to consider that her conduct might sink her in Elizabeth's esteem. A difficult conversation with her friend lay ahead, and she wished to prepare for this, and communicate the news to Lizzy directly, before the rest of the neighbourhood heard it. She therefore charged Mr Collins with secrecy and, although reluctant to comply, he could not argue with the modesty of his affianced.

The next morning, Charlotte arrived at Longbourn for a tête-à-tête with her friend. While anticipating no great pleasure from the conversation, she knew her family would not keep her engagement secret for long, nor should they be constrained to do so. She broke the news to Elizabeth without further ado, who received it with such unguarded astonishment and dismay that Charlotte was momentarily caught between distress and anger at her friend's lack of decorum. But it was no less than she had expected and indeed possibly deserved, and, for a few minutes, neither woman could look at the other. Lizzy, too, seemed ashamed, if not of her immediate response then of the visible pain it caused her old friend, and after her first expostulation of 'Engaged to Mr Collins! – why, this is impossible!' she caught at the reins of her disbelief and tried to utter the necessary congratulations.

Her stammered wishes for Charlotte's happiness gave the latter the strength to speak honestly, rather than pretend to the joy of a bride-to-be. To Elizabeth, she would not dissemble. 'I see what you must think of me,' she said. 'You must be very surprised, especially as only a few days ago, Mr Collins was wishing to marry you. But Eliza, I hope that upon reflection, you will understand what I have done. You know I am not romantic. I never have been. I ask only a comfortable home, and shall endeavour to do my part to ensure that whomever I share it with shall have no grounds on which to reproach me. Mr Collins may not be a star in the firmament of intelligent thought, but then neither am I; we know of no blemish or stain of disgrace on his character; and considering his connections and situation in life, I do not see that my chance of happiness is any less of a gamble than most take upon entering married life.'

Lizzy had by now gained control of her tongue, and

murmured agreement and further congratulations, but it was clear from her face, always expressive, that she was disappointed in and even repelled by her friend's choice, and doubted her prospects for future happiness. Charlotte understood that her response was driven by affection and concern – nothing less could have made her judgement bearable.

A small canker of resentment niggled, too. She, Charlotte, might be accused of disinterested calculation, but while she did not begrudge her friend her moral scruples, surely Lizzy could understand that her insistence on romance was a luxury available only to the young and the lovely?

For now, though, seeing the dismay and shock that marked Elizabeth's features, Charlotte's heart ached. Their friendship was a bright band that stretched back across otherwise unremarkable years, and she feared she had struck it a mortal blow. She reached out a hand as hoofbeats could be heard advancing up the driveway: 'That is my father. I asked him to visit your family to convey the news, but I wanted to speak to you first. I beseech you, Eliza, do not judge me too harshly. Try to understand why I have acted as I have. I believe I have been guided by prudence, not avarice, and shall do my best to make a good wife. Once I am married, I shall regret the loss of your companionship more than anything else.'

Her friend's eyes mirrored the tears in her own, and the young women exchanged an awkward embrace before Charlotte set off home, wishing to escape before Sir William could make any formal announcement.

Her father joined her back at Lucas Lodge a little later, mopping his brow. He had endured harsh treatment at the hands of Mrs Bennet, who insisted that he was mistaken in his announcement of his daughter's engagement, while Lydia had freely exclaimed, 'Good Lord! Sir William, how can you tell such a story? Do you not know Mr Collins made an offer to Lizzy?'

Charlotte had to smile at the thought of her father sitting through such abuse with his usual complaisance, and took comfort from the fact that Lizzy had corroborated his news, which she had been swift to follow with earnest compliments and congratulations. Jane, after a minute's surprise, had followed Lizzy in uttering good wishes, congratulating the proud father not only on the happiness that would surely follow, and the excellence of Mr Collins's character, but the convenient distance of Hunsford from London. This account of the generosity of the elder Bennet sisters cost Charlotte more pain than the frank disbelief and scorn of the mother and younger girls, and the rest of the morning passed in more tears than might be expected on the part of a woman newly affianced.

CHAPTER XVI

T HE LAST WEEKS OF HER maiden life were awkward ones. While preparing to leave all that was familiar and dear behind, Charlotte not only longed for the companionship of her friend, but for the blend of calm and spice the two eldest Bennet girls had provided her over many years. Yet Mrs Bennet could hardly tolerate the sight of her, so visits to Longbourn were not easy. It did not help that Lady Lucas, after years of enduring her friend's pointed remarks on the beauty of her own daughters, never lost the opportunity to call on Mrs Bennet to solicit congratulations on the good fortune of having a daughter well settled, steadfastly ignoring the sour looks and ungenerous remarks of her less lucky friend.

Far worse, while there was not exactly a coldness between herself and Lizzy, there existed a constraint that made the comfortable conversation and confidences of old impossible. This was most unwelcome at a time when Charlotte longed for reassurance and the cheerfulness of friends as she prepared to leave her home to live among strangers.

To further stir the currents of uncomfortable feeling, there was a fresh blight on the fortunes of the Bennet family. The Netherfield party had returned to London, bringing to an abrupt halt Mr Bingley's courtship of the eldest Bennet sister. While at first Jane and the rest of her family believed that this cessation of attention was temporary, a letter now arrived from Mr Bingley's sister suggesting something more serious. She wrote that she and her brother would not be returning to Netherfield Park that winter, and in terms that did not suggest that the acquaintance would be renewed.

Jane bore this blow with the steady sweetness and patience for which she was a byword, but one day, she admitted that her mother's constant bewailing of the fickleness of her suitor caused her immense pain.

This conversation took place while Jane and Lizzy were at Lucas Lodge, helping Charlotte sew garments for her trousseau and table- and bed-linens for her dowry chest. There was a great deal to finish before the wedding, and Charlotte, with her bridal costume to make, as well as the other new outfits and under-garments she would require as a newly married woman, was genuinely grateful for their aid. She, her mother, and Maria were sewing as fast as they could, as were some of the more solicitous ladies and housekeepers of the neighbourhood, but the elder Bennet sisters, Jane in particular, were known for their competent and speedy needlework.

To aid them in their labours, they were seated in the parlour with the best light, and Lady Lucas had once again solicited their compliments and congratu-lations – which were very good-naturedly given. She had then laid a hand on Jane's arm, but fortunately restricted herself to shaking her head and sighing, 'Ah Jane! A great pity indeed! And you such a beauty!'

After the proud maternal parent had quit the parlour, and Charlotte had earnestly thanked the Bennet sisters for their kind attendance and help, Jane had confessed that the outing was a relief, giving her brief respite from her mother's incessant grumbling at the cruelty of fate and young men. Charlotte, who had heard snatches on her brief visits to Longbourn, thought one might easily be mistaken in thinking that Mrs Bennet had been the one thrown over. But Jane was all fortitude: 'Mr Bingley shall be forgot, and we shall go on as before. Let me take it all in the best light possible, and endeavour to achieve a tranquil heart as soon as possible.'

Charlotte's needle stilled. The late-angled winter sun streaming through the windows made a nimbus of Miss Bennet's ringlets, creating an ethereal frame for her lovely features and roses-with-cream complexion. Gazing at Jane, the quintessential picture of feminine beauty, goodness, and diligence as she bent her long white neck over her sewing, flawless stitches flowing from her fingers, Charlotte could scarcely credit their reversal of fortune. By rights, it should have been Jane's trousseau they were preparing; that they should be assembling *her* wedding costumes and linens – she who had neither beauty, youth, nor riches to tempt – seemed incredible. She was struck once again by all the good luck of her situation, and the contrast between her position and that of her exquisite neighbour brought her some comfort, strengthening as it did her conviction that she had indeed made the right decision – the only decision.

She tactfully turned the subject to the superior quality of Jane's stitching and the happy memories of her friends the sight of these tablecloths and quilts would bring once she made her home at Hunsford; and the afternoon passed, if not entirely unclouded, in an atmosphere of diligent goodwill.

※❧

With the gracious permission of his patroness, Mr Collins soon returned to Lucas Lodge to conduct the necessary wooing of his affianced. Now followed the ungainliness of a courtship between two near-strangers, neither of whom had any especial affection for one another beyond growing mutual gratitude: Mr Collins for the balm ministered by Charlotte's acceptance of his hand, and Charlotte for an avenue of escape.

Lady Catherine had apparently interrogated Mr Collins on his choice of spouse, expressing some surprise that he had not been inclined to look towards any of his cousins. This was not a topic he wished to dwell upon, which had necessitated an insistence that his feelings had run away with him upon encountering Miss Lucas's charms and excellent qualities. It was only a matter of days spent repeating this before he himself believed in the truth of this version of his Hertfordshire romance; and after much probing of the future Mrs Collins's habits of economy and industry,

Lady Catherine declared herself satisfied with his choice. This was licence for Mr Collins to give way to flights of imaginary devotion, and his time with Charlotte was coloured by no small amount of self-congratulation.

With no experience of how a couple about to wed should conduct themselves, Charlotte turned, as always, to practical matters. She questioned Mr Collins closely about his living and establishment at Hunsford, topics that had him waxing even more verbose than usual. Every description of the house, its furnishings, its gardens, trees, pastures, and livestock, ended with a treatise on the glories of Rosings park across the lane, and the privilege of her impending acquaintance with Lady Catherine. Charlotte learned to smile and nod while taking mental notes on what fruit trees the orchard held, which flowerbeds were south-facing, and which nearby coppices and brakes were good sources of firewood.

She was pleased to hear that she would soon be the mistress of leeks and marrows, gooseberry bushes and raspberry canes, and a Chinese mulberry tree, along with the usual damsons, pippins, and pears. Apparently, Lady Catherine had lemons and oranges in her hothouses, and was not averse to sharing this bounty. Charlotte felt that she could endure what sounded like a considerable amount of unsolicited domestic advice, and even interference, in exchange for the treat of oranges at breakfast.

Mr Collins's habit of recounting the furnishings of each room was also welcome, although here Charlotte did not trust his enumerations quite as much as she did when he listed the contents of the garden and orchard. She knew that in this regard, she would have to wait until she entered the Parsonage as a bride before fully comprehending the extent and quality of the plate, silver, and glassware of which she was to become the keeper.

With the bustle of Christmas over, and her trunks filled with her new-made costumes and linens, there could be no further delays, and Charlotte's wedding day loomed. The day before, she paid her farewell visit to the Bennet family, with Elizabeth her object. She could not bear the continuing awkwardness between herself and her old friend, and made strenuous attempts to impress upon Lizzy her wish that their intimacy should continue, even if on a different footing.

First, she sought a promise that Lizzy would write to her regularly – that much, surely, she could depend on. Sir William and Maria were due to visit the bridal couple in Kent in March, and Charlotte found herself pressing, almost begging Lizzy to join them – as they descended the stairs as two maiden friends for the last time, she admitted that Lizzy's presence would be as welcome to her as her own father and sister's. She understood but chose to ignore Elizabeth's reluctance to take up the invitation, and pleaded her case with such fervour that Lizzy agreed at last.

This gave Charlotte some relief on her last day as a spinster; with momentous changes ahead of her, there would be some continuity between her old life and her new one. In the unknown that lay ahead, there would still be familiar faces and voices, bringing news of home and the community she was leaving – for which she felt a surprising amount of affection now that her departure, with many long years before she might return, was imminent.

There were moments when the enormity of what she had managed rendered her breathless: never before had she been so aware that, as a woman, she was little better than a parcel to be lodged where first a father and then a husband decreed. But there was no use in hankering after the independence of a man; she was better off than many women, with a family overjoyed by her imminent nuptials, and an ostensibly comfortable home to anticipate.

The wedding day dawned bright and clear, her family, friends, and neighbours filled the pews of the church, and she trod the aisle on her beaming father's arm to where her groom waited, all smiles and no little relief. She spoke her vows like a ventriloquist's doll, and her path was chosen, her fate sealed. What her life would be now depended largely on her capacity to meet the terms of the contract to which she had just assented. And she was determined to make the very best of it she could.

1819

CHAPTER XVII

CHARLOTTE LOOKED AROUND THE FRESH green, white, and gold furnishings and papering of Miss Darcy's apartments. The sun had settled on the tops of the hills as she had spoken, and it was time to wake Laura. She felt exposed: had she been too candid in her account of how she came to be the wife of Mr Collins? But she could not deny the relief she had also experienced. 'I must apologise for speaking at such length – I confess to surprise at how the hours have flown,' she said. 'I hope my account has not been too tedious.'

Herr Rosenstein shook his head. 'I have seldom been so entertained. You are a natural teller of tales, a skill you have no doubt formed as a sister and a parent. We are all children at heart when there are stories to be heard – none of us can resist the lure of a story well told. But yours is far from complete. You have said nothing of your life as a clergyman's wife in Kent, and I am eager to hear more. But perhaps another day?'

'I am glad I have not burdened you. It is not often that I am able to speak so freely.' Too late, she realised her words could be misconstrued as marital disloyalty, rather than a general comment on the role of a clergy-man's wife more accustomed to listening than speaking, but her companion seemed to understand.

'It is always a solace to speak without first consid-ering whom we might offend or how we might be misunderstood. But enough! I am sure this little Fräulein needs her bread and milk.'

Charlotte shook her daughter gently, murmuring as the flushed child made the transition from sleep to wakefulness. The next few minutes were spent getting Laura to her feet, assuring her she had missed no events of importance, and persuading her to with-draw from the luxuries and novelties of Miss Darcy's quarters.

Before they left, the musician extracted a promise from Charlotte that she would soon return to continue her account of her life: 'I warn you, Frau Collins, I am like the Arabian king whose bride was required to tell him endless tales in order to remain alive. Although I am more merciful than in his case – no spectre of beheading awaits you – but I assure you I am eager to hear more.'

His words were playful, but his gaze was warm on her face, and she felt all the force of it as she escorted Laura out of Miss Darcy's apartments and down the wide corridors. At the head of the stairs, she turned back to see him standing in the doorway looking after them, and was glad of the spontaneity with which her daughter waved at him.

The next day, Elizabeth unearthed a pile of sheet music that had been ordered from London, but which she had been too busy to play. 'By which I mean, too idle. Somehow there is always something else to distract. But now I shall ask Herr Rosenstein if he will be so kind as to play some of these pieces for us tonight while you and I attend to our letters, dear Charlotte.'

Charlotte was happy to agree to this plan; she knew Lizzy was a diligent correspondent, who wrote to her sister Jane nearly every other day, and to the party at Longbourn almost as often. To add to this regular programme, she was also writing frequently to her husband. Moreover, Charlotte had letters of her own to reply to. That very morning, along with a rambling communiqué from her husband – much concerned with the early fruiting of their cherries and the slower progress of the Rosings orchard – she had received a letter from Anne de Bourgh.

Now, as Lizzy seated herself at one of the grander desks in the saloon, and while Herr Rosenstein leafed through the pieces of music with which he had been presented, testing out a few bars or melodic lines here and there, Charlotte reread the heiress's letter.

Dear Mrs Collins,

I wonder how you and Mrs Darcy are going on at Pemberley. Mr Darcy passed through Kent very briefly on his way to business dealings in London, and he said you had all settled well, including the girls, although I doubt he had much to do with their arrangements.

Here time goes by as always: my mother pronounces, at length, on how the world should wag, Mrs Jenkinson clicks her tongue or her knitting needles, and I read or retreat into the spaces of my own mind. Fortunately, nobody expects me to pay them much attention, so I can muse freely.

I do wish my father's library was rather less fusty; I would be grateful if you would see what modern productions are in the Pemberley library, and we shall make plans to procure some new books. My cousin's expensive education surely prompts him to select the best and, if not the best, the most fashionable publications. Nailed as I am here at home, I am particularly interested in writings by travellers, such as those by the Frenchman François Levaillant, their accounts of mountain ranges, deserts, lakes and shores, flora and fauna new to me, exotic peoples and interesting hardships; from the furthest poles of the earth to the next county, I do not mind, as long as the particulars are intelligently and fluently expressed. I found Lady Mary Wortley Montagu's published letters from her time in Turkey engaging, and could wish for more.

What shape does your day take now that you are enjoying what must be a sort of holiday from your usual responsibilities? I fear I must press for a reply to this letter as a small measure against the tedium of life here: I miss your contribution to conversations at Rosings.

As the days lengthen, my prison expands – it is

much harder to go night riding on these evenings of golden light, even though the softness of the air and the lengthening shadows of the trees tempt me tremendously. I have to wait for full dark before venturing down to the stables. But on the rare occasions I manage it, the sensations are delicious: the night air is perfumed not just by the blooms of the day, but all the scents of the soil and grass as they give up the day's warmth. The stars hang closer than ever, the barking of foxes carries over the hills, and Bruno and I swing along the tracks more languidly than usual. Poor creature, he does seem puzzled when I tiptoe into his stall in the middle of the night! But we have had no misadventures, and I store up the sensations to relive during the days that creep by. These excursions have the added benefit of leaving me sleepy and yawning, which is noticed, and serves as an excellent excuse for retiring from company – not on account of the frailty so easily ascribed to me by my companions, but because of the need to catch up on missed sleep.

Other than that, there is absolutely nothing of note to report. Mr Collins seems well cared for by the Parsonage staff, but he is dining here rather more frequently than usual, and seems unusually downcast. There is no doubt that he misses you and his daughters, and all my mother's advice on how he should take this opportunity to rewrite his sermons cannot cheer him.

I hope your daughters are thriving – they are of

an age to benefit from all the pleasures of
Pemberley while yet being too young to be over-
awed by the experience. You will of course pass
on my compliments to Mrs Darcy, which compliments are also due to you.

Yours, etc.,

Anne de Bourgh

Charlotte was not unmindful of the tribute paid to her
discretion by the contents of Miss de Bourgh's letter.
But while she was relieved to hear that no alarming or
even mildly disturbing events were taking place in her
absence, she was seized by the memory of the almost
oppressively opulent drawing room at Rosings, with its
superfluity of heat and ornament, the incessantly ticking
clock, the scents of polish and tapestry fabric and smoke
and roses mingling with the slight whiff of mould.
Anne's account of the tedium that lay several hundred
miles to the south rose up to choke her.

She must have made some small sound, because
Herr Rosenstein caught her eye: 'Frau Collins, may I
trouble you with a request for assistance? Would it be
possible to set your letters aside and turn my music
sheets for me?'

Here was escape, and Charlotte sprang to her feet
to oblige the musician.

'Thank you, Charlotte!' called Lizzy from her station:
'Mr Darcy sent for some German *lieder* by a new
young composer, a Mr Schubert – barely more than
a boy, I understand – and I should like to choose some
that fall within my poor ability and rehearse them for

his return. But I fear I rely on the pair of you to carry out my purpose.'

Charlotte sat down at the pianoforte beside Herr Rosenstein, who showed her the songs he had selected, and began to sight-read them. Her role of turning the sheets was much less onerous, and she was able to lose herself in the gentle ripple of the notes he played, and his voice as he sang. Now and again he paused to repeat a phrase with a slightly different emphasis or more confident accompaniment on the keys, and Charlotte shut her eyes to better allow the music to fill her head and heart. This close to him, she became aware of the faint scent of his body, the spice of it, with a tang not unlike that of Dobbin's coat.

She wondered if their proximity now, along with the cascade of music, might cause him to recollect their maze excursion, of which they had never yet spoken; and as if reading her mind, he wove into the piece he was playing the air from the variations he had performed for her first in the schoolroom, and then in the maze. The phrasing was so slight and subtle, she wondered at first if she was mishearing, but he repeated the brief sequence of notes and, as she turned to look at him, he lifted his eyes from the music to flash a smile at her.

She sat more upright, breathed more deeply. The sensation of stifling fell from her like hands releasing her throat. Perhaps Anne's account of her nights, if not her days, indicated that there were indeed means of escaping daily routine – that it was possible to suspend the demands of duty rather than abandon them.

CHAPTER XVIII

THE PICNIC CONCERTS, AS LIZZY began calling them, proved so popular with all, especially the children, that they were regularly repeated; a search of the nursery toys turned up a few instruments, including a drum that Laura seized as her own. Herr Rosenstein also gave both girls rudimentary singing lessons, teaching them to clap rhythms and warble breathy tunes.

On one such occasion he spent half an hour teaching them German folk ballads, notably the one about the Lorelei. The children were rapt at the tale of the rock in the River Rhine, the beautiful maiden who sat on it combing her golden hair and singing for her lost love, attracting sailors whose crafts foundered on the rocks and drowned.

'I want to be the maiden, Mama!' cried Laura. 'I want to draw sailors and ships onto the rocks with my song! And when they crash, I want to dive off the rock into the river and save them all.'

The grown-ups present could not hide their laughter, and Jacob said, 'In that case, you need to be word-perfect with your song, Fräulein. Let us rehearse it again:

Ich weiß nicht
was soll es bedeuten
daß ich so traurig bin;
ein Märchen aus uralten Zeiten
das kommt mir nicht aus dem Sinn.

These watery scenes were matched by external ones; Lizzy and Charlotte had fallen into the habit of taking a walk most afternoons, often accompanied by the girls, and a favourite path followed the course of the river. Charlotte was glad that Lizzy felt strong enough for such exertion, but her friend had always been a great walker, climber of stiles and jumper of ha-has, and years of marriage and three miscarriages had not altered this aspect of her character, however much some might think it beneath the dignity of the mistress of Pemberley to ramble the grounds and surrounding countryside like a shepherdess in Arcadia.

Each step along their preferred path presented a nobler fall of ground or a finer vista of the woods, until the circuit brought them to the water's edge. Here the valley contracted to a glen that allowed room only for the stream and a narrow walk alongside the coppice-wood that bordered it. Their object was a rustic and unadorned bridge that allowed only foot traffic, a good spot to rest before retracing their steps back along the opposite side of the river, with its verdant twists and turns.

Herr Rosenstein, once again waiting for a coat of varnish to dry before he could continue his work on Miss Darcy's harpsichord, joined them on one of these excursions. He walked on ahead with the children, who were squabbling over who would get the honour of pointing out to him the trout flicking their lazy tails in the pools along the way. Sarah poked her sister in the ribs, and Laura responded with a push that had the elder child staggering perilously close to the water's edge. Charlotte called out, embarrassed by the boisterousness of her girls, but also feeling the fear that had trailed her ever since Tom's death step up to breathe on the back of her neck. But her warning came too late – with barely a splash, Sarah disappeared into the swiftly flowing river.

There was no time even to feel alarm: in seconds, Herr Rosenstein had toed off his boots and plunged in after her daughter, diving to scoop her up, then splashing back to the bank and depositing her there, soaked but otherwise unharmed. It was only then that the seconds slowed down. Elizabeth called out for assistance, gardeners came running, the usually imperturbable senior nursemaid arrived at a flustered trot, and was dispatched back to the house with the girls – Sarah uncomplaining, but Laura now howling so heartily one could be mistaken for thinking she had been the victim of the accident.

Charlotte moved to follow, but her limbs had turned to wool; to her perplexity, she sank to her knees, snatching for air, her head spinning. She heard Lizzy's voice, high with agitation, and then Jacob's, closer as he bent over her: 'Breathe, Mrs Collins. Sink your head. Yes, like that. Do not try to rise just yet. Breathe slowly and regularly. Mrs Darcy, there is no reason for alarm, but your friend might benefit from your chafing her wrists.'

After a few minutes of such assiduous attentions from her companions, Charlotte felt able to get to her feet, supported by the musician's arm about her waist, and Lizzy's encouragement. Embarrassment began to break like a wave, even as her friends assured her apology was unnecessary.

Lizzy was the first to thank the musician: 'How fortunate that you were with us, Herr Rosenstein, and reacted so speedily and with such courage! Is there no end to our indebtedness to you, sir?'

The enormity of what the young man had done for her, her child, their family, began to dawn on Charlotte, and she turned to him, stammering: 'My child! You saved my child!' It was all she could utter, her mouth dry. In a tempest of unchecked gratitude that would mortify her in retrospect, she clutched at his hands and covered them in kisses, only to be soothed and quietened: 'I did what anyone would have done, Frau Collins, but do not try to speak just yet. Let us get you settled and comfortable back at the house first.'

After a few minutes, she was able to walk unassisted, although Lizzy still held her arm: 'You shall rest before dinner, my dear Charlotte, and a fire shall be made in your room. Warm milk with brandy and sugar, too; you have had a sad shock indeed.'

'Yes, indeed,' Herr Rosenstein added. 'Mrs Darcy is correct; you have been overset by shock and must recover yourself.'

Much later, after everyone had been rendered warm and dry after the afternoon's misadventures, and Mrs Darcy had at last left her, after twice instructing the servants to keep her bedroom fire burning, Charlotte found herself with time to reflect. She had been doubly struck by both terror and the surprise of that terror. A monster had leapt at her and pinned her to the ground, leaving her gasping as if she were one of the fish in the river and had been tossed into cruel air. No matter that she was safe, her child was safe, she was among friends: a giant hand had squeezed her chest, sending panic racing along her nerves. No amount of reasoning with herself, nor the comforting of her companions, could assuage or stop the shuddering that still wracked her body intermittently. Perhaps it was the reminder of how quickly disaster could step into the path, how helpless mortals were in the face of it. Fate could seize them by the scruffs of their necks, rendering them as helpless as fieldmice in the jaws of the fox – indeed, there were few shocks as great as at those moments.

But then had come the rescue: the sight of Jacob wading out of the river, Sarah safe in his arms, Charlotte's worst terror turning to relief in a tumult of feelings so sharply pitched as to be almost un-endurable – the scene was imprinted in her mind, playing again and again.

Her heart was still so full, she found she needed to find some form of expression, and went to the writing-desk to seek pen and paper.

My dear William,

Pray be assured we are all well and in good heart, but what an alarm we suffered today! We were walking beside the river that flows through the valley. The girls were, I regret, not behaving as well as they ought, and as a result of some horseplay, Sarah was accidentally plunged into the stream. The river was running strongly, and the current immediately seized at her little form. Oh, the sight of her head disappearing under the surface! It will haunt me forever. My instinct was to throw myself after her but, as you know, I cannot swim and was helpless to aid her. I believe that was the worst, in thinking back on it: my powerlessness.

By the mercy of Providence, we were not alone – Mrs Darcy and I were accompanied by one Herr Rosenstein, a piano-tuner from Austria here to set Miss Darcy's instruments to rights. He did not hesitate: he dived in at once and plucked Sarah from the torrent – she was too shocked even to struggle – and had her on the bank before we could so much as call out for help.

To my embarrassment, it became necessary to administer aid to me more than our daughter, but we were all got back to the house in due course, where I was pressed to rest in my chamber while fortifying drinks were brought me. Mrs Darcy was all kindness and did not leave my side until I was more comfortable.

I was deeply anxious about Sarah, but the

nursemaids had her dry and warm in a trice, and she seems unharmed in either body and spirit. There is so far no sign of a chill or fever, and she is in fact inclined to paint herself as the heroine of the hour, and her sister (the originator of the accident) as the blackest of villains. I almost feel sorry for Laura, whose habitual boisterousness is subdued, although I have no doubt that this is temporary. Both girls are sleeping now, looking like veritable cherubs: I have been to check several times.

I have of course given fervent thanks to the Almighty for Sarah's safe deliverance, most especially for the instrument of her rescue, the musician who went to her aid with no thought for his own safety or comfort. My dear William, what a debt we owe this young man! No words, no thanks, no gesture can ever repay his gift to our family, the nobility of his deed in saving us from unimaginable anguish.

He has been a most pleasing companion and adjunct to our visit here, lending cheer not only to Mrs Darcy and myself, always amenable to joining us when we grow tired of women's chat and require our small circle widened, but also a great favourite with the girls, to whom he is giving some lessons in singing and musicality. Now of course he leaps even higher in my estimation, as high indeed as the firmament of angels.

I beg you to join me in prayers of thanksgiving for his selfless intervention, and in wishing every blessing upon him. I shall never cease thanking him for the gift he has bestowed on us: the safety of our daughter.

Charlotte paused, and reread what she had written. She considered the letters her husband sent her once a week, in which domestic duty and fondness were equally mixed. Fairly brief, considering his volubility in speech, they rehearsed the essence of his sermon that Sunday, repeated Lady Catherine's glosses, gave an account of the loaves distributed for poor relief, and enumerated the nettles and sow-thistles he was clearing from the garden beds, or the palings he and Mr Brown had replaced where the cows had trampled them down. They always ended with sincere professions of affection for her and their daughters.

She sighed. It would not be an act of kindness to introduce alarm into their correspondence, not even at the same moment of alleviating that alarm. She crumpled the stiff, costly paper in her hand and tossed it into the banked flames of the hearth, where it flared briefly before thinning to ghostly grey flakes.

CHAPTER XIX

OVER BREAKFAST THE NEXT MORNING, Lizzy and Herr Rosenstein showed no lessening of solicitude, and Charlotte was closely questioned as to her and her daughters' well-being. She was able to reassure them that Sarah seemed to have suffered no injurious consequences from her watery mishap. But she was unable to hide the tremble in her voice, and her friends exchanged a glance before Jacob put forward a proposal: 'Frau Collins, would it make your mind a little easier if I taught the young Fräuleins how to swim? Then we need not fear a repetition of yesterday's alarm.'

Charlotte demurred at first, imagining all kinds of unforeseen consequences. Would there not be an element of danger? Might not the girls perhaps fall ill as a result of their immersions? But her companions gradually overcame her initial reluctance. The musician assured her that it would be no trouble to him, and indeed a form of healthful exercise and diversion for them all, while Lizzy exclaimed, 'That is an excellent plan! If we choose fine weather, there can be no danger of chills or rheumatism. Our waters are fresh and clear, and cannot possibly be injurious. You and I can sit by the river and watch as Herr Rosenstein schools your girls to be ducklings.'

Charlotte had to agree, especially once the plan had been broached with the girls, who, far from being daunted by the previous day's accident, were seized by the notion and its novelty. The housekeeper was dispatched to search trunks for suitable garments and, to the amusement of all, she produced the skeleton suits Mr Darcy had worn as a very small boy, which were admirably suited to the purpose, their high-waisted trews held in place by sashes. At first, however, with the arrival of showers of rain, it seemed that the proposed aquatic adventures would have to be postponed, and the girls shook small fists at the clouded sky as they pressed their noses to the nursery windows. But the sun came out warm and bright in the afternoon, and the project grew more appealing to all.

Their party, including the more senior nursemaid, who came armed with an ample supply of towels and cloths, set out for the rustic bridge, and prepared themselves for either sport or spectating. Charlotte and Elizabeth seated themselves on the edge, where they had a good view of the pool below, and Herr Rosenstein removed his boots, waistcoat, cravat and the tooled straps attached to his trousers, then waded into the water. Next, he had to coax the girls, already overcome by the excitement of wearing their strange new costumes, to join him, as they were now as shriekingly desirous of avoiding immersion as they had previously been enthusiastic. Laura at last closed her eyes tight and launched herself at the river as if she were one of

Mr Darcy's spaniels, creating maximum splash and noise as she landed. Sarah was left with no choice but to follow her younger sister, which she did to less spectacular effect.

The musician set the flailing and roaring Laura upright, and encouraged both girls to paddle in the shallows at first, lending a steadying hand whenever they slipped and squealed. Soon they were overcome by that natural human urge whenever two or more gather in a body of water, and began to splash each other and their tutor. Charlotte had to speak stern words when it occurred to them that their mother and Mrs Darcy might also want their share of scattering drops.

The lesson began in earnest as Herr Rosenstein held first one, then the other child steady in the water and taught them first how to float, then how to kick. The sprays raised by their feet caught the sunlight, gold against the green and brown river, and although the mirth of the girls continued unabated, it was punctuated by the demands of breathing and the commands of their teacher.

It was now the turn of Charlotte and Lizzy to laugh at the antics taking place just beneath the parapet of the bridge, and Charlotte felt another knot in her spine slide loose. She shaded her eyes with her hand to watch more closely. The musician's soaked form suggested some creature at home in water; Charlotte had only a vague sense of what oceanic creatures such as seals or dolphins looked like, but the musculature of his arms as the water ran down them conveyed the sense of a glossy animal, the curves of his back and shoulders as he hoisted the children about and directed their kicking bodies not unlike those of the darting fish their sport had driven away.

As if echoing her thoughts, at that moment he dived like the proverbial fish, disappearing underwater, and Charlotte leaned so far forward to watch for his re-emergence that Lizzy was moved to hook a cautionary hand in the folds of her skirt.

The sun went behind the clouds starting to mass on the hills that rose in stately lines towards the Peaks. The girls set up a clamour of protest as their mother called to them that their swimming lesson was over, but it was largely for show – a little breeze was now ruffling the surface of the water and raising gooseflesh on skin.

The children were bundled in linens and ushered away towards the house, where hot water in ewers and a fire in the nursery awaited them, while Herr Rosenstein, drops of water glinting on his lashes, accepted a towel and wrapped it around his neck and shoulders. Charlotte noticed that wet, his brown hair turned a shade closer to black. His bare feet were narrow and the colour of bone. Encased in wet clothes, his body seemed both more solid and sleek than usual, and she found her own skin prickling in sympathy with his. There was a curious sense of having witnessed him stripped of a layer that had nothing to do with clothing and more to do with having watched him at play in the water; she found herself wanting to stare at him at the same time as she was suddenly shy of doing so. For the first time, she wondered what age he was; clearly younger than she had first surmised.

She looked over at Lizzy, who seemed to feel no such curiosity; she was offering Herr Rosenstein the services of a footman to help him out of his wet garments, and he was demurring: 'Thank you for your kind attention, but there is no need, Mrs Darcy. If my fire could but be made afresh, that would indeed constitute luxury.'

Even though Charlotte repeatedly apologised for the encroachment on Herr Rosenstein's time, he willingly repeated this lesson every fine afternoon for the rest of the week – including one memorable day when the trio swam in the grand lake, rejoicing in the spray from the fountain – until both girls could dog-paddle themselves to the nearest bank unaided. Charlotte no longer had to suffer too much anxiety when her daughters chased each other along the banks of the river or around the ponds.

❧❧❧

One evening that week, Charlotte went to bid her daughters goodnight and, to her surprise, found Sarah fretful. Laura, worn out by the day's excitement and exertions, was already sound asleep, but her sister clung to her mother and was inclined towards tearfulness. This behaviour was not characteristic of her dreamy and stoic daughter, and Charlotte, with an internal sigh, knew she needed to get to the bottom of the matter.

Strangely enough, the alarm of the river episode played no role in Sarah's troubles. It seemed that the discovery earlier that week of a dead squirrel in the garden was part of the problem, and the lurid book of martyrs that Charlotte had glimpsed secreted under the bed furnishings was no doubt an aggravating factor. She lay down next to her daughter and wrapped her arms around her.

She did not have long to wait: 'Mama, did it hurt when Tom died?'

Only like being immersed in boiling oil. Over and over again, Charlotte thought, still amazed she had survived the scalding agony of those first months. But that was not what her daughter was asking. She reassured Sarah, yet again, that Tom had felt no pain in perishing, that there had been no suffering – while silently thanking Providence that this had indeed been the case. As she had often done before, she explained that Tom had simply fallen asleep and never woken.

'But Mama, if I fall asleep, will I wake up?' Sarah went to the heart of her anxiety, and Charlotte stroked her daughter's soft dark curls, so like Tom's, in an upwelling of compassion.

'Of course you shall. Tom did not wake because he was not well. We all knew that he was not strong, that he was weak because of his poor head. Whereas you, my treasure, are as strong as the trees in the garden and the carthorses on the farm. You shall sleep and wake every day until you are an old, old woman.'

'The trees in the garden? But what if they blow down?'

'Think of the big chestnut tree at home. The one in which Papa and Mr Brown put up a swing, where you and Laura like to play in the shade in summer, and collect the conkers in autumn. How it stays unmoved no matter how much the winds howl at it. Its leaves may blow off in storms, a small branch here and there might crack in the winter frosts, but the tree stays strong, held safely upright by its firm trunk.'

Charlotte lowered her voice to a murmur as Sarah's lids closed for longer and longer intervals, the tracks of her tears drying. 'And in the spring, think of how the new leaves and flowers burst out like candles, and the squirrels and birds come to play and rejoice in the new growth. You will be like that tree, you and Laura both. Always strong and firm, and always renewing yourselves.'

And God help me, if that is not the truth, I shall perish myself, she thought as she kissed her daughter's forehead once more, then got to her feet, deftly extracting the troublesome book at the same time. She stood for a long time in the dusk, listening to her children breathe, matching her exhalations to theirs, before she left the room.

CHAPTER XX

CHARLOTTE HELD TOM CLOSE, RELISHING the peace brought her by his arms winding around her neck, the weight and warmth of his body. But as she rocked him, he turned to a bundle of red rags, his arms became strangling ropes, and she jerked awake, her heart battering in her throat. She could hear a child crying, she could swear it, and was on her feet, pulses pounding, before she could stop herself.

Slowly, she orientated herself; she was in her handsome chamber at Pemberley, a bar of moonlight lying across the bed and its hangings. All was still; the faint wailing she imagined she had heard was simply a remnant of her dream. She stood, listening, the sweat of alarm cooling on her body, now bracing herself not against fear, but against the wave of grief her dreams of Tom always brought upon waking; those moments when she reached helplessly for the elusive fragments that restored him to her, only to have them run like water through her fingers.

She knew she would not sleep again easily, and flickers of anxiety still nagged at her: perhaps something was amiss with the girls? She would not rest until she had seen for herself that all was well. She fished for her slippers, lit a candle, and found her wrap. Then she set off down the long corridor in the direction of the nursery quarters.

Letting herself quietly into the room where the girls slept, all was peaceful repose. The two slumbering forms, one dark and one light head on the bolster, breathed in untroubled unison. There was nothing to fear here, but Charlotte sank into a chair to watch her daughters nonetheless, and allowed herself that rarest of treats: an indulgence of memory, recalling times when all three of her children had played and romped together, Tom's sisters treating him with that mixture of affection and exasperated tolerance typical of all elder siblings, as well as that special solicitude they afforded him because of his condition.

She remembered a day, nearly a year ago, when the three of them discovered the pleasures of rolling down the new-turfed slopes between the flower-garden and the orchard, and how at first, anticipating the work of scrubbing at grass stains on clothing, she had wanted to halt their game. But their shrieks of delight and glee had stilled her words of reprimand. And then there were the times they had commandeered Mr Brown's wheelbarrow, the girls hoisting Tom inside and then pushing him all around the garden, a game that always ended with their tipping him out onto a soft spot of ground, a liberty to which he never took exception, responding rather with peals of laughter.

Lost in a reverie, Charlotte was startled when the door swung open and the light of another candle bloomed in its frame. It was the younger of the two nursemaids, Ella, a pleasant girl, who was in turn surprised to find Mrs Collins curled in a chair.

'I beg your pardon, ma'am, is aught amiss? Are the bairns quite well?' she whispered.

Charlotte, also whispering, reassured the young woman that she had been unable to sleep, and had come to check on her daughters. Ella in turn explained that sleeping in the antechamber, as instructed by Mrs Darcy, she had been woken by the light of the candle. But now she was all concern: 'Sleeplessness is a terrible thing, ma'am. Shall I heat you some milk or make you some tea? Mrs Reynolds has the keys to the main pantry, and Carruthers the keys to the wine cellar, otherwise I would offer you brandy. But there is milk and a loaf of sugar in the servants' larder.'

Charlotte was about to demur, but the thought of something warm and sweet to drink was suddenly irresistible, and she accepted the offer, grateful for the kindness that prompted it.

'But let me come downstairs with you, and we can both take something hot to drink,' she said. 'The girls are clearly sleeping soundly, and I do not wish them woken.'

The pair of them padded down towards the vast domestic quarters of the building, the light from their candles streaming across the panelled walls, the eyes of the long-dead figures in the portraits following them, gleaming with temporary life.

As they descended in the direction of the Great Hall, they became aware of faint music and a soft glow. They glanced at each other, puzzled, and Ella clutched at Charlotte's arm in alarm, but Charlotte was made of sterner stuff and pursued the sounds, tracing them to their source in the red saloon. Here they found Herr Rosenstein at the piano, playing a quiet and haunting melody, his own candle guttering in the sconce.

It was hard to say who was more startled, and there were many apologies and counter-apologies and explanations before they established that they were all fugitives from Morpheus. The musician explained that he had come downstairs while the inhabitants of the house slumbered, assuming he was sufficiently far from the sleeping quarters to be able to play without creating any disturbance.

Charlotte invited him to join in their plan to imbibe a wholesome drink to encourage sleep, and he readily agreed. They took up places in front of the banked fire in one of the kitchens, resting their elbows on the rough table while Ella prepared the milk.

The drink was every bit as creamy as Charlotte had hoped – Pemberley's Jersey herd was among the finest in the county – and Ella had grated the sugar with a generous hand. She began to enjoy the sense of being on a midnight adventure, the disruption of conventional routine and ritual. Her children were safe, the wisps of her dream had dissipated, and she had all the comfort of convivial company.

'May I ask, Herr Rosenstein, what piece of music you were playing when we found you? I am no connoisseur, as you know, but I thought it very fine, and would like to hear it again another day.'

He thanked her, and explained it was one of his own compositions, one he hoped to adapt for a string quartet and sell to the *Kapellmeister* of a small court orchestra back in his native Austria.

'It is unlikely that I will able to perform it with them myself, but Herr Hummel is a generous and rational man. I do not think he will hold my tribe against me in considering my offering.'

Charlotte was puzzled, and said as much. 'Forgive me, sir, but I do not catch your meaning. I do not understand the allusion to your tribe.'

Herr Rosenstein glanced at Ella, who, having drunk her milk, had put her head down on her arms and fallen asleep as quickly and neatly as a cat.

'Frau Collins, the structures of patronage for us musicians on the Continent are deeply embedded in those of the Christian church. Orchestras and organists are often employed by various cathedrals, or by Catholic nobles. The pieces most regularly commissioned are for performance in church, celebrating the feast days of the Christian year.' He cradled his cup in his hands, his eyes dark hollows in the diffuse light emanating from the embers of the fire.

'No one is going to ask a Jew to compose a Mass for a special occasion, or even a hymn for a wedding or christening. As a craftsman, I am welcome in almost all homes and places of Christian worship: no one considers my Semite lineage when strings snap or go out of tune and must be replaced or repaired. And the musicality of my kind is in fact lauded; in almost every court orchestra, a Jew, or two, or three, sits in the first row of the strings or strad-dles a violoncello. But as a composer, I have to rely on such few crumbs of patronage as are thrown my way by more liberal employers.'

The note of not quite bitterness, but asperity, in his voice caught Charlotte. She felt once again vastly ignorant of the implications of his religion, and indig-nant on his behalf. She had to content herself by assuring him that she had found the piece he was playing beautiful.

'I must say, Herr Rosenstein, that such loveliness as I heard coming from the instrument when you played tonight is certainly productive of spiritual refreshment. I feel consoled having listened to it.'

He looked up at her words. 'Frau Collins, I am sorry that you are in need of consolation. But glad that my humble piece has contributed to the easing of your spirits.'

They held each other's gaze in a silence broken by the soft tumble and hiss of the fire; then Ella sat upright with a little gasp, and knuckled her eyes. It was time for their strange band to disperse back to their natural stations in the great and preternaturally still house, and they took up their candles and parted with mutual expressions of gratitude and good wishes for a peaceful night. Yet Charlotte was wakeful for several hours thereafter, but not unpleasantly so, as the music that had flowed from Jacob's fingers played and replayed in her mind.

CHAPTER XXI

AT BREAKFAST, YET ANOTHER LETTER from Anne de Bourgh awaited Charlotte. This one ran to two sheets, and she unfolded them with some curiosity as to what could have engrossed the other woman's pen to such an extent.

My dear Mrs Collins,

I hope this finds you and your daughters in good health and spirits, and enjoying all the comforts Pemberley has to offer. What follows is certain to come as a surprise: this letter comes to you from the South of France. I have flown the coop, perhaps inspired by your example. And to think in my last, I was begging you to send me the names of works on travel abroad. Now, here I am, in a small and ancient town perched high over the Mediterranean Sea, with vistas as far as Corsica, and tawny stone buildings that date back to times when this stretch of the coast was pillaged by Saracens, and every cottage was a fortress. The air smells of the sea; how strange that these foreign waters are so differently scented to our own – one would think that the ocean would be a constant.

How did this come to pass? My regular physician, the good Dr Pike, visits my mother to be informed of what ailments afflict me; he then attends to me in order to pronounce her diagnoses and lay out her suggestions for treatment, a regime that has not troubled me much in the past. However, Dr P has been laid low by dropsy, and he sent a new sawbones in his place, a much younger man. The fellow is as tractable as his predecessor but, in this case, he attended me without first hearing my mother's recitation of what treatment I required. I was thus able to drop into his mind the utter necessity for me to decamp to a warm, dry climate to strengthen my chest. This was a feat I take some pride in, given the balmy summer weather Kent is presently experiencing.

Poor Mrs Jenkinson! She loathed our last trip abroad – and that was in the winter months. I did suggest that we find a younger and sturdier travel companion for me, but my mother would not countenance this.

So we travelled via packet-boat to Calais, and then by coach to Paris. And now I must confess to you the full extent of my crimes. Prepare to be shocked, and do not judge me too harshly. My mother recently had the family jewellery appraised and, for once, I paid attention. As you know, it is no boast but mere statement of fact to attest to my considerable wealth. Yet vast acres, rents, and an army of faceless clerks who ensure that tradesmen's accounts are settled do not translate into the jingle of cash in the pocket. And I am learning that it is not buildings and crops, but banknotes and coins that translate into opportunities for freedom. So once my rings and fobs and what-nots were returned to me after the notaries had departed, I selected the smallest and ugliest trinkets and sewed them into the hems of my garments, a trick I garnered from a rather gaudy romance. Let it not be said that novel-reading is not instructive.

Once arrived at our lodgings in Paris, it was a moment's work to release the jewels and gold. Then came the more delicate business of finding a buyer or pawnbroker to receive them. I had no choice but to enlist the aid of the proprietor and staff – but with the strictest of injunctions to secrecy. I made it clear I was prepared to pay handsomely for discretion, and indeed the French are accustomed to such requests – in the turbulence following the Terrors, many distressed gentlefolk had to parlay small items of value into the means of keeping a roof over their heads.

Mrs Jenkinson, who was still recovering from seasickness, further aggravated by the motion of our fast coach, lay prostrate in our quarters, unaware of my machinations. The next day, I suggested she rest still further, and solicitously plied her with the laudanum the new physician had prescribed for me. She was soon all but insensible, and I was able to sally forth to the addresses procured for me by our host, accompanied by a stout young man for my protection – robbery at such a juncture would have spelled disaster.

At the first establishment for the sale and exchange of jewellery, the proprietor looked me up and down, and thought he had an easy mark; he offered me a ludicrously small sum. I did not waste time in argument; I refused it, and left at once, even as he ran after me in some surprise and agitation. I had better luck at our next stop, a small, dimly lit shop in the Marais district. The elderly man who pored over my rather dull emerald and ruby rings with a loupe screwed into his eye wore his hair in the strangest style – ringlets curled like a woman's descending on either side of his face. But he was courteous, and offered a reasonable sum, which I accepted without demurral. I slipped my escort a coin, with the promise of another once we were safely back at our lodgings, and it was as easy as that.

I am a bullock with a needle, but soon transferred the money back into the hems of my garments. Meanwhile, Mrs Jenkinson still pays, with notes of credit provided by my mother, for our daily needs, and writes it all up in her account book at the end of each day, knowing that our expenditure will be scrutinised on our return, and that each penny will have to be answered for. I finger the folded notes and solid coins in the linings of my skirts, and remain quiet. They feel like largesse, and they are.

The heat here is so extreme, it should be ener-
vating; it is a solid thing, the sun beating down
like a drum. It even has a sound: the air vibrates
with the scream of insects. But I find it invigor-
ating. Our hostess, a local woman who rules her
large family with an iron hand, has placed her
grown sons and daughter at my disposal. None of
them speak English, but I spell out my wishes in
my rudimentary French, and have made it clear
that handsome gratuities will be paid for
indulging my whims.

Each day, as the sun reaches its zenith, and
Mrs Jenkinson, like most sensible creatures in this
region, retires to observe the siesta custom, I
venture forth, accompanied by one of Madame's
sons, who provides a donkey to convey me.
Armed with a vast bonnet and veil against the
ferocious light, I explore the hills and scrub, the
crumbling ruins of castles and keeps, my tiny
steed picking her way delicately up and down
apparently impassable trails and slopes.

After the first such outing, when my dark
English riding habit all but roasted me alive, I
decided that more sensible attire was required if
I was to survive my forays. I made a withdrawal
from my skirt lining, and approached Marie, the
daughter of the house and a very sharp-witted
young woman. After some initial confusion, she
took my meaning and set to work adapting a
pair of lightweight breeches for me; she also
purchased several muslin blouses for my use.

This costume I now wear when out exploring, and indeed it is most comfortable and convenient. I make a strange spectacle as I go about the hills with my patient steed and equally patient (if puzzled) escort: dressed in the trews and blouson of the local peasantry, which costume is topped by the aforementioned straw bonnet. But English eccentricity warrants little more than a shrug here, and few see me on my explorations. By the time the tiny village is stirring again as much-needed breaths of cooler air waft in from the sea, and Mrs J has roused herself, I am once again languid Miss de Bourgh, reclining in a loose afternoon dress and fanning myself with a book.

I shall write again soon – who knows what surprising adventures I may yet embark on? I might embrace life as a Barbary pirate or take up my path as a purported artist. If truth be told, I am as clumsy with a paintbrush as I am with a needle, which, for once, I regret, as every other vista here demands to be immortalised.

I have no news of Kent to report, I fear – although everyone was well when we left Rosings what feels a lifetime ago, but was indeed less than a fortnight since. The mails from Paris are indeed regular, but here in the more distant reaches of the country, news travels slowly, if at all. It is most restful.

I send my compliments to all at Pemberley, and wish you in particular, Mrs Collins, a summer of repose and restoration. Heaven knows you deserve it.

Yours, etc.,

Anne de Bourgh

As Charlotte looked up from this letter, Lizzy said: 'I must confess, I am surprised that Miss de Bourgh is such a regular correspondent. I do not mean that I am surprised she has chosen and values you as an intimate, dear Charlotte. But she seemed so – faint – to me, almost a ghost of a woman. I can make no claim to know her on the basis of a few visits to Rosings, but she seemed more of an absence than a presence. I cannot imagine what she might have to relate, much less at length.'

Charlotte had to suppress a smile at these words. *If you only knew, Eliza.* Aloud she said, 'Miss de Bourgh is an enlightening correspondent, and she has indeed news of interest to impart – she is travelling abroad, in the South of France at present. For her health, of course. She sends you her compliments.'

'Heavens! The South of France in midsummer? The heat will be scorching. She must indeed be unwell if her doctors believe such a course of action is necessary.'

The musician looked up from his coddled eggs. 'I should be sorry to hear that any one of your friends is experiencing ill-health, Frau Collins. But I am sure that the warmth of which Mrs Darcy speaks will be beneficial. What I remember of Provence is that the heat, while stupefying, is a dry heat, one that penetrates the bones, opens the chest, and relaxes the body.'

Elizabeth was full of lively interest: 'You have travelled in France, Herr Rosenstein? Pray tell us more. It is a country I would love to visit, but of course the last few years have not been conducive, what with the Terrors and that wretched Bonaparte – himself not even a Frenchman, I believe – harassing us like a terrier. Thank heavens he has now been confined to a far more distant island – a rock somewhere near the South Pole, I believe.'

'I have been fortunate, Frau Darcy,' replied the musician. 'My father and I travel regularly to Paris for purposes of our business, of course, although the wars did indeed disrupt these trips. But it is the journeys of leisure to the southern parts of that country that I remember with the most pleasure. The cities of Nice and Avignon – with its famous truncated bridge – the walled towns perched on rocks, the brazen glitter of the sea, the mountains shouldering into the sky – I am lucky to have seen all this.'

He went on to describe ancient Roman ruins and aqueducts, marshes rustling with blond grasses and populated by wild horses, mule-tracks clinging to dry and peppery coastal cliffs where tideless waves washed far below, seaside promenades made exotic by the planting of tropic palms, palaces jealously guarded by apostate Popes, fields of sunflowers turning their heads to follow their parent orb.

Listening to him speak the names of unfamiliar rivers, mountains and villages, Charlotte almost shivered with pleasure. 'Herr Rosenstein, I swear listening to you speak is like taking a trip on a magic carpet, such as are found in the fairy tales my daughters enjoy. As you speak, these vistas unfold before my very eyes. Pray go on,' she said.

Lizzy laughed at her friend. 'It is not like you to be so fanciful, my dear Charlotte! You sound like your children begging for stories at bedtime.' She turned to the musician: 'This is all very poetic, sir, but your travels cannot only have been a matter of picturesque ruins and cathedrals. Your life cannot have been one long Grand Tour.'

'Indeed, Frau Darcy. I have experienced all the perils of bad alehouses and worse victuals, and as a musician, I have seen my share of revelry and dancing girls. The revues of the Quartier Pigalle in Paris require that their instruments be properly strung and tuned as much as does the orchestra of the Académie Royale de Musique.' He added more seriously, 'And there have indeed been journeys through forests or mountains when the howling of wolves has chilled my blood – when I have wondered if I would ever safely reach my destination.'

'Well, I hope the woods of Pemberley are not too dull for you,' said Lizzy. 'We have no wolves here. Or bandits.'

Jacob smiled across at Charlotte. 'And I have discovered no bears, or trolls, or hobgoblins in these grounds. Only a pair of mischievous elves. I am deprived of my regular dose of terror.'

'Well, perhaps you can entertain us all with additional tales of monsters and savage creatures,' teased Charlotte. 'My daughters would enjoy it: I fear they are at that age where the bloodthirstier the story, the better.'

'That sounds like a delightful project, Frau Collins,' said the musician. 'I am accustomed to spending my breath and effort performing on the sterner mistresses of strings and keys, wood and ivory. This is a holiday for me, to entertain you with my memories and words only.'

The following day was one of those almost unpleasantly soft grey ones peculiar to English summers, in which green foliage and grass shone with an almost unearthly light. Laura was engrossed by a new project in the garden: the construction of a fort made from rocks found in the underground caves that ran below one of the garden grottos. Here she commanded a valiant battalion, and her military duties demanded for the time being the sacrifice of such gentler interests as music, and even the excitements of aquatic activity.

Charlotte was reluctant to allow her daughter to undertake such an enterprise unless she personally kept watch over her, in case of crushed fingers or toes, and she took up her sewing basket, along with some cushions, and settled herself nearby, after Laura had first shooed her away from what was apparently a potential battlefield, with bees and starlings on aerial patrol.

Sarah went along with her sister's scheme good-naturedly enough, but then spied a nearby ants' nest, and became absorbed by the traffic of its tiny denizens. She duplicated her sister's efforts in miniature by constructing the ants a new home made of leaves, and then attempting to divert them in its direction by placing obstacles such as fences (made of twigs) and walls (made of gravel) in their path. Upon finding her new friends obstinately unwilling to change their routes, she found a dimpled stone that held water in one of its hollows and used it to create a lake – which led to the further discovery that ants could travel underwater as long as their almost invisible feet maintained a purchase on the surface below. These zoological exploits kept her content while her sister presided over her more elevated and martial post.

The doves throbbed in the trees that forested the upper part of the gardens, and the air was heavy with pollen, heat, and somnolence. Charlotte abandoned her stitching and stretched her legs out on the grass. Gazing down the slopes of the sheep-nibbled lawn, she saw Herr Rosenstein out strolling, and beckoned to him to join her and the girls. He climbed the hill towards them willingly enough, and after commending Laura on her fortification skills, and suggesting that she turn a cannon made of bark to face possible raiders from the valley, he took his place beside Charlotte and Sarah.

'I see we have here an incipient Duke of Wellington and a naturalist,' he said, wiping his brow with a handkerchief. 'And how wise they are to seek outdoor pursuits! The atmosphere inside the house is close today, and I suspect a storm is brewing. I find myself in need of fresh air. The odours of the glue I have been applying have my head swimming.'

He leaned back on his hands. 'I require diversion, Frau Collins. I am tired of strings and tuning forks and varnish. At this moment, I am more interested in the daily round of a clergyman's wife. If you are willing, I should like to hear more of your life in Kent. So many stories stop at the church or chapel door, with the vows said and the rice thrown – as if life did not begin afresh at that point, with new adventures ahead. Pray continue the narrative you were good enough to share the other day – I confess to no small curiosity as to how you managed the formidable-sounding Lady Catherine, for instance.'

Charlotte smiled somewhat wryly, remembering her first encounter with that lady, and indeed her relocation as a bride from Hertfordshire to Kent. 'Well, Herr Rosenstein, if you insist, I shall not demur. As Mrs Darcy likes to say, I shall save my breath to cool my porridge – or in this case, tell my story.'

CHAPTER XXII

T HE WEDDING JOURNEY FROM MERYTON to
Hunsford, a distance of close to fifty miles, was
tiring and awkward: Charlotte had never yet travelled
so far from home, and when they alighted at an inn
on the outskirts of London, to refresh themselves and
change horses, she was conscious of her bridal costume
attracting stares and whispers. Modest and practical
as her outfit was (it had been created with the double
duty of travelling in mind), it was still finer than her
usual garb, although she had left the veil she had worn
in church behind with her mother, content with the
narrow lace trim on her new bonnet of white straw.

Unaccustomed to travel, she was anxious that her
trunks might be left behind, and that she might have
to begin her new life sans trousseau or the china and
linens she had so carefully packed; a further worry was
that her new dove-grey reticule, a carefully stitched
gift from the housekeeper at Longbourn, might tear
as it dangled from her arm. Moreover, she had the
bursts of chatter by her nervous husband to manage.
It took all her patience to listen with every evidence
of attentiveness to prattle on topics long rehearsed.
Luckily, unlike her, he was familiar with the route and

all its landmarks, and settled to reciting these to her as assiduously as if she were unable to see out the coach window herself.

She was nevertheless disappointed when dusk robbed them of her first views of Kent, and was entirely reliant on Mr Collins's excited announcements that they were now in the lane to Hunsford – now travelling beside the Rosings park palings – now approaching the Parsonage – now stopping at their very own gate. Charlotte was unable to gain more than swift impressions in the darkness: looming hedges, the crunch underfoot of a short gravel driveway, a respectable-looking building perhaps not quite as generously proportioned as Mr Collins had described.

But no dwelling looks unappealing when the windows are warm with light, and someone had clearly prepared for their arrival with ample fires and candles. At that point, chilled and tired to the bone, Charlotte was so grateful to Lady Catherine (who had instructed both their and her servants most minutely in every detail of preparation), she would not have cared if that lady was an ogre with two heads. She was more than happy to echo her husband's praise of her ladyship's magnanimity, although grateful that the dark and damp precluded her new spouse from dragging her into the garden so that she might admire the aspect of Rosings that could be glimpsed through a gap in the trees, an excursion that would have to wait until the morning.

The trunks were brought in, the postilion tipped, the staff (a respectable-looking married couple and a round-eyed young girl) introduced, and the necessary curtseys and bows made. Charlotte could at last look about her new home, beginning with a narrow entrance hall from which led a somewhat precipitous flight of stairs. Mr Collins ushered his new bride into the front parlour and began to list, yet again, each item of furniture the room contained. Fortunately, he, too, was fatigued by the journey, and cut short the tour to revert to the dining room, where cold meat and cake had been laid out as a wedding supper and the housekeeper was bustling in with hot water for tea.

Charlotte gained the impression that although the rooms were smaller and less grandly appointed than Mr Collins had claimed, his representations, allowing for his natural tendency to exaggeration, had been fair nevertheless. She had little doubt that she could be – would be – very comfortable here. And even tired, anxious about what lay ahead, her bones still aching from the jolting of the coach, she felt something like excitement.

This was *her* home. *She* was mistress of all she saw, even if that amounted only to these rooms and their appointments. She was already noting that some of the glasses were cloudy, and would need soaking in spirit vinegar; that the dining-room fireplace smoked a little and might require the services of a sweep; that the silver, although old-fashioned and heavy, was of good quality, and would respond to more assiduous polishing.

Her ears hummed with the quiet after the noise of the journey, and she heard an owl hoot, a familiar sound that for an instant transported her back home to the bedchamber she shared with Maria. But no, this was now her home, and she would be sharing sleeping quarters with a husband. A countrywoman to the bone, she knew what this entailed. She felt neither anticipation – beyond a mild curiosity – nor repugnance. During their brief courtship, Mr Collins's amorous gestures had been restricted to squeezing her hand from time to time and occasionally, very daringly, brushing her fingertips with his lips, but she had felt no desire to draw away from his supporting arm in the walks they had taken. What would be, would be. And in time – the thought made Charlotte glow – there would be children.

She stood at the foot of the stairs, longing for nothing more than sleep. She hoped the mattress and bedding that awaited them had been properly aired. Then she straightened her spine, drew her shoulder-blades together, and began to mount the steps.

❦

The next morning brought a renewal of anticipation for Charlotte. The fatigue of the journey behind her, it offered the first daylight views of her new home, and now it was her turn to be eager to explore all that the house and grounds offered, and Mr Collins who demurred. He was expected to present his new bride at Rosings as soon as breakfast was over, and there could be no delay. His urgings on the subject of Charlotte's dress, which had to be the best she could manage while also being sufficiently plain to mark the distinction in rank, and repeated strictures on how she might avoid being overwhelmed by all she would see and experience, revealed an almost pitiable state of nerves on his part.

As the weather remained clear, they walked across the park to the main dwelling, an imposing building of red and blue brick set on rising ground. The parkland, with deer cropping the frosted grass in the distance, offered glimpses of leafless copses that promised verdant vistas in the summer, and the wilderness area through which they passed on their way to the house was eerily wreathed in old man's beard.

On their approach, Mr Collins, by now scarcely pausing for breath, pointed out the many features of the house that inspired his awe, not least the cost of glazing its forty-five windows. Charlotte tried to be patient: she knew he was minutes away from being judged on his choice of bride, which meant that she, the new Mrs Collins, would be on trial. It was daunting indeed; not so much because Charlotte feared Lady Catherine's disapproval, but because so much of their daily happiness depended on that lady's goodwill. She had the power to make their lives very uncomfortable if she so wished.

At last they were ascending the steps and being ushered into the lofty entrance hall by servants; there was hardly time for Mr Collins to demand that Charlotte admire the dimensions of the room and the grandeur of the furnishings found there before they were escorted into the morning room to meet Lady

Catherine, her daughter Anne, and Mrs Jenkinson, Miss de Bourgh's companion.

Lady Catherine was a tall, statuesque woman with strong features that had no doubt once been striking, if not actually handsome. Charlotte, as she sank into a deep curtsey, noticed that their benefactor had the same dark eyes as Mr Darcy, but there was no resemblance between her and the slight figure of her daughter, who was so pale as to look almost transparent.

'So, Mrs Collins, you are older than I thought you would be.' These opening words, uttered as soon as the formal introductions were completed, were spoken in the decided tones typical of all statements by Lady Catherine, and Charlotte, startled by her ladyship's rudeness, thought them not worth replying to. This left her husband almost on the verge of apologising for the advanced age of his bride, but fortunately the entry of servants into the room with tea-things spared his blushes.

'But then I suppose we must be thankful that you are not some green and idle young girl,' Lady Catherine continued. 'You must have been very useful to your mother? I assume from what Mr Collins tells me of your situation that you helped her with the running of her home.' This statement was followed by a thorough inquisition as to Charlotte's family, education, and life in Hertfordshire.

Charlotte did her best to answer all questions, no matter how impertinent, without agitation or embellishment, restricting herself to providing the facts. She was well aware that she had no especial talents or charms that might engage or delight on a first encounter; winning the favour of the mistress of Rosings would be a long game. But she was fairly confident it was one in which she would acquit herself well.

Her first duty, as soon as they had returned from their wedding visit to Rosings, was to write her letters home, even though she was eager to explore her new domain. Mr Collins was at first disappointed, as he was wishing to show her around the garden and grounds, but when she explained that she wanted to assure her parents as speedily as possible of the kind condescension Lady Catherine had shown her, he was full of smiles of approval. She duly wrote them a short note, in which she encompassed her sister Maria, and then penned a more dense missive to Elizabeth.

Mr Collins raised his eyebrows at the direction of this letter, but no doubt thought his bride would wish to give a full account of the delights Miss Eliza Bennet had spurned, not omitting the attentions flowing from Rosings. Charlotte kept her true motives to herself; still regretting the loss of intimacy between herself and her long-time friend, she was determined to maintain as frequent a correspondence with Lizzy as possible. She depended on the liveliness of her friend's letters to give her a true picture of events in Hertfordshire, which place loomed larger in her affections than ever before now that she had quit it.

These tasks accomplished, Charlotte took advantage of the few hours of daylight remaining to roam her new demesne with her husband, eager for him to point out every feature of the garden, and the two meadows that ran down towards the river. But first they retreated down the drive so that she could admire her new home in the whole. The house was built from grey stone in an old-fashioned style, with steepled gables and many-paned windows. A gilded weathercock topped a small cupola that perched over the front portico rather like a helmet. Smoke rose arrow-straight from the chimneys into an unclouded sky, suggesting a hard frost the next day.

A thick hedge of laurel bounded the front of the property, which was surrounded by a few acres of garden under cultivation, and a small wilderness that led down to the meadows where their livestock grazed. The thin winter sunshine revealed acres starkly black, white, and grey, with only the bright green of the holly and its blood-drop berries offering any colour. But all was neat, and not without cheer; the paths were lined with box and lavender hedges, hard-pruned and tidy. Charlotte was pleased to see that the vegetable garden, hooped about with cages and trusses silvery in the afternoon light, and with spidery trees pleached to the walls, showed signs of orderly planting and good management. She could do much here.

She was equally interested in the well, byre, and pigsty, the small barn for storing hay, complete with a resident tom to keep mice at bay, and the snug chicken coop behind the house, noting what improvements might be effected little by little.

As dusk drew in, with the chill air nipping at her fingers and face, she was at last ready to retreat indoors, and undertake a more thorough tour of the Parsonage itself. Although the building itself was old, the interior had been modernised, smartened up, and secured against damp and rot first by Sir Lewis de Bourgh and then his widow, with handsome oak stairs, banisters, and panelling on the walls, and fireplaces of stone cladding the older brick. Pocked flagstones still covered the floor in the domestic parts of the building, but the public rooms and bedchambers boasted wood floors, with Turkey rugs creating pools of red and blue.

Content with what she had found both outdoors and indoors, Charlotte was more than happy to praise her husband for the contents and contrivances of the home he had made hers, and the next several days were given to minute exploration of every corner and cranny of the house, its attic and cellars, and every appurtenance it boasted. She was especially delighted to find herself the mistress of a bacon safe, which emitted a pungent and pleasant smell of smoked meat and aged wood when she opened it. And while she regretted the absence of a pianoforte – she had hoped that music might sometimes take the place of conversation of an evening – it was not as if she would have leisure for practising.

CHAPTER XXIII

AND SO THE FIRST MONTHS of Charlotte's married life passed. To her joy, Elizabeth replied promptly to her letters, and answered them at great length. The old confiding tone was sadly absent, but she was faithful – and as spirited as ever – in rendering all the news gleaned from Longbourn, Lucas Lodge, and Meryton.

One thing pricked Charlotte to anger; Lizzy wrote lightly of the officer Wickham's sudden attention to a young lady who had until her inheritance held no charms for him. Far from criticising his mercenary ambitions, Lizzy excused her former admirer with the observation that handsome and charming young men needed something to live on as much as plain young men.

And what are plain young women supposed to live on? thought Charlotte, remembering the frank dismay, even disgust, that had passed over her friend's features when she first broke the news of her engagement to Mr Collins. It took some reflection on the connubial disharmony to which Lizzy was exposed at home, and which had rendered her perhaps thoughtless on the topic of marriage, to make peace with this painful memory.

Meanwhile, the winter was a mild one, and Mr Collins was able to be assiduous in his care of the garden. Charlotte encouraged, hinted, and sometimes downright insisted that he follow one or other project aimed at improving his modest corner of Kent, arguing for the benefits to his health, but welcoming the respite from his chatter. As the eldest of a large brood of children crammed into a house that had always felt too small, she found the luxury of an unpeopled establishment one of her greatest pleasures.

She hit on the happy plan of commissioning her husband to build a sundial, a project that began when an obelisk commissioned by Lady Catherine for the lawns at Rosings had been too small to suit. It had been made a gift to the Parsonage, and Mr Collins was dispatched to spend his days outdoors, engaged with stakes, ropes, and much checking of his pocket-watch and listening for the chime of the church clock striking the hour. A few fine days, and the hours were marked by stakes, and the business of choosing stones and plants and carving the numerals ensued, giving hours of harmless and happy occupation.

Their most cheerful conversations in fact revolved around their plans for their home and land. Charlotte, having spotted a few disused skeps in the barn, was determined to install beehives in the orchard, not just for the honey, but so she could be independent of the grocer's for candles. She was grateful that her husband's income permitted their purchase, sparing her the labour and odour of making rushlights, but she was determined to be as frugal as was consistent with comfort. She ordered and pored over almanacs and beekeeping guides, considering the blending of garden and husbandry, imagining lavender-flavoured honey and bumper russet crops next autumn.

Sometimes she and Mr Collins sketched out plans for a conservatory, an object closer to pleasant fantasy than reality, but it was not out of the bounds of possibility (although Lady Catherine would have to agree). And they both studied seed and plant catalogues with interest, Charlotte confessing to a weakness for peonies and dahlias, those foreign and gaudy interlopers amid the usual foxgloves, stocks, and hollyhocks. One project they did put into motion was the establishment of a nuttery; they envisaged walnuts and hazels alongside the ancient sweet chestnuts that meandered down one side of the orchard, and much comparison of varieties and calculation of costs ensued.

Meanwhile, there was a great deal to do. Although it was the worst time of year for stocking the pantry, exotic fruits and plants were sporadically sent over from the Rosings hothouses, for which Lady Catherine seemed to require only the tax of unending gratitude. Mr Collins provided this in such quantities that it was left to Charlotte only to echo complaisant agreement. This meant she had to find receipts for such delicacies as Seville oranges, which she turned to marmalade, a welcome addition to the table at breakfast time; there was also the unexpected gift of much-prized lemons, which needed to be preserved.

There was goose-fat to render, butter to churn and wash, late apples to lay down, cider to brew, horseradish to grate, and she did not trust the flour and barley bins – their contents would have to be sifted in case of weevils. Although it was Mr Brown's job to dispatch a chicken or duck once a fortnight, it fell to her to pluck the birds and save the feathers for pillows.

The entire house, although neat and in a good state of repair, had that patina of cheerlessness that suggested a bachelor establishment, and Charlotte could not rest until it was as clean and comfortable as she and the servants could make it. This meant that she spent her days in an apron, its pockets filled with beeswax polish and blacking, hung about with dusters and cloths, conferring with the housekeeper and working alongside the maidservant.

This joint labour was prefaced by the need to cultivate the staff, particularly Mrs Brown. Charlotte's relationship with her housekeeper was a somewhat peculiar one: although as the mistress, and therefore possessed of the power to dismiss – without a reference – any of her servants, Charlotte was aware that the staff served the Parsonage rather than its incumbents. If, for some reason, the living was taken from them and given to another, the Browns and Katie would remain, at least for a time. In other words, regardless of who paid the wages, they served the establishment – and that meant Rosings, rather than herself and Mr Collins. This transitional passage was nevertheless the one at which the housekeeper and her husband were most at risk – the new chatelaine might take it upon herself to dismiss them and install servants known to her. Promises had perhaps been made to others. So all was wary courtesy and exaggerated formality at this awkward stage.

Charlotte was also aware that a steady stream of reportage flowed from Mrs Brown to Rosings in indirect turns and twists as the servants of the two households exchanged news. It was safe to assume that no aspect of her husbandry or the minutiae of her household was private, down to the pennies spent on shoe-blacking. It was therefore necessary to enlist her housekeeper as an ally or, at the very least, maintain with her a cordial détente. This required care and tact; Charlotte had to show impeccable management stratagems alongside a healthy respect for routines already established and tenaciously clung to. After one taxing morning spent inventorying the household plate, glass, and silver, trying to strike the correct balance between encouragement and admonishment as she uncovered mottled gravy dishes, tarnished candlesticks, and cracked china, Charlotte felt that no diplomat in the Indies had ever faced so delicate a task.

Then there was the tithe of marital patience extracted by her husband. She did not need Mr Collins dogging her footsteps, demanding her attention as he rehearsed such small items of news as enlivened their days. Happily, he appreciated her industry almost as much as her role as audience, and here Charlotte found an unexpected ally: Lady Catherine, who openly sent over her servants as much to spy as to carry messages, approved of the new lady of the Parsonage's bent for domestic organisation.

At first, this was not evident; in her unscheduled inspections of the Parsonage, Lady Catherine found fault with much: the arrangement of the furniture, the dilatoriness of the housemaid, even the size of their joints of meat – which her ladyship considered too lavish for their small household. It took some time and considerable forbearance for Charlotte to realise this bent for interference and advice was habitual, and that Lady Catherine would have found fault with the domestic arrangements of Paradise itself. In truth, at their regular dinner engagements at Rosings, his patroness repeatedly praised Mr Collins for the wisdom of his choice of bride, almost to the extent of claiming credit for the courtship.

'I was the one who told him to marry, you know,' was often heard: 'I was the one who advised him to find a wife in Hertfordshire. I told him to choose a gentlewoman, an active, useful sort of person not brought up high, but able to make a small income go a long way, and he obeyed me completely.' Mrs Collins could never hear these words without wondering at Lady Catherine's assumption that they comprised some sort of compliment, but she could not disagree with the bald truth that this description did indeed fit her perfectly, however impertinently it might be expressed.

The lucky husband placed the arrangement of the Parsonage's rooms at Charlotte's disposal, and she soon encouraged him to take the parlour with the best aspect and light for his study, while choosing for her own workroom a small chamber at the distant end of the house, where he might be less inclined to disturb her as she sat over her accounts, or hemmed curtains, or apportioned out the day's work between herself and Mrs Brown.

Their life settled into a pattern; Thursdays to Saturdays, Mr Collins, with much throat-clearing and frowning, would write his sermon for Sunday, often coming to Charlotte's door to read her extracts. At first, she paid close attention, thinking he sought her opinion, but he simply required approbation; so it was easy to nod with every indication of approval, even if it meant that by Sunday she could have entered the pulpit and recited his sermon by heart herself.

Sundays after church were usually given to the pleasures of Rosings, where they drank tea and listened to Lady Catherine's minute examination of the sermon, and suggestions for improvement. Charlotte was sometimes tempted to ask whether her ladyship envisaged her husband repeating the same sermon each week, but with the embellishments put forward by his patroness, but held her peace.

Monday was ostensibly Mr Collins's day of repose, but Charlotte insisted that such rest was best taken in the form of healthful exercise, whether joining (and sometimes interfering with) Mr Brown's work in the garden, or walking abroad. On days when the weather made outdoor excursions impossible, she encouraged him to refine his plans for redesigning and gravelling the garden paths, refashioning the shrubbery, and shifting the palisades fencing the meadows. Tuesdays and Wednesdays he went about the parish on pastoral business or did the work of poor relief, leaving Charlotte to get on with her domestic duties, and by Thursday he was once again attending to his sermon. They dined at Rosings at least twice a week, and although her husband found these visits far more thrilling than she did, the difference in their station in life (of which Lady Catherine could be relied upon to remind them) meant that she could benefit from this hospitality without anxiety about reciprocating it.

She soon grew popular with her husband's parishioners because she did not meddle, but attended to suffering and want promptly, effectively, and quietly. She had no interest in lecturing the recipients of her charity, and the care of their souls she left entirely to her husband. She did not hector like Lady Catherine, who was assiduous in sallying forth into the village to scold the cottagers into harmony and plenty, but focused instead on practicalities, tactfully drawing her husband's attention to cases of real need or tied cottages in need of repair.

One day as she stood checking the contents of her pantry, Charlotte remembered a dinner she had prepared with special care – for the Netherfield Park party, in fact – at Lucas Lodge, only a few months previously; and yet another lifetime ago.

She remembered the pains she had taken, curling her hair, spending half an hour rubbing a cut lemon over her hands to erase the tell-tale red hue that revealed her hours in the kitchen. As she went downstairs to welcome the company alongside her mother, her cuticles stung slightly, as did the knowledge that she was responsible for the home baking and preserving, as well as some of the churning and cheese-making on those days when Jenny had to help the washerwoman with the household laundry.

The evening had proceeded pleasantly enough, although in the middle of it, the dining room filled with the scent of roasted meat and wine and candlewax, the chink of silver on china and conversation about taxes and hunting, Charlotte experienced an unprecedented moment of exhaustion. *What is this for?* she found herself asking, she, who was never given to philosophical musings. *No one has uttered one word that I have not heard before, multiple times. There are no new topics of interest, and even the novelty of new faces has worn off.*

She had shaken herself, attributing her lapse into introspection to the imminent onset of her monthly bleeding, a short stretch of time in which she invariably found herself snappish and adrift from everyday concerns. *I will soon feel better*, she had told herself, noticing that the fringing that edged her napkin was coming loose, and mentally earmarking it for mending the next day.

Now as she stood, hands at her waist, seeing her wavering reflection in glinting jars, she realised that such ennui and exhaustion had not plagued her for some time. The daily repetition of labour, her management of kitchen, board, and hearth brought a sense of completion to each day. There were times when she found her chores and duties tedious or unpleasant; she hardly enjoyed manufacturing soap or gutting poultry, for instance; but these and other labours never felt pointless. She realised she had the answer to her question: *It was for this*, she told herself.

CHAPTER XXIV

THE DAYS GREW IMPERCEPTIBLY LONGER, with first snowdrops and then celandines filling the woods with sheets of sparkle and soft light not yet reliably seen in the sky. Charlotte had set as a goal the task of making the house as comfortable as possible by the time of the much-anticipated visit by her father, sister and Lizzy in March, three months after the date of her marriage.

By then, she would have dealt with the tendency of the local bakehouse to scorch the bottoms of her loaves, repaired all the household linens that had suffered from the carelessness of the village washerwoman, smoked a sufficient store of pork, and populated the shelves of the pantry. It would take a full summer and autumn before the glinting jars these displayed would hold her own produce, but she found her husband's income sufficient to allow the easy purchase of supplementary foodstuffs, and she soon gained a reputation as a generous chatelaine, able and willing to buy the occasional rabbit, trout, peck of chestnuts, and other titbits from the villagers to whom her husband ministered. The supply of potatoes, turnips, pippins, and quinces in the cellar was ample for their needs, and

211

she was able to set an apple tart with cream or Cheddar before her husband most days. She learned first-hand what family life had already indicated to her: that a man who could anticipate a good dinner every day was also a man of good temper and humour.

The woods were buttery with primroses, and the visit by the party from home was due at last. Charlotte went about the rooms of the Parsonage with satisfaction: all was shining and comfortable. Bedchambers had been aired and linens scented with lavender; her larder held tongue, cold chicken, and a game pie for hungry and fatigued travellers; she had brewed cider and small beer for refreshment, and the pantry was fragrant with the scent of coffee beans sent for from London. The garden, although still winter-bare, was neat, with promising knots and tips of green in most beds. Now there was nothing left to do except hover in the entrance hall, imagining the sound of hooves and carriage wheels every five minutes.

At last the sounds of arrival were unmistakable, and Mr and Mrs Collins stepped out into the driveway to welcome their first guests. Charlotte's heart lifted with real joy at the sight of well-loved faces at the carriage windows, wreathed in smiles, hands waving in greeting. There was Lizzy, alert and glossy as a starling, head tilted, Maria nodding and craning, her father's ruddy face split by a grin. As they climbed down from the carriage, Charlotte picked up her skirts and ran to them, and the next few minutes were given to embraces and cries of welcome.

To Charlotte's relief, Lizzy's responses were as warm

and affectionate as always, and she seemed truly delighted to see her old friend. Mr Collins wished to detain the entire party while he enquired after every member of the Bennet and Lucas families, but he soon acquiesced to his wife's insistence that everyone come indoors and make themselves comfortable after the fatigue of their journey.

Once in the main parlour, he formally welcomed the party, and repeated Charlotte's every offer of comfort and refreshment at length, in between inviting their admiration of every aspect of the room and its furnishings. Charlotte saw Lizzy, never good at dissembling, turning with open wonder to see how she took her husband's flood of words, and could not help blushing. But what Lizzy did not understand was that Mr Collins was at his worst in company, and this company was indeed awkward: his new father- and sister-in-law, along with the cousin who had only four months previously spurned his proposal.

While husband and wife were both desirous of showing Elizabeth that she had been mistaken in her responses of the previous winter, Charlotte's object was to show Lizzy that she was occupied and content; that her decision was not one that *she* regretted, other than what it cost her in terms of their friendship; and that she was capable of happiness in her new marital home and state. She took real pleasure in ushering her family and friend around the Parsonage, attending to their needs, offering them plentiful food and drink, not out of any desire for display, but in all the beneficial glow of willing hospitality. She had a home and a welcome to offer those she loved, and she took no small amount of joy in this.

Once the visitors had eaten and drunk, and been shown their accommodations, Mr Collins was eager to take them on a tour of his garden. Once again, as they processed around the grounds, Charlotte noticed the glance Lizzy threw her when she spoke of her approbation for her husband's attention to, and work in, its plots and beds. Likewise, she was a little uncomfortable with her friend's penetrating look when she showed off the somewhat gloomy back parlour in which she sat at a remove from her husband's study. But such inevitable moments of awkwardness were all soon over, and she could focus on the business of being a hostess.

At first she was a little anxious at the prospect of their establishment swelling in number; it was strange to have the house full of voices and bustle, especially as Mr Collins spent the first day shadowing his guests, telling them of the marvels in store for them – the opportunity to lay eyes upon Lady Catherine in church, the likelihood that they might be invited to drink tea with her thereafter. However, things soon settled down. Her husband was determined to show her father all about the neighbourhood, its farms, woods, roads, and rivers, and his gig would take only the two of them, and that at a pinch – neither were small men. They thus spent all the hours of the day that first week, which was the duration of Sir William's visit, out exploring. For Maria, who had taken over Charlotte's role in the running of the Lucas household, the stay was a real holiday; although assiduous in lending herself to her sister's domestic projects, she had leisure for reading and embroidery, as well as all the novelty of new walks and excursions into the village.

Lizzy was an ideal guest; quick to praise, happy to entertain herself with handiwork, reading, or rambling, equally willing to join in excursions and or stay quiet at home, and a welcome companion both at the dinner table and more privately, on account of her wit and vivacity. Charlotte remembered with pleasure how they used to laugh together, and indeed the Parsonage rang with far more mirth than usual.

Only once in the next few days did she and Lizzy disagree: in response to Charlotte's expression of disapproval at Mr Wickham's alteration of affection once he had discovered that poor Miss King was poor no more, Lizzy had flashed: 'What is the difference in matrimonial affairs, between the mercenary and prudent motive? Where does discretion end and avarice begin?'

Where indeed, thought Charlotte. I wish you had been half as understanding and generous to *me* last winter. But then she considered that Lizzy was indeed generous; here she was, under a former suitor's roof, as sunny and merry as always, lightening Charlotte's days, helping with the hemming, providing company on long walks, as willing to show all the outward signs of friendship and affection as ever.

A few days after the arrival of the Meryton party, the Parsonage was gripped by a fever of anxiety and anticipation; Lady Catherine had invited their entire party to dine at Rosings, and Mr Collins was beside himself at the prospect. Charlotte thought that the pitch of his nerves better belonged to herself, as it was her relatives and friend she would be presenting. She had no anxieties on her father and sister's score: Sir William's passion for rank and his obliging manners, both of which qualities Maria shared, would no doubt make them acceptable to her ladyship. Lizzy – there, she was not so sure. She had nothing to fear from her friend's public manners, and took great personal delight in her liveliness, but she was not sure Lady Catherine would be entirely enchanted by Lizzy's habitual vigour and wit. And her concerns ran in the other direction as well; imagining the intrusive questions her ladyship would feel free to ask her friend, she could only hope that Lizzy would keep her patience and her countenance.

But there was no help for it, and they all walked over to Rosings across the park, admiring and exclaiming at the views, particularly appealing at that time of year, with enough unfurling green and bobbing daffodils to soften the crustiest heart, but not yet such a cloak of growth as to obscure the more distant vistas.

Once indoors, and escorted into the presence of the ladies of the house by the footman, Charlotte undertook the introductions, and all was civilly performed without the long speeches Mr Collins was clearly itching to make. The dinner, as always, was excellent, although Charlotte could have wished for more plain cooking and fewer courses, but it served its purpose in that the visitors could admire and praise every item. It was not until coffee that Lady Catherine's interrogation of Elizabeth got properly underway. Lizzy bore it patiently at first, but eventually she began to be sportive in her responses, and Charlotte closed her eyes as she heard her friend defend her education, and refuse to tell her ladyship her age.

'Upon my word, you give your opinion decidedly for such a young person,' Lady Catherine said, which response to Lizzy's teasing answers was comparatively mild, given how seldom her ladyship was trifled with. Charlotte was nevertheless relieved when Lady Catherine offered them the use of her carriage, and accepted more promptly than usual. Mr Collins's raptures at the condescension of their hostess lasted long past their arrival back at the Parsonage, but fortunately, Sir William, who had spent the evening storing noble names and anecdotes of the mighty in his memory, was more than happy to echo his son-in-law's praises, sparing Charlotte the need to do so herself. All in all, she considered, the excursion had been a success, even if those in attendance would no doubt give very different reasons for the pleasure they had taken in it.

CHAPTER XXV

THE APPROACH OF EASTER BROUGHT a surprising alteration to their quiet society; Mr Darcy and his cousin, Colonel Fitzwilliam, were to visit their aunt at Rosings. Lady Catherine repeatedly trumpeted their arrival, congratulated herself on her nephew's impending match with her daughter, and seemed almost angry that Mrs Collins and her guests had met him in Hertfordshire, thus denying her the opportunity of introductions. Charlotte noticed that Miss de Bourgh showed no interest in the imminent arrival of her intended, nor any expectation that anything might arise from his visit.

Mr Collins could not resist walking over to Rosings to pay his respects to the visitors the first day after their arrival and, to the wonder of all at the Parsonage, the gentlemen accompanied him back home to call on the ladies of the house. Charlotte saw them approaching from a window, and ran to alert the others, adding, 'I may thank you, Eliza, for this piece of civility. Mr Darcy would never have come so soon to wait upon *me*.'

Her friend seemed genuinely puzzled by her observation, but Mr Collins was ushering in his august visitors, and all was bustle. After paying his compliments to Mrs Collins and congratulating her on her marriage, Mr Darcy spoke too little, and Mr Collins too much. Happily, the Colonel's manners were perfectly pleasing, and he entered into conversation with an ease and grace much appreciated by the rest of the party.

These additions to their small circle, particularly of the charming Colonel, meant that engagements at Rosings promised to be a great deal more enjoyable. However, as the occupants of the Parsonage were now less necessary, it was almost a week before Lady Catherine invited them to spend the evening of Easter Day in her company.

Colonel Fitzwilliam was especially glad to see fresh faces and hear new voices, and he clearly found Elizabeth appealing. He took his seat alongside her as tea and coffee were served, and their chat flowed so entertainingly that the rest of the party remained quiet so that they could listen. Lady Catherine, accustomed to directing conversation, had to insist on her share of the discussion, but the Colonel was not a military man for nothing; he reminded Lizzy that she had promised to play for them all, and encouraged her to sit down at the piano, drawing up a chair and offering to turn her sheets.

Charlotte could not help noticing that both he and Mr Darcy were struck by Elizabeth's vivacity, especially when she spoke to their aunt. Both were clearly surprised by her lack of servility, but they did not seem in any way disapproving of Lizzy's merry tone. She also noticed that while the Colonel openly showered Lizzy with attention and praise for her performance,

Mr Darcy was no less absorbed, even stationing himself at the instrument where he could best study her face.

As Lizzy remained at the piano for the rest of the evening, with the gentlemen insisting on her continuing to play each time she rose from her seat, Lady Catherine was left with nothing to do other than point out all the faults of her execution and insist that she practise with greater regularity, concluding that Miss de Bourgh would have been the superior performer – had she ever learned to play. There was no answer to be made to this, and Anne herself appeared deaf to this maternal compliment, a stratagem Lizzy also adopted. Charlotte, who found the evening both far livelier than was usual at Rosings, but also productive of anxiety, was relieved when it was announced that her ladyship's carriage was ready to take them home.

The next day, Charlotte and Maria walked to Hunsford village on an errand. On their return, Katie met them at the front door, her eyes even rounder than usual: 'Mr Darcy is here, ma'am, alone. He is in the front parlour with Miss Elizabeth. I thought you should like to know right away, ma'am.'

Maria immediately ran upstairs to attend to her toilette before facing their formidable visitor, while Charlotte stepped towards the sounds of voices, Mr Darcy's grave and measured baritone, and her friend's swifter and more musical tones.

'Mr Collins seems very fortunate in his choice of wife,' she heard Mr Darcy say. This was gratifying, and Elizabeth responded almost as satisfactorily: 'Yes, indeed; his friends may well rejoice in his having met with one of the few sensible women who would have accepted him, or made him happy if they had. My friend has an excellent understanding – though I am not certain that I consider her marrying Mr Collins as the wisest thing she ever did. She seems perfectly happy, however, and in a prudential light it is certainly a very good match for her.'

This time, Charlotte overheard what gave her mostly cause for satisfaction; it was no small thing to gain the approbation of a man such as Mr Darcy, and she was glad to hear Lizzy give a softer account of her marriage, one that seemed based on conviction brought about by the evidence of her own eyes. But she did not wish to risk hearing something to her detriment, so she entered the parlour with all due speed and no small amount of curiosity. Neither party seemed quite easy, although Mr Darcy rose to his feet and made his bows with courtesy and conviction. Lizzy seemed flustered, and Mr Darcy was at pains to explain that he was under the impression all the ladies were at home, otherwise he would not have disturbed Miss Bennet at her letters. He apologised for having come and, having come, he further apologised for staying. But this did not last long; shortly after Maria tripped into the parlour, almost as wide-eyed as the maid, he made his excuses and left.

Charlotte turned to her friend, eyebrows raised: 'My dear Eliza, he must be in love with you, or he would never have called on us in this familiar way.' But Lizzy herself argued against this case so strongly that in the end it seemed safer to attribute his motive for visiting to boredom; the lack of any sports the gentlemen might pursue outdoors at that time of year, and the ever-present threat of quadrille with Lady Catherine indoors.

Nevertheless, as the days passed, it became increasingly clear to Charlotte that Mr Darcy was entranced by Elizabeth. Not that he paid her anything like the gallant attentions lavished on her by Colonel Fitzwilliam; but he constantly sought opportunities to be in company with her. He repeatedly visited the Parsonage, creating minor storms of domestic havoc as the household had to stop whatever task was in hand to offer him comforts and refreshments. These he always declined, but his sudden appearances nevertheless meant the reception rooms had to have their fires continually stoked and the woodbaskets filled, the pantry stocked with fresh dainties. No one could quite relax, never knowing when his august presence might manifest itself.

Charlotte could scarcely credit it that all around her seemed oblivious to Mr Darcy's infatuation; one with potentially significant, if not devastating, implications to almost every member of her immediate circle. It amazed her that Lizzy herself counted herself puzzled by his constant insertion of himself into her presence: 'What can he mean by it? It makes me quite out of countenance. He sat here for half an hour in the parlour, but did not speak more than twenty words. I cannot make him out.'

Charlotte shook her head. Elizabeth, who prided herself on the quickness and acuity of her perceptions, could not see what was as evident as the emerald sprays shooting from the branches of the trees outside: that the man was deeply mired in love. Even as she confided to Charlotte the substance of a most interesting conversation with the Colonel – who, in the course of a private walk, had gently warned Lizzy that he was required to marry money – she seemed blind to the fact that a man with the liberty to marry where he pleased was revolving around her as steadily as the moon circled the globe.

After her first observations, Charlotte gave up dropping hints to her friend; she did not want to excite undue hope, especially after the debacle of Jane Bennet's terminated courtship. Mr Darcy might be smitten, but he did not strike Charlotte as an impulsive man, and he had no pressing reasons, either of vanity or practicality, to enter into the matrimonial state.

But Charlotte did take an unseemly amount of pleasure in imagining the hullabaloo that would ensue if such a proposal was indeed made. Lady Catherine would be incensed, Rosings thrown into uproar. She dwelt upon the scenes that might follow with some amusement: while Mr Darcy showed his aunt the respect that was due to her as an older relation, he did not seem to value her advice as most did, much less hang on every word of it.

Lizzy's family would be in no less uproar, even if delight would surely make up a great part of their responses. Mrs Bennet would be in danger of expiring with joy, at the same time as having to scramble to reverse her opinions of a man she claimed to detest.

Charlotte would not allow herself to be so disloyal as to smile at the idea of her husband's dismay if such a proposal came to pass, but she had no doubt he would be badly shaken. Always submissive to the closest and most pressing superior force, he would no doubt throw in his lot with Lady Catherine, and support all her reasons for deploring the match; it would not occur to him that a close association with Mr Darcy might be better in the long term for *his* prospects. No matter how wealthy and powerful his patroness, Mr Darcy was yet more wealthy and powerful; he was also young, had considerable influence in the church, and – most compelling of all – he was a man. Mr Collins would consider none of this, and she had to commend him for his hypothetical stead-fastness, at least. If such a situation ever came to pass, she would have to steer him judiciously.

Would she envy her friend if indeed she became the mistress of Pemberley? She looked about her, at the ordered room, the logs releasing their scent of apple in the grate, the early eglantine framing the window. A rich beef soup was bubbling on the kitchen range, and a rhubarb fool was setting in the larder. This was manageable. She could no more imagine running a household like Mr Darcy's – she had heard tell they employed sixty servants indoors alone – than she could imagine riding in the Epsom Derby. It was a prepos-terous notion, the stuff of thieves in oil jars and genies emerging from magic lamps. No, she wished Lizzy joy of her conquest – should it come to pass. She felt certain she understood Mr Darcy's heart, but she claimed no special insight into his mind; such a grand man might yet consider the opportunity to unite the estates of Pemberley and Rosings the most prudent path to follow.

❦

The last few days of Lizzy's visit, she seemed unusually subdued and preoccupied; one morning when she came down for breakfast, it was clear from her swollen eyes that she had been giving way to tears. Charlotte made sure to be more than usually attentive, both as an indication of her regret at her friend's imminent departure, and in case she wished to exchange confidences. However, no explanation was forthcoming, and Charlotte held her peace. Perhaps Elizabeth's heart was not as disengaged as it seemed.

On the morning of her departure, Mr Collins made Lizzy a lengthy speech on the topic of his marital felicity, with many smiles at his wife. Charlotte had to smile in turn at his confident claim that the pair of them were always of one mind. But she was pleased at the eagerness of Lizzy's agreement, and to hear her friend's compliments on her evident contentment.

Charlotte *did* consider herself content: her husband's initial attraction to her might have been a matter of invention, but few ardent lovers could subsequently have been more uxorious; and while her husband might not often speak sense, he always spoke kindly – at least to her. He boasted freely of her talents, skills, and amiable nature, a form of complimenting she did not take amiss, and beamed with pride at the smallest scrap of approbation she earned from Lady Catherine.

No small amount of self-satisfaction made up his view of his choice of bride, but the crux of it was that he *was* satisfied, and he made certain that Charlotte – and all who would listen – knew it. He might be fatuous, but he was never cruel, and lacked the wit for sarcasm. Sadly, Charlotte had to consider that she had heard more barbed words fall from Mr Bennet's tongue in addressing *his* wife than she was likely to hear in a lifetime of marriage.

Besides, her few months' tenure as the wife of a clergyman had exposed her to the miserable state of many marriages and families behind cottage doors within their parish. She was learning that it was no small thing to have a husband who did not drink himself into a sodden or sullen stupor at dinner every night, who was neat and fastidious in his person, who did not grab idly at the buttocks of the scullery-maid as she passed in the corridor.

And it was unthinkable that he would ever strike her. At first, Charlotte had been mystified, then horrified, to see the marks of knuckles on the faces of the women to whom her husband ministered, their split lips and blued eyes. But after a few weeks, it was as if a gauzy veil slipped, and her vision adjusted, revealing to her afresh scenes from her life in Meryton – those women of the neighbourhood, high and low alike, who seemed unusually clumsy – whose arms were always gingerly wrapped around their ribs, who limped too often, whose faces bore traces of their many slips and falls.

As Mrs Collins's wife, Charlotte was safe, appreciated, and occupied; and her marriage had brought other benefits, some of which she was still learning to value. When Mothering Sunday approached, and she interviewed Katie to make arrangements for her to visit her mother that day, she was surprised to learn that the young maidservant came from a large family nearby. While it was convenient that she lodged in a tiny attic room under the Parsonage roof, it was by no means necessary – her home was but a half-hour's walk away.

'Do you not miss your family?' Charlotte enquired. 'I had no idea they lived so close by. I would have given you some hours off to visit, had I known.'

Katie gaped at her. 'Ma'am, I am the eldest of ten. Every year, there is another baby brother or sister when I visit. Until I came here, I helped my mam care for them all. There was never any—' she paused and thought for a moment: '—peace. Here I have my own bed, *my own room*, ma'am.' She leaned forward in her earnestness to convey her sense of good fortune. 'My own room!'

Charlotte remembered the bed she had shared with Maria at Lucas Lodge, the hustle and press involved in living in a house crammed with slightly too many people, and she thought she understood. The cramped and dark space under the eaves must seem a haven to Katie.

The new Mrs Collins considered herself more than content; she knew that she was fortunate.

CHAPTER XXVI

As THE MONTHS OF HER first summer in Kent passed, Charlotte was extremely busy preserving and bottling as much as she could from the kitchen garden, and not as attentive as usual to news from Hertfordshire. She had caught a whiff of some terrible scandal concerning Lydia Bennet and Mr Wickham, but it had culminated, surprisingly and mercifully, in their marriage. The new Mrs Wickham was bouncing around her old neighbourhood, demanding congratulations from all in a fashion that was curdling the tempers of many. Charlotte could only imagine what Lizzy thought of such careless behaviour.

However, the most startling news of all concerned Lizzy herself. One day, both the Collinses were summoned to an urgent meeting with Lady Catherine. They presented themselves, a little uneasy, both examining their recent conduct to try and discern if they had unwittingly displeased her ladyship. To their astonishment, their patroness informed them of a rumour that Mr Darcy was on the verge of proposing to Miss Elizabeth Bennet.

Lady Catherine's rage at this information, and her desire to blame someone for it, was such that she railed at the bewildered pair as if they were somehow agents of the impending match. Certainly there seemed to be considerable resentment of Charlotte, who was responsible for introducing the audacious Miss Elizabeth Bennet as an interloper at Rosings and, worse, a thief who had carried off Miss de Bourgh's rightful fiancé.

'Mr Darcy is engaged to marry my daughter,' exclaimed her ladyship. 'Now, what do you say to that?'

Mr Collins, at first rendered speechless by this turn of events, had resorted to repeated apologies of a general nature, but had not much of sense to contribute otherwise, and it was left to Charlotte to attempt to reason with Lady Catherine.

'Your ladyship, surely if Mr Darcy and Miss de Bourgh are engaged, neither you nor she have anything to fear from what is doubtless a mischievous report, or a grave misunderstanding?'

Lady Catherine hesitated. 'Theirs is not the usual sort of engagement: it is an understanding shared by the family. His mother and I planned it while both were still in their cradles. It is an expectation that has become fact, a union that will be most satisfactory, correct, and necessary. I will not have it overturned by a pert girl with ideas above her station. Mrs Collins, I charge you to use your power to dissuade your friend from a step that will cost her *all* her friends. It did not escape me last Easter that you have influence with Miss Elizabeth Bennet. I insist that you write to her at once.'

She turned to the goldfish-mouthed Mr Collins: 'And I insist that *you* travel straight away to Longbourn, bearing your wife's letter, to speak most sternly to the Bennets, and warn them against spreading such wild and malicious rumours. There can be no truth in them. They must be contradicted at once. You must impress this upon your cousin.'

This was going too far. Charlotte had no intention of writing such a letter, or allowing her husband to cross two counties on a fool's errand. 'But Lady Catherine, we know of no such predisposition on Mr Darcy's part.' She paused, remembering the rapt expression on Darcy's face as he watched Elizabeth during their evenings at Rosings. She felt private delight and even triumph at this intimation of her friend's conquest; of Mr Darcy's feelings, she had never been in any doubt. *Eliza, I hope this is true.*

However, now she needed to dissemble: 'Your lady-ship cannot wish for me to excite Miss Elizabeth Bennet's hopes in this regard. This would be foolish in the extreme. If Mr Collins were to visit, especially to speak on such a topic, surely this would confirm or harden reports of such a match? Would not the Bennets begin to speak of it abroad? We could hardly hope for discretion, and it seems that discretion is our friend in this matter.'

Lady Catherine was not disposed to be soothed by any of this, and it took Charlotte's most strenuous efforts to explain that no letter from her, or visit by Mr Collins, could be productive of anything more than added evil to the situation, which might in any case be entirely imaginary.

It was the closest to open defiance of her ladyship

she had yet shown, and it greatly distressed her husband, but even he had to agree with her point that he had no special influence with his cousin, and no evidence that she would not act wilfully against his counsel.

'Very well,' Lady Catherine snapped. 'I see I am to have no aid from you. I am most disappointed in you. But your feebleness does not inspire confidence that you could indeed intervene effectively. I shall have all the inconvenience of travelling to Longbourn myself to attend to the matter. You are dismissed from my presence.'

Mr Collins was by now almost weeping with distress and, all the way home, his wife had to dissuade him from returning to Rosings to throw himself at Lady Catherine's feet and promise any service he could offer. It was only by dint of impressing upon him the unlikelihood of such a match (she argued for this robustly while privately holding the opposite view) and the equal unlikelihood that his cousin would obey any instruction of his (this she had no trouble believing) that she got him home. She kept murmuring the words 'headstrong' and 'wilful', hoping Lizzy would forgive such calumny, but it took the entire evening to calm her husband. They eventually settled it that after Lady Catherine's visit to Hertfordshire, he would write to Mr Bennet, giving an account of the rumour, and advising him to take all steps necessary to contradict it, explaining that even if such a match might be thought of, Lady Catherine would never consent to it.

Charlotte now decided the time was right to distract him with a piece of news she had been saving: she was certain she was with child, an infant, as far as she could calculate, who would be born at the end of the year. This had the desired effect: Mr Collins was overcome by joy, pride, and solicitude, and began to revolve around the room with feverish good spirits rather than anxiety, unable to decide whether to call out the news to the servants and invite them to take a celebratory glass of Madeira, or to tuck a quilt over his wife's knees and make up the fire afresh. The rest of the evening was spent in speculation of a happier kind, and Charlotte privately enjoyed the sense of double anticipation: a child on the way, and perhaps a match between her friend and Mr Darcy.

Lady Catherine's visit was paid, and Mr Collins's letter written, but, within days, there came the following reply from Mr Bennet: 'I must trouble you once more for congratulations. Elizabeth will soon be the wife of Mr Darcy. Console Lady Catherine as well as you can. But, if I were you, I would stand by the nephew. He has more to give.'

Charlotte winced at the casual cruelty of this note, but truly rejoiced for her friend. Fortunately, her husband seemed to take the advice it contained at face value, and after a few days of listening to Lady Catherine rage with unpleasant bitterness, he proposed that they pay Charlotte's family a visit until the storm had passed, a plan she agreed to with alacrity. She did not anticipate much pleasure from the journey, nauseous as she was, but she welcomed the thought of resting at Lucas Lodge, and partaking of the festivities and general joy that accompanied the news of the elder

Bennet girls' engagements – Mr Bingley had returned to pay his addresses to Jane, and requested her hand in matrimony only days before Mr Darcy and Elizabeth announced their betrothal. Jane and Lizzy were well loved and valued in their neighbourhood, and Charlotte looked forward to being able to give free rein to congratulation and celebration.

They were all soon reunited, and Charlotte's sincere delight in the match was met by the equally sincere delight Lizzy took in sharing her joy with her old friend. They both had moments of discomfort: Sir William's studied compliments, Mr Collins's obsequiousness to Mr Darcy, and Mrs Bennet's tendency to prattle on about exactly how much pin money Lizzy might expect to enjoy; all exacted a tax of mortification. But unlike the previous winter, neither woman – nor indeed Jane – had anything to fear from their relations and connections. They had done their worst; and yet Charlotte was safely married, and Jane and Elizabeth were soon to enter that state.

CHAPTER XXVII

CHARLOTTE LOOKED AROUND THE VARIETY of vegetal greens offered by the grounds of Pemberley; clouds had advanced overhead, and while the air remained warm and soft, a few spits of moisture promised rain. It was time to detach the children from their pursuits and take them indoors.

'I hope I have not been too dull in my recounting, Herr Rosenstein. I seem to have spoken as much of Mr and Mrs Darcy's courtship as my own.'

Herr Rosenstein smiled as he helped her to gather cloths and cushions. 'It is certainly of interest to learn how my kind absent host and Frau Darcy came to marry one another. But your own story is no less interesting, Frau Collins. You must not underrate yourself, or your capacity to captivate.'

He scooped up her sewing basket with one arm, and offered her the other for the walk back to the house. The girls ran on ahead, darting here and there as various objects caught their interest – a lizard drawing up warmth from a stone, a water-lily closing against the darkening sky. Laura, puffed up by her military prowess, turned a few celebratory cartwheels and, once upright again, she planted her hands on her hips and called out, 'I am so happy here! Look, I am a horse!' before prancing on, snorting and whinnying.

Charlotte smiled as her elder daughter ran back towards her to reach for her free hand. 'And you, my treasure? Are you happy here among our kind friends?'

'Oh yes, Mama! So very happy. But I wish Papa were here, too.' Sarah leaned her head against her mother's side. 'And Tom.'

Charlotte was once again amazed that she could still be surprised by the stab of pain her son's name occasioned, but contented herself with stroking her daughter's hair and murmuring endearments. It also struck her, not for the first time, that here in Derbyshire she found she missed her son more than she did her husband. But this was not a productive line of thought: Mr Collins was alive and well in Kent, and she had received from him only that morning a letter boasting of the success of their marrow crop. No repining was required, whereas the knowledge that his sisters also felt Tom's absence, even in the midst of hearty outdoor pleasures, was bittersweet.

Herr Rosenstein drew to a halt as she attended to Sarah, but pressed her arm more firmly against his side, a gesture of comfort she did not take amiss. As her daughter wheeled away in pursuit of her sister, Charlotte was once again grateful that the musician did not speak or ask questions. She did not trust her own voice at that moment, and they walked on, now more swiftly, as it was no longer clear whether the moisture on their faces was blown from the lake fountain or descending gently from the sky.

※❀❀❀※

Midsummer approached, with the northern dusk glowing until late in the evening, and the sky never turning quite black, but intensifying to a warm Persian blue. On the eve of St John's Day, Lizzy, the musician and Charlotte ambled along the main avenue that bisected the garden in the long twilight, the garden tickling and rustling around them. One could almost hear the plants growing, and every insect had a minute voice to add to the star-speckled night. Only a few sleepy birds still murmured, but small bats fluttered about like flakes of ash caught on an invisible breeze, and the air was heavy with the scent of lilac and green sap. On the surrounding hills, midsummer bonfires glowed like jewels.

'Does all this not suggest magic?' said Lizzy. 'One can understand why Mr Shakespeare wrote his play full of fairy folk for this night.' She had become an avid aficionado of the theatre during her winters in London as a married woman, and now recited the words:

> *If we shadows have offended,*
> *Think but this, and all is mended,*
> *That you have but slumber'd here*
> *While these visions did appear.*
> *And this weak and idle theme,*
> *No more yielding but a dream.*

Charlotte, content to listen and enjoy the match between the bard's words and the whispering velvet dusk, thought not for the first time how strange it was, the way intractable, incurable grief could live alongside so much that was beautiful and tranquil, that inspired and soothed; how pain and comfort did not necessarily cancel each other out, but co-existed instead.

A few days later, news of a joyous kind came to Pemberley from Hartscrane: Mrs Bingley was safely delivered of her third child, a little girl. The proud father, with two tumbling sons, was delighted to have sired a potential replica of his beloved wife, and the small boys were already fighting one another for the honour of protecting their brand-new sister from assorted imaginary dangers. Kitty, who was in residence to help Jane during her confinement, wrote in her own letter that the infant showed every sign of mirroring her mother's looks, and that the family was united in happiness as they welcomed the new addition.

That evening, at another informal supper around the pianoforte, the party charged their glasses and drank to the health of mother and new daughter. Herr Rosenstein played a celebratory march, and Laura and Sarah paraded up and down, swinging their arms and singing a tuneless welcome to their new cousin.

The news, although bringing happiness in the main, was not without some cost to the two ladies of the house. Mrs Darcy could only sigh at the thought of what might have been, and hope for what might still come. Charlotte feared for the impression the news would have on her friend's spirits, and found that she, too, was unsettled. The thought of a new infant stirred memories that were painful in retrospect, and she sought to banish them from her mind and support her friend.

The musician surely could not have failed to notice the lack, after several years of marriage, of any occupant of a cradle at Pemberley. But his concerned glances encompassed not only Mrs Darcy but Charlotte as well, and he played louder and longer than usual, pieces marked by their bravura and liveliness rather than yearning melodies. The girls skipped about, revelling in his performance, which allowed Lizzy and Charlotte the respite of being able first to sit thoughtful and silent, and then to talk privately under the cover of the music.

Charlotte invited her friend to speak freely, and Lizzy confessed that the news had indeed caused her mixed feelings. 'It seems ungenerous not to feel untrammelled pleasure at such glad tidings, but I cannot help giving way to envy. Three live children in six years! What good fortune some women do have!' And then, seeing her friend's face: 'Oh my dear Charlotte, forgive me! Your daughters are precious beyond price, but I spoke carelessly. You lost a child only last winter, and this news must surely scratch at that wound. I beg your pardon.'

Charlotte assured her friend that she took no offence, as none was intended, and insisted that the news of the new child, which was hardly unexpected, was cause for congratulation, even if it did cause her some pain.

'But I would rather have that remembrance than nothing. Where we have once loved, there will always be a tender spot. But we must strive to be rational, and to look forward with hope.'

The party broke up soon afterwards, and that night Charlotte found herself afflicted by her old tormentor – sleeplessness and the accompanying hot itching that had subsided since she had come to Pemberley. Her own words to Elizabeth notwithstanding, it was hard to be rational in the face of the twin burdens of grief and wakefulness, and she found herself wetting with tears a pillow that seemed to have turned to stone. This in turn meant that the next day began with a leaden sensation in her heart and limbs, as if she was on the verge of a headache.

Sarah, who had been much struck by her sister's accounts of the delights of Georgiana's chambers, now declared that she would like a turn to watch the piano man at work. And so, once again, Charlotte found herself knocking at a door, holding a child by the hand, requesting admittance. This time she was sure of her welcome, and indeed the musician ushered them in with every indication of pleasure at their company.

Sarah soon spied Georgiana's books and hung over them longingly, eventually requesting permission to look at a translated copy of the French fairy tale, *Beauty and the Beast*. After checking that her daughter's hands were clean and that the work, along with its illustrations, was indeed suitable for a child, Charlotte agreed. Sarah took herself and her new treasure across the room into the window embrasure, where she curled up behind the curtains and gave herself over to a fantastical world.

Once her daughter was settled, Herr Rosenstein turned to Charlotte with great compunction: 'Frau Collins, I am afraid that you are not well. You look pale.'

Charlotte confessed that she had slept little the previous night, and was now troubled by the beginnings of a headache.

'I hope no disturbing accounts from home were responsible for your troubled night. It seemed that neither you nor Frau Darcy were quite easy yesterday evening.'

'Oh! All is well at Hunsford, I assure you. No, it was the news of Mrs Bingley's safe delivery and the new child. Joyous as it was, it – it brought back memories.'

He waited, and when she added nothing further, he invited her to seat herself. Then, with only one hand, he picked out a melody on the upper register of the instrument, where the notes were still in tune. It was vaguely familiar and infinitely sweet, and Charlotte found to her surprise that her cheeks were wet. Herr Rosenstein did not comment on her silent tears, but continued to play. It was not until the air was finished and the room silent for a few minutes that he remarked, 'That was a movement from Herr Gluck's "Dance of the Blessed Spirits". I hope it was apposite. I cannot help but notice you wear a mourning ring, Frau Collins.' He reached for the hand that bore a ring in which Tom's soft dark hair was enclosed, and pressed it gently.

At this gesture of kindness, Charlotte gave up the struggle for control. 'I had a son. He was beautiful and good and loving – so loving! He was a veritable angel. Oh, he was not well, Herr Rosenstein; we were lucky to have him as long as we did – or so everyone told us. He died just before the onset of last winter. There was no worsening of his condition that we could see, but one night . . .' She could barely speak. 'One night he went to sleep. And he never woke. My husband found him in his cot, unmoving. I never got to bid him farewell. I thought I was prepared, but I was not.'

Mindful of her daughter on the other side of the room, she tried to muffle her sobs, but the curtains did not stir, and she spoke, at first stumbling, and then with the words pouring out along with her tears. It was somehow easier to tell the story of Tom's short life to a stranger who had never known him than to speak of him to those who had loved him, and who had shared her loss.

It all came out: the weight of his chubby body in her arms, the scent of his skin, the adoration in his eyes as they fixed on hers as she fed or bathed him, the pleasure of watching him learn to crawl and walk, of encouraging him in achieving these simple milestones. The day she found his sisters feeding him spiders, and the hullabaloo and scolding that ensued before she began to see humour in the situation. His delight in the simplest of things: a sparrow splashing in the water trough, the quacking of ducks – which would have him honking back in return – a battered rattle he got from Laura in exchange for a tin soldier, his hearty appetite for sweetmeats. Most treasured of all, the way his face would light up every time she entered any room in which he was present, his cheeks pinking and his eyes shining, his gurgles of glee, the way he would call 'Mama!' as if they had been parted for weeks, not minutes or hours. The way he would run towards her, arms outstretched, the enthusiasm with which he would clamber into her lap.

'For three and a half years, he gave me nothing but joy. Every moment with him was a shining one. And then he was gone. Just gone. Snatched away by a thief in the night. And I, a clergyman's wife, had to accept my lot as best I could. The loss of a child is something many families, high and low, have to bear. I could not be seen to repine or rail against fate, no matter how much I might wish to do both.'

She looked again at the ring, remembering the scent of her son's damaged head as it nestled into her neck, the silkiness of his hair tickling her face. And gave herself over to a fresh bout of weeping. It was only after the long storm of grief had passed that she realised Herr Rosenstein was still holding her hand, his long fingers passing over hers, retuning her own inner strings.

At last Charlotte made use of first her handkerchief, then the musician's. He turned and rummaged in a pocket of his coat, slung over a chair, extracted a pewter-coloured chased flask, uncapped it, and offered it to her. She accepted, grateful to have something concrete for which to thank him, then took a cautious sip. The liquor was not something she recognised –

both fiery and spicy, with a tang of fir. Calmer now, and comforted by the presence of her companion, she found herself remembering Tom's birth, which, after the relatively easy deliveries of her daughters, had been difficult and prolonged.

CHAPTER XXVIII

BEYOND EXHAUSTION, YET CHARGED WITH wild instinct, Charlotte reached for the bundle in the midwife's arms. There was no sound of infant crying, as there had been with the births of Sarah and Laura, only a faint snuffling. Mrs Talbot had not announced the baby's sex, an omission that frightened Charlotte. Instead, she turned to her charge and presented her with the small slick body of a son, amphibian limbs waving feebly – but what was clear, even by candle- and firelight, was that the baby's head was grotesquely swollen, giving him the appearance of a mushroom. Mrs Talbot did not speak. She laid the damaged infant down with exquisite care, swiftly double-wrapped a cloth around both hands and put them to the child's mouth and nose. Then she paused and looked to Charlotte, her posture and face a silent query.

A roar burst from Charlotte, stranded on her back like a beetle, blood still pouring from between her thighs. Her arms sawed at the air as she stretched them towards her newborn son.

Mrs Talbot, with the slightest of shrugs, lifted the baby and settled him on Charlotte's chest, where, after a few anxious moments, he began to root at her breast. At that animal connection, Charlotte's heart flooded: maybe he would live after all. She peered at the lumpy mass in place of what had been the smooth eggshells of her infant daughters' skulls. 'What is wrong with him? Must we not send for a doctor at once?' she asked.

The midwife said that she had seen such a case before. 'The doctor said it was a condition known as water on the brain. It cannot be cured, but sometimes a surgeon can drain it.'

'Is it painful? Will he suffer?'

'I believe it is not painful, nor an ailment that causes physical suffering. But Mrs Collins, such children do not develop as others do. Your son will always be a child, and delicate. I have been told that conditions such as this make the afflicted susceptible to other illnesses. He is unlikely to live to adulthood. I speak bluntly, but this is preferable to giving false hope.'

Charlotte looked past the puffy mass that swelled above the baby's ears and brows. These same brows were delicate pencil arches, the ears were tiny pink shells, as were his eyelids, threaded with thin violet lines. His mouth was the perfect definition of a kiss and, as she watched in fascination, it clamped gently around her nipple, comforting them both. She had enjoyed the immediate physical connection all her children had formed with her upon birth, and the sensation of love and protectiveness was not new to her, but this time it churned through her almost violently. She would raise and protect this baby. He would survive.

She spoke firmly. 'Mrs Talbot, please inform Mr Collins that he has a son.'

After tidying Charlotte up somewhat, and calling for Katie to help dispose of stained linen and to build up the fire, Mrs Talbot went to announce the tidings to the anxious father, who entered the room shortly thereafter, prayer book and jug of water in hand, ready to meet and baptise his progeny.

A variety of emotions rippled over his face: satisfaction at having at last sired a son, concern about his condition (for which Mrs Talbot had prepared him), a different species of concern for his wife. After ascertaining that she did not seem distraught and was in tolerably cheerful spirits, if clearly physically weak, he congratulated her warmly.

He bent over to hear her response: 'Thank you. My dear Mr Collins, I know we agreed, in case of a son, to name him William, paying both you and my father proper respect, but I should like him christened Thomas William. Would you be so kind as to indulge me on this point?'

At such a moment, it would take a husband with the heart of a stone gargoyle to demur, and Mr Collins baptised his first-born son according to his wife's wishes. Perhaps he feared that the child would not live long enough to make the matter of his name one of significance.

And so Tom and Charlotte passed the next weeks in her chamber, warmed by fires and proximity. Apart from his deformed head, he showed every sign of health; his colour was good, he rarely cried, and he fed hungrily and often. Their only visitors were Mrs Talbot, Mr Collins, and Tom's small sisters, who were ushered in to see their mother and brother twice a day by Maria, who had arrived a fortnight earlier to run the household and care for the little girls during their mother's lying-in.

A doctor recommended by Lady Catherine arrived to confirm Mrs Talbot's prognosis, and over at Rosings the topic of the new baby's prospects, ranging from imminent expiration to a future in the workhouse, were canvassed with gloomy vigour by Lady Catherine, who never missed an opportunity to commiserate with Mr Collins on the misfortune of producing such a frail heir. Fortunately, Charlotte was safe from all such prognostications, and Mr Collins had the good sense, for once, not to repeat his patron's opinions on the matter to his wife.

Perhaps it was the difficulty of the labour, or the fragility of her new infant, but Charlotte remained immersed in an animal world of suckling and sleeping, her hand always on her small son. She kept him swaddled alongside her, resisting all attempts by others to place him in a cradle. As long as she could see his chest rise and fall, she was content.

Sarah and Laura sensed the change in their mother, but her maternal preoccupation made room for them also: her favourite times of day were when the girls were brought to visit her. She permitted them to clamber onto the bed alongside their new brother, and the four of them would huddle languorously together while the girls babbled about their day's adventures, anticipated or experienced, or Charlotte told them stories, or Maria, in a chair next to the bed, read or sang to them.

The rest of the world fell away; Mr Collins receded to a distant benign presence whose visits never really impinged on Charlotte's world of warmth, the smell of wet wool and infant skin, the hours spent staring at her baby's perfect fingers, the long dark lashes on his milky skin, the lustre of his eyes as they cleared from blue to dark brown as the weeks passed, the pleasure and relief they both gained from nursing. It was only years later that Charlotte would realise that these months – which could so easily have been a period of sorrow and anxiety – were possibly the happiest of her life.

1819

CHAPTER XXIX

T HE CHIMING OF THE GILDED clock on the
mantelpiece brought Charlotte back to Miss
Darcy's rooms, to Herr Rosenstein's gaze on her face.
She scrubbed at her cheeks with her fists, and glanced
over to where her daughter's feet could be seen peeping
out below the curtains of the window enclosure. Their
motionlessness suggested that Sarah was either asleep
or lost in the world of her book, and Charlotte could
relax and allow herself to feel all the luxury of having
both wept and been comforted. There were no words
of thanks she could utter; she had to depend on the
musician's innate sensibility to comprehend the extent
of her debt to him.

This time, as they parted, with the now-familiar
ritual of detaching a sleepy child from her temporary
refuge and shepherding her away from Miss Darcy's
airy nest of light and colour – a small bustle that
covered any innate awkwardness between the adults
or reluctance to leave – Charlotte felt exhausted, yet
cleansed. And beyond either of these sensations, she
felt understood.

At breakfast a few days later, Mrs Darcy, who had
been in consultation with the head gardener, proposed

a strawberry-picking expedition. In the vast vegetable gardens that served the estate and its many souls, the fruiting beds had reached that state of plentiful glut where there was so much excess, no one could begrudge even the birds – who had grown too bold for the scarecrows and too greedy for the bird-scarer – their share. She thought both children and adults might enjoy such an excursion. The little girls should surely not find such a task too onerous if they could eat as much fruit as they wanted while filling their baskets. Charlotte suppressed a qualm at the thought of the impact on their digestions, and agreed enthusiastically to the plan.

'Will you join us, Herr Rosenstein?' asked Elizabeth, turning to the musician, who had long since become a welcome fixture at the breakfast table. 'Or do the demands of your work make such an excursion impossible today?'

'I have almost finished the glue-work and varnishing necessary to repair Fraülein Darcy's harpsichord. Another day of further drying would be of benefit to the instrument before I retune it. So I will be happy to join your band of strawberry-pickers. Simply allow me an hour to complete my portion of work for the day – and I shall bring a surprise for Snow White and Rose Red here,' he said, nodding affectionately at the children.

Charlotte's daughters clapped their hands at the news, and submitted with good grace to having broad bonnets tied on, although both were already as freckled as hen's eggs from the amount of time they spent outdoors.

Armed with trugs lined with rushes, the women and girls repaired to the fruit beds and set to. Charlotte enjoyed sinking down, her skirts spreading around her, and feeling for the fruit under the leaves, revealing their stippled ruby hearts, the edging of white around the frill of green where the stem attached. It was as if the strawberries blushed in reverse.

She could hear her daughters chattering as they competed to find the biggest unblemished fruits, with no tell-tale beak-shaped cavities, but she knew the sweetest strawberries were the small ones, no bigger than her littlest fingernails, bred from the wild varieties. These, dense in jelly and containing not too much liquid, made the best jams and preserves, and she concentrated on filling her basket with these tiny treasures.

Then they all heard a bird piping, except that the notes were too regular and tuneful to be any bird, and there was Jacob walking up the slope towards them, wearing a wide-brimmed hat that gave him a Bohemian air, his recorder at his lips. Sarah and Laura squealed with delight, dropped their baskets, and ran to meet him, an approach to which he responded with the greatest cordiality, sinking to his haunches and sere-nading first the one child, then the other, playing snatches of the folk tunes he had taught them to sing.

There it was again, striking Charlotte with physical force: a moment of pure happiness. Such instants were beyond price to someone paying a toll of grief every hour of the day, and she inhaled deeply, taking in every sensation almost greedily: the febrile scent of the soil, rich, friable, and almost warm to the touch; the subtle distinction between the peppery scent of the leaves and the deep sweetness of the fruits themselves as their juice stained her hands; Lizzy's peal of laughter at the scene before them; the light glancing off the polished wood the musician held to his lips. It was like opening a grey oyster and finding a pearl within, and she shut her lids once again, although the scene was fixed in her mind's eye – the musician and his flute, the hills a blue blur behind him, the green spreading beds around him, her daughters leaping like puppies at his knees.

When she opened her eyes again, she noticed a hawk swirling above Jacob's head, riding the currents of air brought about by the fine weather, the way it turned the same way as the corkscrew wielded by the wine steward at Pemberley, but more elegantly and effortlessly. She knew it was prosaically waiting for some small rodent to panic at its shadow and make a fatal scuttle, but it was hard to believe those lazy sweeps were not done for the pleasure thereof, that the bird was not somehow aware of its airborne grace in the face of gravity.

Herr Rosenstein put away his pipe and came towards her as she sat back on her heels, the girls dancing behind him. He caught her eyeline and turned to follow it. She pointed, feeling sure that he would understand her delight in that small arrow holding steady on the wind.

'Ah, a falcon. I wonder if it is one of those that belongs to Pemberley? It is too high, and the sun too bright to see if it has a jess attached. Did you know they had a hawk house here in the grounds, Frau Collins?'

'Heavens,' said Lizzy, 'I knew that and had quite

forgotten. Mr Darcy took me to see it when I was first a bride here. It is very striking, you know, all those birds in their hoods. They put one in mind of knights of old. You should see it, Charlotte. It is something of a novelty. Perhaps Herr Rosenstein will take you and your daughters on a tour.'

Charlotte confessed her ignorance, and it was explained to her that hunting birds, like hounds, were kept in special quarters on estates such as Pemberley. They slept in cages or on leashes, and were released into the sky by their trainers, who gentled them and taught them to return to their human masters.

'But is that not a pity?' asked Charlotte, her eyes still fixed on the chevron holding motionless against the silver sky, pressing its strength against all the currents of the upper air, and winning.

'Indeed, some might say so, Frau Collins,' said Herr Rosenstein. 'But what are we all but tamed animals, grateful for the safety of our homes and our benign captivity therein? Birds such as these will never know savage hunger or buffeting storms; they have a measure of protection against such ills. And yet they are still able to fly, to hover, to hunt, all things instinctive and functional to their very being. Just not always of their own free will. This is not very different to the way our own civilised societies function.'

'Oh! I wish Mr Darcy was here to listen to you, sir,' said Lizzy with real warmth. 'You have a talent for expressing philosophical things, for putting them just so, without sounding too clever or dry. Does he not, my dear Charlotte?'

Charlotte concurred wholeheartedly, and it was agreed that after the strawberry-picking was done for the day, Herr Rosenstein would take them all back to the main demesne via the hawk house. But at that moment, the welcome spectacle of servants carrying picnic hampers and cloths appeared at the gates of the vegetable garden, and the party moved to the shade of the nearest orchard trees to enjoy haymakers' punch, pork pie, and jellied eggs. In spite of having already consumed a superfluity of strawberries, everyone ate with good appetite: 'I swear I am always hungrier on a picnic than at table,' Lizzy opined. 'It is perhaps the lack of ceremony that makes the dishes more tempting: no bringing and removing of courses, but everything laid out as a collation.' Nobody was inclined to disagree, especially not when the little girls discovered that a kind-hearted cook had sent up figs from the hothouse – their first encounter with such fruits, which rendered the now-scorned strawberries merely commonplace.

After eating, the little girls fell asleep in the shade, and the adults sat quiet too, speaking now and again, the women reminiscing about their lives in Hertfordshire, telling the musician stories from their girlhood there. At last the punch was finished, the sun at an angle in the sky, and the girls stirring. They were a little fretful upon waking, but Herr Rosenstein distracted them by reminding them of the proposed tour of the hawk house. With everyone on their feet again, the little party made their way further up the hill, around and behind a grouping of trees that ran along the skyline.

They arrived at a building about half the size of the stables, built of dark wood with a roof of thatch, and fronted by a porch that supplied uninterrupted views of the estate and the distant hills. Here stood a bench encircled by arms of box, and they all rested on it and gazed downwards. It offered that magical combination of privacy, even secrecy, while also providing a bird's-eye perspective on all happening below: the insect figures of gardeners far beneath them, the imposing bulk of Pemberley reduced to the size of a wedding cake, its great lake a silver puddle.

After sitting a few minutes to take in the scene below, they ventured inside. In the gloom pierced by shafts of light from narrow windows, the birds of prey stood silent, occasionally scratching at their heads and necks with taloned feet. The dominant impression, for Charlotte, was of dormant force; all that ability to soar housed in the soft dark, tethered to the stalls, biding their time.

She left it to Herr Rosenstein and Lizzy to answer the girls' questions about the birds and their habits, content with looking around, her nose twitching at the sharp combination of smells, catching the gleam of topaz eyes here and there. They did not go too close to the stalls, as the birds grew disquieted and stamped their feet or rattled their wings, a susurration of feathers and claws.

Back outside, she sank down on the box bench once more and sighed deeply. She must have made some sound, of satisfaction or longing or both, and the musician's head turned in her direction. He fixed his eyes on hers for a long minute, then nodded, as if they had entered into some compact.

Then they set off back down towards the cascade for which Pemberley was famous, and to which Charlotte had taken such a liking. It began as a fountain spilling from a shallow temple-like structure, with a tiled Italianate dome and arch that cupped a series of fountains. These fed a stream running down a stone staircase in an undulating sheet before being pumped back up to begin the journey again. It was a favourite object and point of admiration for visitors, and Charlotte walked there almost daily, but now Herr Rosenstein explained something she had not noticed before: that each of the twenty-four stone steps down which the rills of water ran produced a different tone or note, creating a musical scale.

Sarah and Laura were distracted from water that could sing by the opportunities for sport offered by the slope, and proceeded to roll down the grassy hill, shrieking with delight, while Lizzy, who had had the musicality of the cascade explained to her many times before, ran down the hill after them, laughing at the dizzy circles in which they staggered every time they got to their feet before lying down and propelling themselves downhill once again. Herr Rosenstein and Charlotte followed on behind at a less precipitate pace.

'Your daughters are a delight, Frau Collins. They have been a bright part of my visit here. I commend you on being an excellent parent. I speak from observation, of course, but your children are not merely happy. They have a facility for happiness.'

'I must thank you for these kind words. Nothing else you could say could give me half as much joy.'

'Of course I know nothing of your late son, other than what you have told me. But looking at his sisters, I have no doubt that he too was a happy child. Your love and care would have made this a certainty.'

Charlotte looked out over the glowing scene, the late light saturating the greens, blues, silver, and gold of the scene before them, its lawns and liquids, hills and trees, all now wavering as her eyes filled. She did not attempt a reply, but the musician offered her his arm with solicitude as they trod down the slope towards where Lizzy was now applauding the girls as they attempted to turn somersaults on the lawn above the lake.

As they watched, Sarah and Laura galloped indoors, Mrs Darcy chasing them with as much energy and gaiety as if she too were a child. Charlotte laughed aloud before turning to her companion to thank him for his role in their day. As he had taken to doing before they parted, he kissed her hand, a mark of attention and courtesy she enjoyed, but did not attach any special meaning to – he did the same for Lizzy before they all retired for the night. But this time, perhaps intuiting the warmth, the unexpected happiness that flooded her, he turned her hand in his, and impulsively pressed his lips to the transparent skin on the underside of her wrist.

A small gesture, but it transfixed Charlotte. Her husband had always been a clean-shaven man, so the brush of moustache was a novelty to her, as was the combined softness and firmness of Jacob's lips.

She halted, unable to move for the tumult in her body, and he snatched his mouth away and flushed deeply, rose coming up through the golden ivory of his skin. His eyes dropped, throwing into relief the half-circles of his dark lashes on his cheeks, and she was momentarily reminded of Tom. For the first time in their acquaintance, he looked uneasy, and as he began to stammer, she interrupted him: she could not bear to have an afternoon of such rich contentment marred by apologies or explanations, or to see him discomforted. Momentarily feeling the difference in their ages, she set about speaking in calm tones of the beauty of the vista before them, while moving on as sedately as possible, once again taking his arm with both formality and friendliness. He took his cue from her, equally eager to regain their footing of ease and affection, and they processed into the grand house once again apparently comfortable with one another.

But upstairs, in the privacy of her chamber, Charlotte first leaned against the door, then looked at herself in the glass. Face flushed, her chest was rising and sinking as if she was the hapless heroine in one of the flimsier novels Anne de Bourgh liked to read. But no amount of self-mockery or chastisement could stop her sinking onto her bed and replaying the incident again and again, reliving the frisson that had flooded her body with warmth at that moment, raising gooseflesh and, to her mingled dismay and delight, tightening her nipples.

Her unruly mind ran in pursuit of more intimate details: she flashed back to the musculature she had seen as his wet shirt had clung to his skin after he rescued Sarah, and her fingers tingled, anticipating touching, stroking: what would it be to caress his body, to feel his skin against hers? What might it mean to recline for him, to part her legs, open herself up to him, to bear his weight on her body, to melt and blend with him?

She groaned with both the shock of desire and the hammer-blow of guilt: such wicked thoughts were forbidden, more than forbidden; their very existence was iniquity. The Bible from which her husband read to their family every day barred not only actual adultery; it inveighed against mental adultery too. She was as scarlet a woman for entertaining such scandalous fantasies as any Magdalene.

But her heated body led her down still more prohibited avenues: was there not perhaps a world in which she, Jacob, and the girls could make an alternative life together, one in which she would be free to enjoy his caresses? She knew too little of geography to imagine his home country of Austria, as much a fairy tale to her as the stories she read her daughters, but a picture pushed into her mind: herself and Jacob, strolling in a foreign fir-smelling forest, hands interlocked, pausing to kiss: what if he gently opened her mouth so she could feel the moisture and press of his tongue? What would those lips and tongue feel like on her breasts?

At this, Charlotte sat bolt upright in horror at her own thoughts. She was a married woman, the wife of a clergyman, outwardly and inwardly respectable. Her vows had been explicit: to be faithful until death parted her from her husband. But that set off a far worse train of thought: if she were to be widowed, then perhaps . . . and the illicit images began their shadow-play on her inner lids again. Again she felt Jacob's mouth on her skin, and now it was compounded with all the other times he had supported her physically, his supple, strong arm around her waist, his warmth, his slightly peppery scent as she took his arm while walking: what would these translate into, if they could be alone together? She had a vivid memory of his laughter in the garden, the brown of his skin transitioning sharply to white at the borders of the V formed by the neck of his shirt, the notch like a thumb-print at the base of his throat. What if she could press her lips to that inch of his skin?

She lifted her hand and gazed down at the subtle tracks of blue at her wrist, her pulse visibly thudding in the veins. There his mouth had rested, there it had pressed. She found herself kissing the same spot, placing her mouth where his had been, a means of returning his kiss. One last lasting kiss – and then she caught at herself. Such fantasies entailed wishing her husband – her harmless, oblivious, loyal husband – dead. They meant wishing her daughters fatherless; and at that, she slid to her knees by the side of her bed, and prayed most heartily for forgiveness. What if some imp, some evil embodiment of fate, caught her ignoble thoughts and struck her husband down?

And then came the blasphemous prompting: *I was a good wife. I kept every promise I made, fulfilled every part of the bargain I made. And still my son was taken from me. What point is there in fidelity, then?* Swift on its heels came the response: *The girls. My girls. I cannot risk their happiness, not even here in the privacy of my chamber, the secrecy of my own heart.* She got to her feet and shook herself, fighting back both the tremble of want and bludgeoning guilt.

Even more than a wife, she was a mother: she could do nothing, not even in thought, that in any way imperilled Sarah and Laura, or their happiness or station in life. That night, she would read her daughters improving tales, and then she would write her husband a diligent account of the innocent pleasures of the day. And they *were* innocent – barring that brush of skin and hair and warmth across her pulse. Which she was determined to put from her mind.

CHAPTER XXX

THE NEXT MORNING, THE USUAL tranquillity prevailed at the breakfast table, and Herr Rosenstein was as courteous and friendly to both Charlotte and Lizzy as always. If his colour was slightly heightened, Charlotte could ascribe it to any number of things, and she herself was assiduous in speaking as pleasantly as possible of general matters. She was fortunate to have both a distraction for herself and a topic of conversation for her companions: another, briefer, missive from Miss de Bourgh awaited her, and she opened it with some anticipation. Who knew what further surprises Anne might deliver?

My dear Mrs Collins,

I have not joined the piratical profession – yet – but I write this from the Île Sainte-Madeleine, a tiny island (one can perambulate its circumference in a morning) populated only by nuns of the Cistercian Order, who live in austerity and grow sufficient to meet their needs in between their prayers. They take in visitors such as myself to pay for necessities such as tea, coffee, and flour; I discovered this thanks to a chance encounter with the local *père*. His English matched my French, and so we were able to cobble together a conversation – which led to the happy discovery of this refuge.

Mrs Jenkinson was utterly confounded by my declared intention of retreating to an island off the coast to lodge with cloistered nuns for a few weeks: I think she had visions of having to break the news to my mother that I had taken the veil. I had to play my hand carefully; the poor woman is, as I have mentioned, a terrible sailor, and the only way to and from the island is by fishing boat, rowed by rough men, and stinking of the day's catch. I suggested she remain behind in our lodgings and rest, given that she remained debilitated by the rigours of the journey and the heat. It was wrong of me to tempt her, but I explained that the Mother Superior of the establishment would send sisters to meet me on the quay and accompany me on my short voyage. She did not have the strength to oppose me, and so I am here alone, unless you count the good sisters, who are so silent, but for their singing and prayers, that I might as well be sharing this island with corporeal ghosts.

This will be a shorter note than my last, because although I have leisure to write, there is little to report. The shape of each day is determined by the prayers recited at set hours in the small but rather fine cathedral – which luckily escaped demolition during the Terrors – and punctuated by meals and readings from the Rule of this Order. In between, the sisters work in the distillery, vineyards, lavender fields, and vegetable rows. I am excused such labour and left to entertain myself through the long, hot hours of the day.

It might seem that I have exchanged my life at Rosings for a foreign version but with habits and hymns – yet here I answer to no one but myself. Each day I walk for hours alone in heat made almost delicious by the wafts of cool air from the watery surrounds, circumnavigating this little island like the Portuguese navigators of old circled the globe. I have my objects – one of them a ruined castle where the wind whistles around the keeps and walkways, and whips at my clothing. The rocks below are black and sharp, and the waves froth about them, and I feel a rather pleasant tremor seeing them beneath my feet as I perch on the edge of a battlement.

The island is also supplied with a number of small chapels, cool, dark caves against the burning sun – welcome places to rest and drink from the bottle of water I carry, which I refill from the spring as I pass its mossy green bubble. More bellicose are the cannons pointed out to sea against the depredations of Boney, and the oven for casting the balls.

One consequence of all this exercise and air is that I am perpetually as hungry as a hunter, and the meals here, while not entirely Spartan – this is still France, after all – are plain in the extreme. But although the bread is coarse, it is served with honey almost ruby in colour and cherry-flavoured, and there is always an array of cheeses, along with speckled and musky grapes, to follow the soup that makes the main meal most evenings. On Fridays, as is consistent with the Roman tradition, we eat fish in the form of a thick and tasty broth called Bouillabaisse, and there is meat on Sundays and feast days.

The first day I turned my steps towards the centre of the island, I came across a sight I shall not easily forget – it was as if a sky purpled by thunder had fallen to the earth. Lavender fields spread before me, creating a swathe of blue stronger than either ocean or sky, and the scent – I swear it was the odour of Paradise itself. I know I wax lyrical, but believe me, it enlivened my nerves and blood. I have purchased a bottle of the distilled oil as a keepsake, and shall bring you some as well on my return. Which creeps closer – I cannot leave Mrs J abandoned in a French hostelry forever. But knowledge of the necessity of adventure is now engrained in me for good, and if subterfuge is required for the pursuit thereof, so be it.

I send all at Pemberley my compliments and good wishes for continuing health. And I pray once again that you are experiencing both comfort and diversion. I think we underestimate the bene-fits, not so much of repose – I am, after all, mostly an idle creature – but of escape. New experiences are a form of freedom, and I hope the peaks of Derbyshire offer you at least some opportunity to follow new paths.

Yours etc.,

Anne de Bourgh

Charlotte was able to give Jacob and Lizzy almost a full account of the contents of this letter, which were met with exclamations of interest and, on the musician's part, reminiscences of his travels in that area. He was able to describe in more detail the contents of the fish soup Anne had eaten, and to confirm her rendering of the colour of lavender fields of Provence, and their brazen contrast with fields of golden sunflowers.

'I declare, you make me wish to travel abroad myself,' said Elizabeth. 'I can see I shall have to work on my husband. We did not think of the Continent for our honeymoon journey, given the wars, and there were distant cousins in Scotland and Ireland to be visited. But you make me yearn for such hot skies and colours.'

Charlotte also felt a yearning that was somehow intensified by Miss de Bourgh's account of her unorthodox adventures, but she could not put a name to her restlessness. She knew only that their time at Pemberley was spinning by faster and faster, and something needed to happen – but what?

Her imagination could supply no answers; she only knew that soon Mr Darcy would return, bringing with him her own husband to conduct them back to Kent;

and that they would all return to their usual demesnes and lives, and that this suspended summer would be over. There was no denying she missed her home; at the same time she dreaded that the grief she had been able to dress in different colours here might resume its usual blacks and greys.

❧

The pianos were all tuned, and the harpsichord repaired and set to rights at last. Herr Rosenstein declared himself satisfied, and invited the ladies of the house to Miss Darcy's rooms so that he could give them a little concert, an occasion that was much enjoyed. Sarah and Laura, who had never heard a harpsichord played before, were particularly intrigued by the differences in tone and volume between the exquisite little jewel of an instrument, with pastoral scenes painted on its sides, and the larger and more sombre-looking piano-fortes they were accustomed to hearing played.

Now only the harp remained to be tuned, and that would take but a few days, according to the musician. Fortuitously, Georgiana Darcy was about to begin her journey homeward from Switzerland, so one of the Pemberley coaches would take Jacob as far as Dover, where it would await Miss Darcy and her companion, and convey them home.

That night, as their group ate their usual picnic supper of fruit and cheese in the saloon, Charlotte was seized by a sense of urgency. She could not stop fidgeting, so much so that Lizzy asked her what was amiss. Charlotte looked around the room, its deep windows framing vistas of the hanging woods and hills. Laura was under the piano, pretending to be a leopard stalking its prey, growling to herself. Sarah was lost in another no doubt unsuitable book, the tabby cat curled in a knot of sleep on her lap. Lizzy herself sewed with her usual swift darting movements, and only Charlotte rumpled the shawl she was supposed to be repairing. 'I shall miss this. You, my dear Eliza, this place – these evenings.'

'Oh, but you must visit again! All of you!' said Lizzy. She turned to the musician: 'You too, Herr Rosenstein. Your companionship has been a boon. We have had such gaiety together, such entertainment – Covent Garden and Sadler's Wells must look to their laurels. I think Georgiana and I must roundly abuse the instruments in this place until they all go out of tune, and we are forced to summon you again. But perhaps you would not wish the arduousness of the journey or the retirement of this place again. Our pleasures, while satisfying, have been of a small and domestic kind. It is not what you are accustomed to.'

'Ah, but I have benefitted greatly from the peace of this place and the pleasure of the company,' Herr Rosenstein said with a gallant bow, neatly dodging Laura's attack on his ankle. 'I do not mean that idly; my time here has replenished me. I feel like one of those falcons we saw a few days ago; rested and ready to fly on possibly intemperate winds, at the mercy of weather, hunger, danger. But for now, content to enjoy your presence and fellowship.'

He smiled at Charlotte, and her hands pleating the shawl stilled: a surge of surmise rose up in her, staggering in its certainty. She had not so much an idea or plan as a sense of appointment: she needed only to appear at some juncture or special spot, and her destiny would unfold before her.

For the third time in her life, Charlotte rose before dawn in a slumbering house and went out to present herself to fate, to see where it might take her. The day was so new the sky had not yet cleared from pink and pale yellow to blue, and the birds in the garden were all yelling like hoydens.

As she hastened up the last slope and around the hedges that guarded the hawk house, she had a moment of terrible doubt: but there he was, sitting on the bench in its enclosing arms of box as if waiting for her. He *was* waiting for her; she had not been mistaken. Relief washed through her bones.

She stood before the musician, panting as he rose to his feet. It became necessary to speak. 'Mr Darcy and Mr Collins arrive tomorrow.'

It had to stand for everything she could not say. *We have one day left. One day.*

For a long moment, time spooled to a halt as each stood on the other side of a precipice. Then Jacob spoke with great formality. 'Frau Collins, we have already breached all rules of propriety. We did so that morning we spent in the maze, we have done so a score of times as you have vouchsafed me the great honour of showing me your heart. And yet we have broken no rules of God or man, have not really said or done anything for which outsiders can reproach us.

'But I am only human. I am seconds away from risking, for both of us, our security, our reputations, our peace of mind, the happiness of our families. The risks are far greater for you, and I must be clear: I can make you no promises. I can offer nothing more than my admiration, even devotion, for the time we are both here in this place, and ever after at a distance. And this with only the thin assurance that I will shield your reputation by maintaining utmost secrecy of any special connection between us. But I assume – no, I believe – that you are a rational, intelligent woman, one of fortitude and character. You chose to come to this place of your own volition. You now have another choice to make.'

Charlotte met his eyes, the deep brown of streams flecked with mica, the faint latticing at their corners, the fine bones of cheek and socket framing them. He returned and held her gaze steadily as she felt the framework of her moral universe – her life as a dutiful eldest daughter, the wife of Mr Collins, protégé of Rosings, chatelaine of Hunsford, a mother – her girls, Tom, her *girls* – yaw beneath her. A sensation not unlike rage boiled up from her feet: she had stowed away all the hopes of girlhood, settled for the sensible and the possible, kept every promise she had ever made. And now there was something potentially fatal, potentially a source of ecstasy, before her. She knew herself to be Eve in the garden, and understood the inevitability of the coming bite.

She stepped forward, close enough to smell the faint spice and sweat of Jacob's body. She knew that whatever movement she made would be enough, but what should that movement be? Should she reach for one of his hands, hanging loose and tense at his sides? Lay her hand on his chest? She dropped her eyes from his at last, to his mouth, then brought up a finger, knowing she had only split seconds left to change her mind, to make a different choice – and then she brushed it slowly across his mouth, electrified by the softness of his lips and the wiriness of his beard combined.

With little experience of such matters, she nevertheless understood that the next move would be his, and he did not fail her. He gathered her into his arms, and stood holding her, his jaw pressed against her cheek, his arms sliding up and around her back and trunk, meshing their bodies together. The embrace felt rough and comforting rather than romantic, although each could feel the other trembling violently.

'Charlotte,' he murmured, and a piercing flare ran to earth in her groin at this first use of her name. She desperately wanted to kiss and be kissed; at the same time that she was fighting so hard for breath, she was relieved to wait. But nothing compared with the relief of his mouth seeking hers, covering it, opening it, at last: it was *this* that she had been waiting for.

For long minutes she stood clasped in his embrace, head tilted back, returning the movements of his lips and tongue hesitantly at first, then with increasing greed and ardour, giving herself over to inhabitation only of that moment, and the next, and the next. She twined her arms around his back, his neck, almost sobbing as their bodies swayed.

At last they paused, drawing back slightly to scrutinise each other's faces. And then Charlotte did what she had to do: she stepped out of the comfort of his arms, took another two steps back. Then another. They stared at each other wordlessly, the only sound their harsh breathing. Her eyes filling, she turned and stumbled away, her soul tearing.

And then, like Lot's wife, she looked back.

CHAPTER XXXI

THE DAY DAWNED THAT WOULD bring the homecoming of the master of the house, and formality once again settled over Pemberley like starched linen. The girls were taken upstairs to eat in the nursery, while the adults donned evening dress and assembled for a rather more lavish meal than the ones they had grown accustomed to. Lizzy prepared to meet her husband dressed both fashionably and elegantly in a gown of green silk, wearing a choker of emeralds and a matching ornament in her hair, which her maid had piled into a heap of pomaded curls. Any other day, Charlotte would have felt drab and countrified by comparison; but she was still humming like a rung bell, richness emanating from within.

She had spent the day trying to make sense of her feelings and actions. She was almost dismayed by her lack of guilt. She was at last able to pinpoint her most acute sense of distress: it was the prospect of her husband and Jacob meeting and spending time together in company. Not, she discerned, from any alarm at the prospect of suspicion, much less outrage or disgrace: it was Herr Rosenstein's judgement of Mr Collins she feared. She knew she would see no triumph on the musician's face as he sat across from her husband at the dinner table, but she could not bear to see pity on her behalf.

The arrival of the gentlemen shortly before dinner, leaving them only time to change, meant that the happy reunions between spouses took place in the general company. Charlotte was not so engrossed in her own feelings as to miss a degree of anxiety in Mr Darcy as he made enquiries about his wife's health, and a slight relaxation of his stately demeanour as he observed her general high spirits. But it was her own husband who presented the most unexpected change in his general deportment and behaviour.

Mr Collins approached her with expressions of warmth and affection that were marked by their sincerity and enthusiasm, claiming to have missed her inordinately, both her hand at the helm of their household and her companionship as a spouse. He would never again agree to such a parting, he told all who would listen, never again agree to be deprived for so long of his dear Charlotte's company. It had been their first separation of more than a few days in over seven years of marriage, and he had felt it sorely.

As dinner progressed, it became apparent that he had, in the soft and lonely evenings of lengthening days, embarked on a programme of reading designed to entertain and impress his wife. Rosings had gone some way to fill the empty hours after dinner, but Mr Collins was uncharacteristically reticent on the subject of the de Bourghs.

Among the first items of news he presented were

greetings from Lady Catherine, which were gravely imparted to the Darcys and to Charlotte herself. Those accustomed to Mr Collins's partiality for his patroness braced themselves for a half-hour rehearsal of all that had been said and done at Rosings in the last two months, embellished with the usual effusions; but no such account was forthcoming. Instead, he explained that before leaving on her excursion to the Continent, Miss de Bourgh had been gracious enough to introduce him to the delights of the novel. On this subject, he, Mr Collins, had undergone a rare sea-change: he knew his wife and cousins to be admirers of this form of reading, and had therefore undertaken to investigate what it had to offer, with the view of reading aloud to his family once the winter evenings drew in.

'To be sure,' he opined, 'there are works that are, while morally sound, not sufficiently wholesome in terms of subject for sharing in the family round, especially not while my daughters are of a tender age. But I confess there have been times that I found myself impressed by the representation of the human condition and its dilemmas in the pages of make-believe. It is not that different from a sermon, perhaps: to choose a topic that delves into good and ill and the choices we face as we strive towards the former and are tempted by the latter. The task of the author of both is to create hypothetical situations in which our inclination towards the good is encouraged, while evil choices are discouraged by presenting the consequences thereof.'

This, although stated in Mr Collins's habitual verbose

form, was very far in opinion from his previous views, and no one knew quite what to say in response, but Herr Rosenstein, with no prior direct knowledge of Mr Collins, was caught up: 'Indeed, Herr Collins, what you say is true. But there are some romances now abroad that leave such moral discernment to the reader. In Germany, *The Sorrows of Young Werther*, by Herr Goethe, is the subject of much debate at present, as it presents a convincing account of the almost necessary despair of a young man who is eventually led to self-harm by his observations of the world. Some theologians and clergymen are condemning this, and other similar works, for failing to provide guidance needed by disordered younger minds.'

Mr Collins was delighted, as while not having read the work to which Herr Rosenstein referred, he had happened upon an essay in *The Morning Chronicle* on this very subject. 'Indeed, as a man of the Church, and thus charged with a particular responsibility to lead the way when society leans in this direction or that, I would agree. Novels, plays and romances, to be sure, can misdirect. But judicious guidance by wiser minds can prevent such dire consequences as have followed Mr Goethe's publication.'

Mr Darcy was following this conversation, which he could hardly have anticipated when he sat down to his soup, with some interest: 'But Herr Rosenstein, do you recommend this fiction by Mr Goethe? And has it been translated into English?'

Herr Rosenstein asserted his belief that the work was well worth reading, supported by Mr Collins, who announced his intention to read it as soon as he could lay his hands on a copy.

'It seems, then,' said Mr Darcy mildly, 'that I shall have to purchase a copy for the Pemberley library. I only hope that the elder works on the shelves are not thrown too much into the shade by such modern writings.'

Charlotte spoke at last: 'Herr Rosenstein, perhaps we could impose on your kindness, and pray that you would send us a copy once you return to your homeland? I cannot read any word of German but, as Mr Darcy says, there may be translations. And Mr Collins can read it to me, I think, and explain the meaning to me.'

'Oh, I do not pretend to be any great scholar of the German language and its literature, I assure you,' cried Mr Collins. 'But for you, my dear, I shall be spurred on to attempt my best, and even to make humble efforts at improvement. If the subject matter is unsuitable for children, I can read it to you in the evenings after our girls go upstairs. Herr Rosenstein, we would indeed be most grateful for such a gift, and indeed any further recommendations you might make. I am determined to conquer my old prejudice against fables,' he added, nodding earnestly around the table, 'if only the better to entertain my dear Charlotte.'

Charlotte raised her head and met Jacob's eyes, and saw there only warmth and generous hope for her future happiness. She did not think she would ever again experience such a strange commingling of pain and pleasure. She could not help a smile breaking through, and she noticed Lizzy's glance flickering her way.

After the ladies left the gentlemen, Mrs Darcy lost no time in commenting on the strange alliance between Mr Collins and the musician they had just witnessed: 'Mr Collins, a partisan for the novel! And discussing Teutonic romance at dinner! I did not think to see or hear such a thing. But Herr Rosenstein seemed very eager to aid and abet the programme of family reading for you all. He seems to value *you* highly, as indeed he ought, my dear Charlotte.'

Charlotte made sure her voice was light and even as she replied, 'We have indeed formed a friendship which – for my part – I hope will survive the vicissitudes of distance, time, national origin, and religion. I will always value Herr Rosenstein's good opinion.'

The gentlemen soon returned, but the party did not sit long together after dinner, as Mr Collins, who was no great rider, had been much fatigued by the journey, and was prompted by violent yawns to excuse himself early. Charlotte, with so much to think of, was grateful to have time to sit alone in her chamber and try to reorder her world.

The next day, Mr Darcy proposed that the reunited couples take a walk in the grounds after breakfast, keen to be renewed by reacquaintance with the familiar outlines and vistas of the estate of which he was master, and to feel the slight weight of his fleet-footed wife on his arm. As the party gathered in the foyer of the great house, somehow the question of the piano-tuner accompanying them arose, and a servant was sent to invite him to join them. 'He will probably decline,' said Mr Darcy; 'we do not wish to keep him from his work,' but indeed Herr Rosenstein came that moment down the stairs, seemingly eager for exercise and company.

Charlotte did not know whether to be dismayed or relieved when her husband attached himself to the musician, keen to continue the conversation of last night, and to beg the names of works of literature he might recommend not just to his wife, but to Lady Catherine as the doyenne of the Rosings library. At some point, the path they were following narrowed so that she was obliged to slip her arm from that of Mr Collins and, at that moment, Mr Darcy looked around and beckoned for her to join him and his wife. She had little choice but to step forward and join the couple ahead, but the Darcys made her welcome, and there was no sense of intrusion on marital communication as Lizzy included her in the scope of her remarks.

'We have enjoyed ourselves, have we not, Charlotte? Who would have thought a small gathering of women and children could be so rowdy! Indeed, Mr Darcy, you have returned in time to civilise us once more, and not a moment too soon. We have been picnicking, both indoors and outdoors, picking fruit like gypsies, dancing with the children – such song and noise and games, Pemberley has at times resembled a bear garden.'

'I am sorry you feel my absence is required for such debaucheries. Perhaps I too might be persuaded to make my dinner from sandwiches or dance the horn-pipe in the company of such charming girls as the young Misses Collins.' A fondness in Mr Darcy's eyes as he looked at Lizzy robbed his words of any potential sting, and Charlotte glowed at the compliment to her daughters.

She felt light-headed. In the background, the conversation between her husband and Herr Rosenstein had moved on to German philosophy, on which topic Mr Collins seemed to be discoursing with more enthusiasm than knowledge; and yet she was able to take pleasure in thoughts of her children, the lush summer views that stretched in all directions, the support of a strong masculine arm when the path grew uneven. She kept waiting to be wracked by guilt and anxiety, but these emotions arose mostly from their *lack*.

Their walk took them to the principal bridge over the gleaming river, where they paused to look back over the handsome property, the stonework of the main house turning gold, then biscuit-coloured in the fitful sun, the plume of the lake fountain falling in a lazy arc. Mr Collins was in raptures, having learned that none other than the famous Mr Lancelot Brown had landscaped the grounds under the stewardship of Mr Darcy's grandfather, and had turned from discussing philosophy to explaining the principles of landscape architecture to all who would hear him, with a long disquisition on Mr Brown's motto concerning the 'capabilities' of a property. Mr Darcy was drawn into this conversation, and was now engaged in pointing out sightlines and horizons to her husband.

Charlotte found Jacob standing beside her. 'Frau Collins, would you not agree that to truly appreciate some things of great beauty, as in the case of this view of the buildings of Pemberley, perspective is required?'

His question coincided with the party striking out on the return journey, and he offered Charlotte his arm with an ease and naturalness for which she was grateful: she could not have borne awkwardness or distance. His arm felt like an extension of her own body, and they moved automatically in step.

'As you know, Herr Rosenstein, I am an ordinary and ignorant Englishwoman, with no special insight into the art of landscaping. I simply know what I like when I see it. And everything I have seen in my time here, I have liked.'

They walked in silence for a minute, then she added: 'I am no romantic, as all my friends – and I hope you are one – know. I rely on consistency for my contentment. I like to see the same things, to follow the same routes, each day. What is familiar to me is what is also dear to me.'

'Ah!' he cried. 'I comprehend you. There is indeed comfort to be found in knowing, in a world in which we have little say over our destiny, that some things remain unchanging, that their beauty or worth will not decline, or very little, over the passage of years.'

Charlotte's heart overflowed. Every word they spoke to one other was laden with exquisite meaning, and she was confident they understood each other. There would be no recriminations, no false promises or hopes. They would part as friends and resume the patterns of their separate lives. But – and she had to consider the particular irony of this – Jacob and Mr Collins might correspond in future; indeed, she had heard the two men make such promises earlier that morning, with every token of earnestness. Letters would arrive from Austria, carrying news, perhaps addressed to the both of them. Her husband might read the words of her beloved to her; she might add snippets of information and compliments to letters he would pen in return. And all without any sense of underhand stratagem. It seemed a delicate thread had been spun that she could take forward into her life.

CHAPTER XXXII

A CONCERT WAS PROPOSED FOR AFTER dinner that evening. 'It will be our last opportunity to enjoy the talents of Herr Rosenstein before his departure,' said Lizzy. 'It can be his farewell gift to us. And our applause can be ours to him.'

The little girls were granted permission to attend, on condition they did not run wild, and indeed they sat solemn and still through the grand sonatas Mr Darcy requested, which the musician played with skill and aplomb. He was praised for his performance, his patron expressing deep regret that his sister was not present to listen, and Mr Collins contributing many expressions of gratitude and admiration. Then it was Lizzy's turn, and with her accompanist she sang several lighter airs that gave general pleasure. As she sang with her characteristic unaffected brio, Charlotte noticed the play of feelings on Mr Darcy's face: anxiety, pride, tenderness. *Eliza, you deserve a son*, she thought. *You both do.*

Mr Darcy even asked whether or not Herr Rosenstein could play any music suitable for dancing, and upon being assured that their merry band had indeed rehearsed for such an occasion, he gravely requested the honour of his wife's hand as his partner. She assented with alacrity, he swept into a deep bow, and the musician struck up a Scotch reel. To the joy of the little girls, before giving her husband her hand, Lizzy invited Laura and Sarah to tread the floor as a couple as well, and Charlotte united with her husband in beaming at the sight of their daughters processing around the drawing room of Pemberley, none other than Mr and Mrs Darcy dancing alongside them.

Stranger things have happened, thought Charlotte, but not many. And then she remembered the encounter at the hawk house with a shudder of joy and shock: she had to close her eyes and hold herself still for a minute before she could go back to smiling and nodding at her daughters.

The dances came to an end, the girls made their curtseys, kissed their parents, and were dispatched upstairs. 'What about you, my dear Charlotte?' said Lizzy, flushed from exercise and gaiety. 'Shall you not also entertain us? Have you not been practising these past weeks?' Mr Darcy gallantly added his request to hers, and Charlotte was obliged to explain that she did not sing, and was not enough of a performer to play in company.

Jacob came to her rescue: 'Shall I play on your behalf, Mrs Collins? But you shall choose the piece.'

She smiled back at him. 'I wish you to play that air – the one with variations – by Herr Mozart, if you please.' She was proud of pronouncing the composer's name properly, the way he had spoken it to her the day they first met.

The room settled into quiet, and Herr Rosenstein laid his hands on the keys as tenderly as if he were laying them on her skin. The first pure notes filled the room, as warm and clear as the candles in their sconces. Charlotte leaned back and tried to absorb every note, commit them to perpetual memory, to hold time still. Tears slid down her face unchecked, and she hoped those present would attribute them to her old grief – which assumption would not be far from the truth; that which comforted her for the loss of Tom would also always bring thoughts of him back to her.

Sure enough, her husband reached for and squeezed her hand affectionately, causing her a further storm of feelings and counter-feelings, many of them uncomfortable, some exquisite, but none of them unpleasant. She was among friends, and could speak of her heart to no one; she had two happy, healthy daughters, and her son was dead; she had a devoted husband, and was sitting alongside him in the presence of a man with whom she was deeply in love – a state she had never expected to experience.

❧

The next morning, the entire party gathered to bid Herr Rosenstein adieu. Now that the horses had rested, one of the Pemberley carriages was to take him, his instruments and his tools as far as Dover, where it would await the arrival of Miss Darcy from the Continent.

Charlotte had somehow thought that the two of

them might contrive a moment alone together before his departure, but then dismissed this as absurd: what purpose would this serve? They had said all that was necessary two days before, and she was not so brazen as to wish a repetition, not with her husband on the very same property – and indeed, their last day together had already taken on the quality of a particularly vivid and intense dream.

Standing before him, preparing to dip in a curtsey of farewell, it seemed impossible that she would never see him again. There was no trace of regret in her heart for what they had shared during this spell of blended pain and pleasure, but she pursued no fantastical endings in her imagination. The very notions of running away with him, going to live in a foreign land, abandoning her children and her religion, living forever on the wrong side of all laws of state, society, and God, were not to be countenanced. Her very fantasies had taught her that. She understood that divorce did occur among the rackety aristocratic set, and had heard that remarriage was permitted in some Continental countries, but such impossible adventures were not for the likes of her. Her roots ran too deep into the soil of her native land and familial connections, into the conventions of her class, faith, and education.

All was affability, smiles, and nods abounding. Mr Darcy made his gratitude plain to the man who had played no small part in lifting the spirits of his wife, and was almost jovial in his expressions of appreciation, while Lizzy showed no restraint in her affectionate farewells to the musician. Then came the turn of the

Collins family, and Mr Collins was eager to step forward and wring Herr Rosenstein's hand, with promises of correspondence and earnest thanks for his many kindnesses, his interesting hints on philosophy and literature, his good-natured attentions and service to Mrs Collins and their children.

The girls had requested permission to be present and to say goodbye to the piano man, but now that the moment of parting had come, they were overtaken by shyness, and hung about their mother's skirts. It remained to Charlotte to offer Jacob her hand, and her thanks – for the gifts he had given them all. She made her way through a speech of gratitude without stumbling, and hoped her eyes and smile would compensate for what she could not say before others. He listened and said public words, and then lifted her hand to his lips with great tenderness, and she felt the brush of his mouth and beard: the last time they would touch.

At the last minute, as the servants trooped out with his belongings, and the jingle of harness could be heard from the drive, Sarah and Laura broke from their mother and ran at Jacob, flinging their arms about his legs, Laura setting up a wail. Charlotte fought tears of her own, but found that in comforting her daughters, she herself caught at fortitude: 'We shall always be grateful for his kindness, shan't we? We shall never forget our friend Herr Rosenstein. We will remember him in our prayers every night.'

'Like we remember our brother Tom?' asked Sarah, and Charlotte hitched her breath in her throat, glad to have an excuse for wet eyes. 'Yes, my dearest, exactly like we remember Tom.' She bent and folded her arms around her daughters as she watched the man she loved walk out the magnificent doors, down the steps, and out of her life.

CHAPTER XXXIII

THE COMPANY AT PEMBERLEY WAS gathered for breakfast a few days later. With the return of Mr Darcy, decorum once more marked the rituals of the day, and Charlotte suppressed a twinge at the memory of the easiness of meals with Jacob and the children present.

Mr Darcy made no secret of his predilection for newspapers rather than conversation at this meal, and Mr Collins had learned to remain mostly silent, his habit of prattling with nerves in the presence of great rank mercifully in abeyance. Elizabeth tapped her fingers lightly on the tablecloth, until addressed by Charlotte. The two women engaged in desultory talk concerning their plans for the day; an hour of reading with her daughters for Charlotte; the morning conference with her housekeeper for Lizzy. Elizabeth invited Charlotte to join her in selecting flowers from the conservatory and their customary river walk in the afternoon if the weather continued fine.

A servant entered with the day's post: on the salver was a black-edged communiqué for Mrs Darcy. Apprehension rippled through the company, and Mr Darcy immediately laid down his broadsheet and went to his wife's side. He used his own letter-opener, and put the missive into her trembling hands. Lizzy uttered a great cry of distress as she read, then dropped the letter, jumped to her feet, and stumbled from the room. Her husband took a swift look at it, then turned to follow his wife, calling over his shoulder, 'Read the letter, if you please. It concerns you both.'

Anxious for her friend, yet curious, Charlotte pushed the letter over to her husband, and requested that he convey its contents to her. But although written in a shaking hand, its message was clear and brief: Mr Bennet had died suddenly, after a day or two of illness not thought to be serious. His lady was beside herself with grief and terror, and Mary, who had penned the letter, was herself evidently too overcome by real sorrow to be verbose.

Charlotte and her husband stared at each other over the coffee cups, trying to absorb the implications; they were now, to all intents and purposes, master and mistress of Longbourn estate. Charlotte's mind began to revolve; she would return to the country of her childhood as the first lady of the modest society it offered. She would not have to labour so industriously. They would be able to afford more staff, a small carriage. They would have stables and horses, grooms and a cook-general. She could take down those execrable curtains in the north-facing parlour, redesign the herb garden. William could settle down – but to what? Perhaps he could collate and publish his sermons?

Mr Collins's thoughts were running along the same lines. 'This means great changes for us, my dear,' he said. 'Far be it from me, however, to congratulate myself on our good fortune when your friend has been made fatherless, and Mrs Bennet a widow. We must proceed slowly and carefully, or be thought to be taking undue pleasure in the sad loss of others.'

Charlotte murmured her assent, and asked to be excused to see if she could be of any assistance to her friend. She hastened down one of the long, wide corridors that linked the various rooms of Pemberley towards Mrs Darcy's private chambers, and met a flustered servant on her way to fetch Lizzy's personal maid. She followed the sound of voices, and came upon Elizabeth prostrate and sobbing on a chaise-longue, her husband kneeling at her side, chafing her wrists and murmuring encouragement.

'I beg your pardon – I do not mean to intrude,' said Charlotte, ready to retreat, but Mr Darcy rose and approached her with alacrity.

'I must write to Longbourn immediately, and also ride down to Hartscrane to communicate with Mr Bingley,' he said. 'And arrangements for travel to Hertfordshire must be made with all due speed. I would be grateful if you would sit with Mrs Darcy. Send for the doctor if necessary; she may be in need of a calming draught.' He kissed his wife on the forehead and hurried from the room, leaving Charlotte to take his place and offer affectionate embraces and words of comfort to her friend.

Sarah, Mrs Darcy's own maid, soon appeared, and was almost as affected as her mistress; she had come to Pemberley from Longbourn at Lizzy's personal request, after serving the Bennet family for years. She had been particularly attached to Mr Bennet, who had generously loaned her books from his library, and now shed nearly as many tears at the news of his passing as his daughter.

Lizzy loved her father dearly, and was deeply affected by the news of his death, but as the sorrowful day wore on, with Sarah coming and going with trays of broth, sherry and other liquids traditionally supposed to soothe those afflicted by great sorrow, a new anguish appeared. 'Oh Charlotte!' she cried. 'I shall have to have my mother come and live with us at Pemberley. Kitty and Mary, too. Them I shall not mind; but think of having Mrs Bennet at dinner every day! I know I sound harsh and unfeeling, especially at such a time; I admit I lack the respect I owe a parent. But I cannot give my husband yet more grounds for reproach. He is so patient and loyal; not a word of criticism, not a hint, crosses his lips. He is too much of a gentleman, and I know he will suffer my mother in silence. I would rather he roared and protested. There is already too much silence between us.'

Charlotte murmured a mention of Mrs Bingley, and Lizzy brightened a little: 'Jane! Yes, Jane and I might manage between us. Lydia – we cannot look for help there, and it would not be suitable for my unmarried sisters to make a home with her.' Then came a fresh burst of tears: 'Oh Charlotte, my poor sisters! How I miss Jane, my dear Jane! She will be so grieved at the passing of our father. I must write to my mother – and to Jane. I cannot think what to do first, my mind is so disordered.'

With a spike of pain, Charlotte remembered how scattered her thoughts had been immediately after Tom's death, how grateful in those first days she had been, for once, for Lady Catherine's interference and advice. She reminded her friend that her husband would know how to proceed, and that he surely had practical matters well in hand. She encouraged Mrs Darcy to begin her letters without delay, leading her to her desk, sharpening nibs and looking out for ink and paper.

Once Lizzy had settled to her letters, with Sarah, pink-eyed, hovering in attendance, Charlotte went in search of her own husband, although she did not have to hunt around much; he was in his favourite room, the library, which rivalled anything he had seen at Oxford and cast even its equivalent at Rosings into shade. He was applying himself to correspondence of his own.

'Ah, my dear, this is a sad business,' he called as he saw her. 'I am writing to Lady Catherine. She will of course already have the news – she is attentive to such events, and indeed her sagacity will no doubt be of value to the Bennet ladies. But it is incumbent upon me to inform her myself, and to seek her advice on how to proceed. Not that there is any doubt about what should follow next, but judicious instructions on the manner in which to advance will be welcome.' He added, 'I am of course also writing my condolences to Mrs Bennet and her daughters, my fair cousins.'

Charlotte considered. The news had clearly jolted her husband into that state where his faith in his own opinions and decisions had faltered, leading him back to the familiar path of obsequiousness. A firm hand was needed.

'My dear Mr Collins, I have a proposal to make. An unusual one, to be sure, but I would be grateful if you would hear it nonetheless, and consider it.' She sat down facing him and leaned forward. 'Do we *have* to take possession of Longbourn?'

At the look on his face, she hurried on, 'The sudden death of Mr Bennet makes what follows very precipitous. I have indeed been thinking of the extra comforts Longbourn offers, the standing, the fact that you would not have to work so hard. But may I say this? I love my – our – home. It is comfortable and completely adequate for our needs, ours and the girls'. It is dear and familiar. I decorated the house myself. I know every tree in the orchard, each hen and how many eggs she lays in a week. And that has made me think of Mrs Bennet. What it will mean to her, newly widowed, to have to quit the home she has occupied for thirty years, to be forced to leave all that is dear to her behind.'

At that, Mr Collins expostulated: 'But we will not be turning her out into the woods! It will be a great elevation for her, coming to live here – with all this,' he said, waving a hand at the cherrywood shelves adorned with calfbound volumes, their gilded titles catching the muted sun coming in through the windows. 'Once her entirely natural grief has subsided, she will be the envy of all her friends.'

'Yes indeed, and there are the Bingleys, too. But neither establishment will be her home. And even in this great and grand place, I find myself longing for our own home at Hunsford, where I am mistress, where even if our meals are much humbler, I myself have proved the bread and bottled the dessert damsons from our own garden, where you have laboured so much, and with such wholesome benefits.'

Her husband looked at her uncomprehendingly. 'But we cannot fight the entail, otherwise Mr Bennet would have done so years ago.'

'Oh!' cried Charlotte. 'No, I do not mean to go up against the law. I am proposing instead that we offer Mrs Bennet a tenancy at Longbourn, now that it is ours, for the length of her natural life. I understand the farm has a very good bailiff, and if he is willing to continue, that need not change. The bulk of the income from the estate would come to us, of course. Mrs Bennet has a small annuity of her own, and Mrs Darcy and Mrs Bingley, I am sure, would supply whatever extra is required.' She crossed her fingers as she added, 'The needs of a widow and two single daughters will surely not amount to much.'

She laid a hand on her husband's knee: 'William, would you like to run the Longbourn estate? Do you wish to give up being a clergyman? I know the hours are somewhat irregular, that your occupation exposes you to mean sights, suffering, and sickness. Would you rather live at Longbourn and discuss crops and cattle and marl pits and rents with the bailiff? Tell me.'

She watched his face, wondering if she had gambled on an innate sense of compassion that was perhaps not as active as she could have wished. It was time to apply a lever. 'And then there is Lady Catherine. She relies upon you so much. You are essential to her company, to life at Rosings. She would not wish you supplanted by a stranger.'

'Do you think so, my dear?' said Mr Collins, clearly struck by this line of reasoning. 'I agree, it would be a great wrench leaving dear Lady Catherine and Rosings behind.'

Slowly, they mulled over Charlotte's idea, with Mr Collins throwing out objections, and Charlotte talking her way carefully through each one. Mrs Bennet might live another thirty years, but the terms of the lease could be reconsidered each year. What about their own daughters, Sarah and Laura – would they not benefit from coming out in the society of Meryton? That was still years away, and what social advantage could Meryton and its surrounds offer compared to the heady proximity of Rosings, and the benefit of Lady Catherine to advise and guide them? Was it not selfish to withhold the Rosings living from another deserving candidate? The decision was not forever. Mrs Bennet, who had always been choleric, might not live that much longer. Besides, with the extra income from Longbourn, a curate could be employed to undertake some of the more tiring and insalubrious aspects of Mr Collins's work. He could concentrate on writing and publishing his sermons, perhaps even his garden notes. He could travel more regularly to Oxford and London to confer with his fellows and use the libraries there, should the shelves of Rosings ever become stale.

'William,' said Charlotte, reaching for his hand. 'I

love our home. I love our life there,' and as she said it, she realised it was true. Love was perhaps not the right word, but it was the first place she had ever experienced deep peace, the satisfaction of knowing she had a place in the world. 'And besides,' she said softly, 'Tom is buried in the churchyard.'

Her husband's eyes shone with tears at that, and Charlotte had to blink back her own. She lifted his hand and kissed his knuckles.

They settled on an apparent compromise, but Charlotte felt safe. The agreement was that they would confer with Lady Catherine, ask her advice on this daring proposal. If she approved – and Mr Collins was not optimistic that she would – then they might consider such an unusual step. But Charlotte knew how to fix Lady Catherine, even though it would have to be done in person. All she had to do was to take steps to ensure her husband made no mention of her suggestion in his letter, in case her ladyship returned a strenuous disavowal of a notion so preposterous. They agreed to say nothing to anyone yet, certainly not in writing, but to wait until they returned home.

Charlotte rose, claiming a need to return to Mrs Darcy's side, but not before bending to whisper in her husband's ear: 'Come to me tonight.'

CHAPTER XXXIV

THE DAYS AND SCENES THAT followed were understandably clouded. Letters had to be written, plans made and unmade. Georgiana Darcy had to be intercepted and instructed to stop in London instead of journeying on to Derbyshire. There was much debate as to whether or not the Collins family should decamp to Longbourn to pay their respects and attend Mr Bennet's funeral. Mr Collins was set on this at first; for reasons of kinship and friendship, his family was doubly obliged to offer condolences and what support they could. They could all travel in the Darcy carriage, and the journey would take them a good part of the way home. Elizabeth was at first gratifyingly keen on this plan, and Mr Darcy was happy to agree to anything that would soothe his wife in all the freshness of her grief.

However, Charlotte could see all the disadvantages of such scheme. The girls would have to come with them, and she was reluctant to let such a solemn and tiring pilgrimage make an end to their holiday; or to descend with her entire family on Lucas Lodge, no matter how welcome they might all be. Someone proposed that the girls be dispatched back to Hunsford in the care of trustworthy servants while their elders stopped at Longbourn, but Charlotte would not countenance this: 'If something befell them, and I was not there, I could not endure it.'

More privately, she considered that the presence of the Collins family at Longbourn might inflame an already sorrowing and disordered household. Mrs Bingley was still unable to travel, a source of great regret to all, but especially Lizzy; and Charlotte was reluctant to risk aggravating the grieving widow without Jane, still recovering from her confinement, at hand to calm and comfort her mother. She was afraid their presence might be seen to be expedient, or proprietary; that they might appear as crows come to pick at the bones, or to imagine new furnishings in the home. Not least, she was afraid that the sight of Longbourn and its grounds and lands, its handsome honey-coloured stone and arched windows, in all the fullness of its summer gardens, might tempt her husband into imagining himself settled there, and thus create resistance to her plans to remain at Hunsford.

Her arguments prevailed, but at least the first and longest part of the journey was undertaken together in the relative comfort and privacy of the Darcys' carriage. Charlotte bade her friend a sad farewell once they reached London – a sombre end indeed to the gaiety and pleasures of the summer.

The Collinses returned to Kent after only one night in town, and Charlotte found her home especially dear, but also disconcerting. Everything reminded her of Tom, and yet his absence seemed more pronounced.

The bronze veins starting in the late summer leaves, the riotous growth of berries in the kitchen garden and hedgerows: all these seemed to flaunt the passage of time while he would remain in memory forever a small boy in ringlets and petticoats. The rooms seemed tiny and dark after the spaciousness to which she had grown accustomed; yet it took only hours to draw the skin of the house about her and feel it fit once more.

As soon as her family was settled back at the Parsonage, Charlotte sent Lady Catherine a note requesting the honour of a private interview, in which she wished to seek advice and guidance – guidance she was confident her ladyship would be able to provide. She also took the risk of asking that Lady Catherine not mention her application to Mr Collins just yet; she did not wish to involve her ladyship in the keeping of marital secrets, but her dilemma was such that she wished to solicit advice before consulting her husband. She did not add that such an approach doubtlessly corresponded with his notion of how matters ought to stand.

Within a half-hour, a servant brought back a scrawled reply, granting the favour; no doubt curiosity played a part in the promptness of the response. Charlotte told her husband a truncated version of the truth – that Lady Catherine sought a tête-à-tête with her – and set off across the park. She had forgotten how gentle the Kentish Weald was, with no hill sloping too steeply, no vista too dramatic. The green of the trees was just beginning to fade like silk in the sun, and haws could be seen among the roses as they dropped untidy drifts of petals.

Soon she was ushered into the presence of Lady Catherine, whose eyes were unusually sharp. But before Charlotte could express more than the usual courtesies, her ladyship had much to say on the subject of Mr Bennet's death, and the imminent move of the Collins family to take possession of Longbourn. Charlotte quailed a little; it was clear that in *her* mind, her ladyship had them already settled in Hertfordshire. She was voluble in her advice on every aspect of the matter, including the return of Sir William and Lady Lucas to court: 'Pray send your mother the name of my mantua-maker; I shall write a line and see she is attended to. Cost is not a factor for *my* family, of course, but I imagine your mother is obliged to economise, and I can assure you that at least in Mrs Rossetti's hands, she will not be cheated.'

Next, Lady Catherine had a great deal to say about Mrs Collins's stay in Derbyshire, but at least she broached a topic Charlotte hoped to allude to: 'I trust you found your months at Pemberley pleasant. You certainly look well, Mrs Collins; your colour is improved, and I believe you are a little plumper, which suits you. But that is Pemberley for you; no one who visits comes away without some benefit. My sister did a great deal to improve the family apartments and their furnishings, you know. I believe Miss Georgiana Darcy's rooms are a byword for beauty and style not only throughout England, but even the Continent. Mr Henry Holland designed them, and I hope you were afforded the chance to see them – the paper for the walls was produced as a special commission in the studios of Mr Chippendale.

Even accustomed as you are to witnessing the style of living at Rosings, I imagine that the splendour of Pemberley was unlike anything else you have experienced. I presume you bring me compliments from Mr and Mrs Darcy. I hope they are in good health. Tell me, is there yet no sign of an heir?'

It now became necessary to speak, and as fast and plainly as she dared. Charlotte laid out her plan: that she and Mr Collins remain at Hunsford for the time being, while allowing Mrs Bennet and her remaining unmarried daughters to remain at Longbourn as tenants, even if only temporarily.

The results were no less than she anticipated: 'Mrs Collins, have you entirely lost your mind? It is not for you to interfere with the settled notions of inheritance, the natural law of this land, all that regulates family and rank! I never heard of such a thing! Mr Collins is the heir of Longbourn, and he is required, by duty and law, to take possession thereof.'

Charlotte, screwing her courage to the sticking-place, rapidly moved to the reasons why such a delay might be both compassionate and advantageous to both families, but Lady Catherine became yet more indignant: 'I understand better than most the pitiable state of many widows in this country, Mrs Collins. You need not try to school *me*. In Sir Lewis de Bourgh's family, proper and sensible provisions were made for myself and my daughter, but, sadly, not everyone is as well prepared. But there is no case to be made for pitying Mrs Bennet! Far from sinking into hardship, she will take up residence at Pemberley, an elevation greater than anything she could have hoped for. She will be the most fortunate of women.'

Charlotte snatched at the opening. She needed to be both bold and delicate. *Forgive me, Eliza.* Aloud, she said, 'Your ladyship earlier made allusion to the fact that there is no heir in the nursery at Pemberley. I have knowledge, based on my intimacy since girlhood with Mrs Darcy, that is of a private and confidential nature. I hesitate to share it – but I must.

'Mrs Darcy has been brought to bed with a stillborn child no less than three times in the years of her marriage to Mr Darcy. Surgeons can find no defect or reason for her travails, so there is room for hope.' She paused, hoping that Lady Catherine might be stirred to remember her own long-lost infant sons, and there was indeed silence in the room.

She went on: 'The medical fraternity is of one mind. Mrs Darcy needs circumstances of peace and harmony – of restful repose – if she is to bring a child safely to life. She needs no additional anxiety or reason for agitation. Yet she has confided in me that she fears for connubial harmony in her home, should she bring her mother under her roof. I have no right to speak so bluntly – I know I sound harsh – but picture your nephew and Mrs Bennet dining together daily. Imagine the – *fret* – of it.'

She stopped again. Was it enough? Had she gone too far? What if Lady Catherine took it upon herself to write to the Darcys on the subject? Lizzy would never forgive Charlotte for interfering in a matter so painful and personal. But it had to be done.

'There are many reasons to delay – merely delay, nothing more – our transfer to Longbourn, many unexpected benefits and advantages.' It was time to spread the butter. 'For one, although he would bear it bravely, it would cause Mr Collins extreme grief to leave Hunsford, Rosings, and yourself. Where will he ever find another benefactor so generous and active, so interested in his fortunes? I include myself in that grief, Lady Catherine. The thought of being distant from all that is beloved here is an evil indeed. To take possession of Longbourn would be cause for congratulation, but no less commiseration.

'It would be an act of kindness to keep Mrs Bennet safe in the comforts of her own home and all that is familiar at this trying time of her life; but it would also allow her daughter, Mrs Darcy, the tranquillity of mind – and body – that might be necessary to safeguard the succession of Pemberley. Once that is assured, we can reconsider the matter of the tenancy.'

I did my best, Eliza, she thought, as she sat back and exhaled. Silence once again, broken only by the ticking of the handsome clock on the Adam mantelpiece. Charlotte was aware of Lady Catherine's scrutiny, of something like sour amusement in the older woman's mien.

'You are a shrewd woman, Mrs Collins. Mr Collins did well the day he married you. Speaking of whom, is he apprised of your scheme to delay his enjoyment of his legal inheritance?'

'Indeed he is, Lady Catherine. But I have said nothing of Mrs Darcy's situation to him. I left that matter until such time as I could discuss it with you, trusting in your feminine discretion. But I know that if you throw your weight behind my suggestion – one which has the best interests of not one, but three families at heart – we might persuade him together.'

Now she was convinced she saw a faint smile. 'Very well, Mrs Collins. Your argument concerning an heir in the Pemberley nursery is unanswerable. I will support this lunatic scheme of yours, at least for a year or two. We shall discuss it further, but let us agree, for the time being, that after we have both spoken to Mr Collins, he should write to Mrs Bennet with this proposal. And then we shall see.'

She reached for the bell alongside her chair and snapped her wrist, clanging its silver tongue once. 'Let us have Blake fetch the good brandy from the cellar. I believe we should drink to the memory of Mr Bennet, to the future of Pemberley, and to the health of your family, Mrs Collins. Your friends and relations have an asset in you. I commend you for that. And it has not escaped my notice that my daughter – she returns from France next week – relies on your company, too. We shall not lose you to Hertfordshire just yet.'

CHAPTER XXXV

THE NEXT EVENT OF NOTE was the return of Anne and Mrs Jenkinson to Rosings. While the latter was sadly haggard and reduced by her spell abroad, the change in Miss de Bourgh's appearance was marked. She was pleasingly improved in plumpness, but most startling was the brownness of her face, in which her eyes were much brighter and her teeth flashed like piano keys. She also seemed possessed of new energy, her steps and movements lacking in their habitual languor. Fortunately, her mother cared for nothing beyond her daughter's improved health, and took full credit for the excursion, now deemed to be her idea. There was talk of such a trip becoming an annual event, and perhaps even finding a companion younger and a better traveller than poor Mrs Jenkinson.

Charlotte's first encounter with Anne after her return was at dinner at Rosings, on which occasion they could not speak other than in generalities of their respective eventful summers. But soon came an invitation to meet in the hothouses again, ostensibly so that Miss de Bourgh could show Charlotte the new plants she had brought back from the Mediterranean.

It transpired that the heiress had stayed several weeks

with the French nuns on their island, before decamping to Nice, then roasting in all the glare of late-summer Provençal heat. Here she had spent the days in a cool stone pension, reading, writing, and trying her hand at sketching: 'You can scarcely have an idea of how poor my efforts were,' she assured Charlotte when the latter expressed an interest in seeing these attempts.

Early in the mornings, in her plainest gown and pattens, she would visit the local markets: 'Such a press of odour and colour and noise!' Amid the clatter of hooves and boots on cobblestones, and the honking of doomed geese and ducks, she would purchase such delicacies as white peaches and goats' milk cheese, and make her breakfast as she wandered, sometimes adding a tin cup of rough red wine to her repast.

Once Mrs Jenkinson had retired for the night, which she often did early, perpetually felled as she was by the heat and her charge's generous offerings of laudanum, Anne would venture out to explore, dressed once more as a man. This stratagem had enabled her to visit taverns and other watering-holes of dubious repute, where any queries were met with a hoarse mutter identifying the speaker as an English native unable to converse in French – a necessary pretence to foreclose discovery. Charlotte marvelled at her companion's boldness, but Anne waved aside her concerns.

'You would think, Mrs Collins, that this involved risk, that I was placing in jeopardy if not my virtue, my modesty,' she said, extracting a tin from a pocket and liberating a small cheroot, which, to Charlotte's amazement, she lit and puffed at. 'An Englishwoman abroad at night, unaccompanied, in the insalubrious quarters of a foreign city! But not even eavesdropping exposed me to anything really dreadful or dangerous.'

Waving her evil-smelling cheroot, she admitted to curiosity as to what men discussed when the gentler sex was absent. 'How disappointed I was! I found that they are the dullest of creatures. My understanding of colloquial French might be imperfect, but I heard no exciting tales of striving, exertion, or battle, whether with forces of nature or other men, no accounts of travels and travails, of broader vistas and horizons. Barely even any mention of emperors and empires, the rise and fall of nations. Instead, an endless litany of complaint: against their employers or employees, their fathers or brothers, their spendthrift or sour wives, their ungrateful children. You never heard such – *whining*. It put me in mind of beagle pups. So there you have the mystery that is men explained, Mrs Collins. Wholly self-absorbed and possessed of a sense of grievance that the rest of the world does not share their sense of self-importance.'

Charlotte, although by now laughing, felt she had to spring to the defence of the stronger sex: 'Nay, how can you say so, Miss de Bourgh? Think of the good men you yourself know . . .' Her voice trailed away as she considered the men of Anne's acquaintance.

'Precisely my point. Colonel Fitzwilliam's charm does not alter the fact that he is entirely self-serving. My cousin Darcy, I would agree, is the very model of moral probity, but he might be more appealing if he were not so very serious and formal in his pursuit of goodness. And I hesitate to speak of your own spouse, Mrs Collins, but even as a partial wife you must own that his greatest virtue is his affection for you and his children. All that is good in his character springs from that source.'

She stopped to peer at Charlotte. 'Am I too frank? Is my lack of varnish discomforting? I certainly do not mean to draw you into marital disloyalty.'

'No,' said Charlotte, fanning the smoke away with a sprig of lavender. 'No, it is not that. I might disagree with your judgement of the three men I do know, one intimately, but I do not feel compromised.'

She hesitated. Could she speak of Jacob without betraying herself? 'What gives me pause is that I came to know a man – no, a gentleman – at Pemberley this past summer. He was there to attend to the musical instruments. And when Sarah fell in the river, he saved her. No doubt this influenced my opinion of his good qualities, but I found him wholly sympathetic.'

'So he told you no tales of hardship, no accounts of the various wrongdoings and injustices he suffered?'

Charlotte paused, remembering the taste of warm milk and the servant's head pillowed on rounded arms. 'He did, once. But that was different,' she said, seeing Anne grimace. 'He was a Jew.'

'Ah, that does indeed alter the complexion of things. It cannot be easy to make one's way in the Christian world as a Semite,' said her companion.

The talk turned to more general matters, with Miss de Bourgh congratulating Charlotte on the accession of her family to the Longbourn estate, although, as she was quick to note, this was a matter of the vagaries of fortune rather than calculation. 'I commend you on your management of the situation: allowing the surviving Bennet females to remain as tenants, while maintaining your home here. But what really has my admiration is that my mother considers this an excellent plan of action. This leads me to all but suspect witchcraft on your part, Mrs Collins. Did our gypsy friends weave a spell, perhaps?'

Charlotte laughed again, and demurred, and talk turned at last to matters botanical, in which she took a sincere interest: most particularly a new and creeping form of rosemary Anne had brought back from Provence, which she hoped might prove resistant to frost.

A few weeks later, Charlotte heard at the front door more than the usual commotion that announced a visitor, and her husband's astonished voice: 'Mr Darcy, sir! You do us great honour! Welcome, welcome to our humble abode. My dear Charlotte, see what a great compliment is paid to us here! Mr Darcy has come to call. What civility! Come in, sir, and accept such hospitality as we can offer, although it will of course be nothing as to what we received at your hands this past summer, or the welcome that no doubt awaits you at Rosings.'

This tide of words carried both men into the front parlour, where Charlotte joined them, deeply curious as to what brought Mr Darcy to their neighbourhood. After the bows and curtseys were performed, compliments exchanged, news of Mrs Darcy given, and enquiries as to the health of the Misses Collins made, their visitor explained that he had business in town, but had heard news concerning Longbourn he wished to have explained to him in person.

'Is it true, Mr Collins, that you are deferring taking possession of the estate for the time being? My wife received a somewhat unclear account from her sister Mary, in which she indicated that by your good graces, she, her mother, and her sister Kitty are to remain in occupancy as tenants, with the bailiff to continue the management of the farm now that Mr Bennet has died. I confess I might not have given this puzzling story too much credit had I not received a short note from Lady Catherine conveying similar information. May I enquire, as one deeply engaged in the well-being of my wife's family, as to its veracity?'

Charlotte held her breath. This indeed was a test of her husband's resolve. Fortunately, Lady Catherine's assent to the plan, and indeed her speeches on the nobility and magnanimity thereof, had fortified Mr Collins to the extent that his enthusiasm for it now matched his wife's. 'Indeed, sir, every word of it is true. There is no need to turn a grieving widow and her daughters out of their home just yet. Let us allow some time to pass.'

'But Mr Collins, legally, Longbourn is now *your* home. Possession of the estate would allow you the life of a gentleman; your family would rise in standing and ease.'

Now Mr Collins looked a little crestfallen, so Charlotte thought it time to slip into the conversation: 'Mr Darcy, all you say is true. But the income from Longbourn will come to us, and it is not forever, you know. Mary and Kitty might marry soon, and who knows how long Mrs Bennet may yet live? Besides, we are not so discontented with our lot here – the attentions of your aunt, the work of the parish and stewardship of our Parsonage – as to wish to quit it at the first opportunity.'

'But you are uniformly gracious to concern yourself with such small matters, sir,' cried Mr Collins. 'We are grateful for your attention and advice.'

'You give me too much credit, Mr Collins. Mrs Bennet is my wife's mother, Elizabeth's sisters are my sisters. Their happiness and comfort is very much my concern, especially at this time of bereavement. But still more important is the happiness and comfort of my wife, and I must own that at a time of great grief and distress, these tidings have made a significant impression on her. She speaks of nothing but your compassion and kindness. Mrs Collins, I have a note from her for you, in which I assume she conveys these feelings to you directly.'

He drew a letter from his jacket and presented it to Charlotte, who hastily tucked it into a pocket lest her husband suggest she open and read it to them all.

'I am glad to learn that Mrs Darcy takes comfort from our decision,' she said, hoping to lead the conversation into a different channel. 'And I am certain Mrs Bennet is greatly supported by the knowledge that she has good friends about her at this time.'

'Indeed,' said Mr Collins, veering towards dangerous territory. 'And think, in all the first distress of widowhood, Mrs Bennet need not give up her home to others, move elsewhere, find herself estranged from familiar scenes and faces.'

Mr Darcy regarded them thoughtfully. 'Mr Collins, yours is certainly not the usual response of an heir, and I would be sorry to see the legitimate process of inheritance disrupted. Are you not being too superfine? Pray do not make such a momentous decision for the ease and convenience of *my* family. We could easily accommodate ten Mrs Bennets at Pemberley.'

Her husband opened his mouth, but Charlotte was there first: 'Oh, sir, do not mistake us for saints! We are, we freely confess, motivated as much by self-interest as compassion. The extra line of revenue will make our lives here more comfortable – we can employ a curate, and Mr Collins can pay more attention to his sermons and his writing, and matters of the land here at Hunsford. We mean no disrespect to the processes of the law, or to the conduct of our superiors, and intend to be guided by them in due course. But the suddenness of Mr Bennet's death has taken us all off guard. There is no reason matters should not go on as before for a little time, while we all make our adjustments.'

Mr Darcy nodded. 'Very well. I shall write to my wife tonight to convey the particulars of your decision. Might I say once again that whatever the reasons that prompted such an unusual course of conduct, she finds it a source of comfort and ease, and speaks repeatedly of the kindness of your family. We are both indebted to you.'

Happily, Mr Collins was so distracted by the notion of Mr Darcy being indebted to *him*, and so determined to contradict this point, his speeches took him all the way to the door to see off their illustrious visitor, with Charlotte obliged only to return his bows with her most gracious curtsey.

As soon as she could, she repaired to her parlour to read Mrs Darcy's letter in private.

My dear Charlotte,

I write in haste, as Mr Darcy leaves for London in an hour, and has just apprised me of his decision to visit you to seek clarity on the matter of Longbourn. I will be frank. I see your hand in this, my dearest and oldest friend. I mean no disrespect when I say that I doubt that Mr Collins would or could have dreamed up such a scheme. Delay taking possession of Longbourn? It is an act of such kindness, Charlotte, such thought and care of the feelings of others, as can only stem from your good heart. Depend upon it, I know that however united a front you and Mr Collins present, this proposal stems from *your* concern for myself and my family. When I think of the times my mother has been less than gracious to you, I am ashamed, and grow even more grateful towards you. Even if this plan does not come to fruition – Mr Darcy is dubious about it, and I cannot imagine how you got Lady

Catherine to agree to it – know that I appreciate your kind efforts to spare my mother and sisters further grief and misery. And, remembering our conversations at Pemberley, I suspect you of wishing to spare me an added burden of anxiety, too. I have not spoken of this point in particular to my husband, and shall not divulge my suspicions that you are behind this plan to anyone else, not even my sister Jane; but I know she joins me in praising your true compassion and friendship at this time of sorrow. I send my compliments and love to Sarah and Laura. I miss having children at Pemberley.

God bless you,

Yours, etc.,

Eliza Darcy

CHAPTER XXXVI

EARLY AUTUMN WAS THE PERIOD most marked by industry and activity in Kent, and the fields were once again filled with travelling labourers, the women's skirts bright splashes of colour against the pale stubble and golden grass of field and meadow. Carts trundled along the lanes, piled with sweet resinous-smelling hops on their way to the oast houses to be stripped, sifted, and dried.

This was, as always, the busiest time of year for Charlotte. Everything in the garden and orchard seemed to ripen at once, and the tasks of digging potatoes and roots, picking and storing fruits, preserving vegetables in vinegar and currants in syrup, brewing perry from the first green pears, seemed Sisyphean. The tinkers were back in their field on the Rosings estate, and her friends there brought her trugfuls of berries, wild greens, or mushrooms wrapped in leaves almost every other day – much appreciated additions to the table, but also requiring preparation or preservation. Outdoors, Mr Brown and Mr Collins were active in the orchards and nuttery, while she, Mrs Brown, and Katie seemed to be in a permanent state of bustle as they shuttled between garden, kitchen, pantry, and cellar.

The apples were ripening rapidly, and Charlotte had collected a bucket of windfalls for the pigs. Carrying it into the yard, she was suddenly intensely aware of the ordinary stink of animal manure, and had only time to turn to the nearest pile of straw before vomiting neatly onto it.

She stood wiping her mouth, considering the familiar prickling in the skin of her breasts, slowly turning dates over in her head. First motionless as she calculated, she almost staggered as the implications darted about like fish in her mind. The bucket was dropped, the pippins rolled across the stones: she was almost certainly pregnant.

The enormity of it was too much to grasp all at once. She abandoned the bucket, went into the kitchen, and, with unusual peremptoriness, asked the housekeeper to prepare her a tray of tea and some thinly sliced bread and butter, even though she knew this would upset the household's morning routine. At Mrs Brown's look of surprise, she blurted out, 'I feel faint,' and saw the surmise in the other woman's face. 'Say nothing of this to the master,' she said, and headed for the front parlour, where she knew a fire was burning.

Here she sank down in a chair, and clasped herself, encircling her stomach. *A child. Another child.* And for the first time since returning home, Charlotte allowed her thoughts to return to that day at Pemberley, the early morning hour she and Jacob had stolen at the hawk house together.

Deliberately, she relived those moments after she had whirled and run back into his arms following their first kiss, clutching onto him like a sailor to wreckage. They had kissed again, and then again, greedily – and somewhere in that frantic clinging to one another, all restraint was swept away and they both knew what would follow.

He had murmured something in German into her hair, and spread a hand across her hips, tilting them so that she pressed hard against his pelvis. Charlotte's knees turned to water in a flare of terror and hunger, and she crumpled against him. Without slackening his hold on her, he walked her backwards until the bench bumped against her legs. She folded down, and he followed her, bending to lay her out on it. His arms cradled her shoulders, supported her back, and his face, inches from hers, was furrowed as if in pain.

He lifted her legs so that her feet rested on the bench, then nudged at her skirt and petticoat so that their fabric slid up over her knees and down towards her thighs. The air on her bare skin came as a shock, but nothing prepared her for the sensation of his hand sliding down between her legs, pushing them apart – and she cried out as his fingers parted and entered her without hesitation. One part of her brain registered the slickness of her own body, the ease with which it welcomed his entry. For the rest, she was a maelstrom of disbelief and overwhelming physical pleasure, a sense of gorging while growing greedy for more as the slow plunge of his fingers mimicked the movements of congress.

What happened next was beyond the realm of her imagination. He was saying her name softly as his fingers slid deep again and again, his face comfortingly close to hers, when his head withdrew and followed the same path as his exploring hand. What was he doing – surely he could not be *looking* at her? She watched in disbelief as his head sank between her legs, and instinctively clamped her thighs tight against his ears. But still he burrowed down, and then his mouth came to rest where his fingers were working, and Charlotte's body was wracked with such intense pleasure, her body cracked against the bench like a bow releasing an arrow.

His fingers kept the rhythm of his penetration steady, but the sensation of soft wet mouth against soft wet opening had her arching and groaning. She felt the firm press of his tongue slide up and hit a spot so sensitive, it was almost unendurable. The world contracted to that slide and press, slide and press, and then burst as she thrashed in a series of convulsions so violent as to be almost painful. She could hear herself crying aloud, could feel that he was grasping her firmly so that she did not roll off the bench, at the same time as the thrust and lap of his tongue kept triggering new spasms. The only physical experience Charlotte had experienced this overwhelming was the labour of childbirth; and indeed, this was a swifter, sweeter echo of that abdication of the mind to the body and its needs.

Slowly, the shocks of release subsided, and his mouth and fingers quietened, as if he could sense the vast peace now flooding her veins. At last his face was above hers again, and he kissed her, and she almost swooned at the taste of her own salt.

It was now her turn to open up again, welcome him into her body, to clasp him, to murmur endearments, all the mysterious and suddenly easy rituals of romantic love, all the allusions of the poets, come to life in her arms. The feel of him sliding in, belonging, stirred her to ecstasy again and again, no longer a sharp release, but an almost tidal sense of overflowing.

Words rang in her as he moved: *Home. Safe. Comfort.* This was the rest she had always sought without knowing it; the purring cat rolling to offer the soft fur of her belly for caresses, the basin of steaming hot water as laces were undone and stays came off, the scatter of fresh drops as the wind shook the branches after the refreshment of rain, the hearth on an icy winter's night.

She shut her eyes and saw again on the backs of her lids that folded triangle of a hawk on the wind, hovering, hovering, then swooping in one bursting moment of beauty.

Afterwards, they lay cocooned in each other's arms and further encircled by the shielding greenery, spending the short hour before they had to part talking and kissing, both without urgency. They did not waste time with declarations; their bodies had spoken that part. They did, however, repeatedly say each other's names, rolling them in their mouths.

Charlotte tried, not very fluently, to explain how Jacob's touch, his words, his friendship had poured balm on a wound all the more grievous for being both invisible and commonplace; how their lovemaking, against every principle and precept she had ever espoused, felt like a secret consolation, a card the universe had drawn from its sleeve: *see, you have lost a child, but not all is lost.* 'You have taught me that happiness is still possible. That it can take one by surprise; that while ruin, loss, disaster, and grief stalk us all, joy can also spring into our path when least expected.'

He clasped her yet more closely, his breeches still unbuttoned, her skirts crumpled as high as her waist, both of them luxuriating in immodesty. 'If I have given you joy, my treasured Charlotte, the pleasure, the honour, has truly been mine.'

He tried to speak further words of love, but she pressed a finger against his lips. She did not require the reassurances of a young lady being wooed; she did not demand that he explain why a young man of unusual intelligence and exceptional education, one who was talented, handsome and kind, should have fixed on her: married, a mother, plain, older, with no special talents beyond the realm of the domestic, no great charms or vivacity to attract notice. It was enough that for this brief moment in the shifting of the spheres and the spinning of the globe, they had overlapped, had found each other.

She could not explain this, so contented herself with murmuring, 'I am the one who has been given a gift, granted a boon,' as she plaited her fingers in his hair.

'But it could be argued that I have taken advantage of you, led you to stumble most grievously, debauched you. These are grave charges against me. I know this is a hard question, but do you not feel guilty?'

'Of course I do. But I do not feel regret. Not one

jot! I never will. Can we ever regret the draught that stills pain, even if it is forbidden? Besides, you were right about the hawks. We are all necessarily tamed. But sometimes there are moments – such moments as we have shared – oh, I cannot put it into words. I have not your facility with them,' and she felt his mouth move into a smile against her cheek. 'All I can tell you, Jacob, is that I will never again see a hawk – any hunting bird on the wind – without thinking of you, of this. Without feeling you close to my heart.'

Now, seated before her own hearth, surrounded by the familiar tokens of her everyday life, Charlotte forced herself to think through the implications of that glorious and forbidden encounter. What was not certain, what would never be certain, was the paternity of the child she was carrying. It was possibly Jacob's progeny. What if it looked like him? What if it did not? What if it was as blameless a mix of her and Mr Collins's blood as if ordained by God? What could she do? How could she protect herself and the child?

The answer came to her almost directly: nothing. She could do nothing. She was helpless in the grip of fate and nature. All she could do was to take care of her family, including this potential new child. She stretched her hands to the fire and tried to tiptoe up to the idea: another baby. She waited, and slowly, from her fingertips and toes, the sensation spread: a creeping, wild joy. Another whole human being, but also a keepsake. He or she could not replace all or even anything that Charlotte had lost, but she would gain more to love, to cherish, to nurture.

She would not share her news with Mr Collins until a little more time passed; she needed to prepare herself to face without flinching the innocent pleasure, the joyous smiles with which he would certainly respond, the congratulations he would claim from family and friends. And yet the coming child might well be his. His conviction of this would be a punishment she would willingly bear. But never was a punishment also so productive of ecstasy. And as Mrs Brown came in bearing a tray, she found Charlotte laughing and hugging herself.

1820

CHAPTER XXXVII

TOWARDS THE END OF THE winter that followed, a servant arrived with what Charlotte had come to think of as one of Anne de Bourgh's coded messages: a suggestion that they meet that afternoon in the conservatory, where the first hyacinths from Holland were blooming. She wrote that she believed Mrs Collins would enjoy taking in their fragrance, and that she might also admire the recently acquired granadilla vine and bougainvillea tree, both exotics from the West Indies. If all was agreeable, she would be happy to send the carriage, given the unsettled weather and Charlotte's condition.

There were a few anxious moments when Mr Collins, as the established horticultural enthusiast of the family, proposed escorting his wife on this occasion, and even bringing the girls along, but fortunately, he remembered Charlotte's role as Miss de Bourgh's confidante, and restrained himself, although expressing hope that in future such invitations might extend to him as well.

Charlotte made vaguely promising noises, and reminded her husband that he had an engagement with his sexton that afternoon, and a funeral to conduct the next day. Duty would have to preclude pleasure in his case. The carriage duly arrived, and it was a matter of minutes to transfer her to Rosings, where Anne waited in the scented hothouse, the air warm and damp as a kiss on Charlotte's skin.

As was her wont, Miss de Bourgh spoke without preamble: 'Mrs Collins, I am once again about to treat you with great injustice. I have two propositions to make to you. You will soon give birth to another child. And you and I both know that the sex of that child determines a significant portion of your future; whether or not you shall be able to take possession of Longbourn in security of succession; what lies ahead for your daughters – whether they will be able to marry according to inclination or affection, or whether they may be driven, by want, to expediency.

'So this is my first proposal: that I settle money on each of your daughters. Not sums so large as to tempt fortune-hunters or make them eligible prospects for that reason alone; but enough that should they wish, they may live respectable lives as spinsters, if need be; in the event of your and Mr Collins's demise, to be able to afford modest but adequately comfortable establishments, with respectable companions, or even one other.'

Charlotte heard a ringing in her ears, and swayed, tears starting in her eyes. She stepped forward to take Anne's hands, spilling with gratitude, but the younger woman stepped back, holding up her palms. 'Wait, Mrs Collins. I said I had two propositions to make. You will like the second much less, I fear. But first, I wish to stress that these are two separate, not intertwined ventures. They are not conditional upon one another. Even if you respond to my second proposal with a determined negative, I will still honour my first promise, to secure a future free of anxiety and want for your daughters. In fact, if your third child is another girl, she will receive a settlement equal to that of her elder sisters.

'But if you have a boy, Mrs Collins – I wish to foster him, and raise him to become the heir of Rosings.'

The ringing continued in Charlotte's ears, but now it took on the quality of a knife being sharpened. Her first thought was *Lose another child? I cannot*. And then she was seated on the edge of a raised planting bed, her head touched to her knees, the foliage on either side of her swaying queasily up and down, and Anne was saying, with great agitation, 'Mrs Collins, I beg you, do not alarm yourself—'

Slowly, the sensation that her surrounds were swirling around her stilled, and she sat up cautiously and cracked open one eye to gaze at Anne, who had gone so pale she was almost blue. 'Dear God, I feared I had brought on a misadventure, that you might even lose the child. Let me call for assistance. You need something sweet to drink.'

Charlotte demurred, sweeping her tongue around her dry mouth. Anne, with no ceremony, rustled down next to her, careless of mud on her skirts. 'Forgive me – I was far too precipitate. Allow me to explain. This is no tale in which the newborn infant will be borne off by a wicked fairy. You would keep him, in your home, no doubt the pet of his elder sisters, for as long as you choose. I ask simply that once he grows sensible, and of an age to require education, that he spends time at Rosings, too; and that I take over the provision of his education. That he be raised with the expectation of inheritance, with all the advantages and responsibilities incumbent on such an expectation. That when he turns twelve or thirteen, I formally and legally adopt him, and guarantee the future of Rosings.'

She stood again and knuckled her hands in the small of her back. 'I have no nephews or nieces, or even godchildren requiring any special attention, for whom I feel any familial affection. If Mr and Mrs Darcy should have children, my little cousins will hardly be in need of anything I can offer. I do not pay children particular notice, but there is no doubt that your girls have admirable spirit, and I like the idea of your son treading these hectares as lord and master of all he surveys, bringing his sisters under this roof. I confess I take pleasure from the thought of my mother's amazement at such a pass – that the son of the clergyman to whom she had condescended to give a living should one day inherit Rosings.'

Charlotte's mind pecked from among her scattered thoughts the seed that there was no guarantee that the child soon to be born could indeed call her husband father; and the mental picture of the son of a pianotuner – one who was a foreigner and a Jew – ruling over Rosings caused a tide of hysteria to rise in her throat. She remembered very well Lady Catherine's railing when Mr Darcy first wrote to announce his engagement to Elizabeth Bennet: 'Are the shades of Pemberley thus to be polluted?' Oh, if she but knew what greater potential contamination was stalking ever closer to home!

She shut her eyes again, and Jacob's face was at once before her, intelligence and compassion in every lineament, every gesture conveying his confident manners, every word his superior education and understanding. She was not certain Rosings was even worthy of the gift of his son.

Anne once again spoke with uncanny prescience: 'We require fresh blood, Mrs Collins. Look at me, a grown woman in a girl's body, neither fish nor fowl, the only living child of my parents after three stillborn sons. No wonder my mother kept me at home, as if in a hothouse like this one in which we stand. And look at *her*, so determined to control destiny in spite of being a woman, so hardened in her insistence on caste and rank that she is unable to acknowledge what she sees, what she *must* see: that I am the end of the de Bourgh line. Unlike my mother, I am pragmatic. I know enough of horse breeding to know that it is time for new stock, a good hardy graft that will enable our family tree to continue branching.'

Charlotte pecked at another seed, and caught up a word: 'Longbourn?'

'I understand you,' said Anne. 'If you bring forth a son, your family's need to look around for protection falls away, as he will eventually inherit Longbourn, a goodly estate. He will not be rich after his father dies, but he will be comfortable and, if he is clever, also respectable. By that token, his sisters should enjoy the same benefits.

'My intention is not to lay temptation before you. I know you are prudent, but you are not a grasping woman. My wish is that yours would be a rational, impartial decision; only secondarily, if you like, a gift to me. Your son would be happy and respectable as master of Longbourn; or he could be all those things, but also possessed of the wealth and power that would come with the Rosings inheritance. He would have the security of not one, but two estates to call his own. One would hope that he would freely house and support his elder sisters – he would certainly have the means to do so. But he would not *need* such wealth. Longbourn alone should provide for him, and them.'

Charlotte stumbled out her next sentence: 'But why then settle money on the girls?'

'Would you have them reliant on fraternal affection or obligation alone? Vulnerable to the whims of a future sister-in-law? Edged aside by the cares and needs of an expanding family?'

Charlotte was silent, remembering her brothers' yells of delight when the news of Mr Collins's proposal was broken to their family, the open joy with which they celebrated her no longer being their charge and burden should she remain an old maid. 'I understand, Miss de Bourgh. You want for my daughters what I have only dreamed of for them: the dignity of independence. Believe me, for that alone, I shall be eternally indebted to you.'

Anne nodded: 'I wish to reiterate that the two proposals are to be considered separately. The one regarding your daughters is an offer, not a bribe; it comes free of obligation, in as much as that is possible – all gifts come with invisible expectations. But I must stress that my proposal should you give birth to a son is a request, Mrs Collins, and you are free to reject it out of hand, much as I hope you will not. It is by no means intended as a sort of command, or even a strong plea, but a proposition, one I leave humbly to your consideration. I ask only that you take some time to consider it, that you do not immediately respond with a negative. Once you have fixed on a decision, you may wish never to speak of it again to a soul; or, if you believe my plan has merit, you will of course wish to consult with your husband. But I repeat, it is yours to make.'

Anne's face cracked into one of her rare grins: 'Do you know to whom I am indebted for all these bold proposals, Mrs Collins? It is Colonel Fitzwilliam himself. Oh, not that I have mentioned any word of this to him, never fear. But it was he who first unwittingly instigated the idea, when he proposed fostering a son, should we marry. And it then occurred to me that I need not marry in order to foster or even adopt a son. I could have my cake and eat it, as the saying goes.

'But I think I have caused enough alarm and shock for the day. Speaking of cake, let us go and drink tea in the house, and ensure that you eat something fortifying. My mother will be glad to see you, and will find some matter of importance to instruct you on, I am sure. And then we shall call the carriage so that you may go home in comfort. I have an interest beyond the usual in the safe delivery of this child.'

Back at home, where all was routine and predictable, Charlotte reclined on a chaise-longue and tried to disentangle all she had heard and felt. The room still rocked a little whenever she tried to imagine her child – Mr Collins's son? Jacob's son? – as the future master of Rosings. But hard as it was to resist wild surmise, she could not anticipate too much: the child right now thudding its feet inside the drum of her belly might well be a girl. She focused on the real miracle the morning had vouchsafed: her girls – including this coming child – would be provided for, and while she did not dare to quite believe Anne's munificent promises just yet, she had no doubt of their sincerity. This brought on such fervent gratitude and relief as to occasion both tears and prayers of thanks: only her bulk prevented her sinking to her knees.

She was glad to be distracted from all that overwhelmed her by the arrival of another letter from Lizzy, and opened it anticipating news of glamorous far-off events – evenings at the theatre in town, balls at court, mingled with accounts of less exciting but more interesting events among their mutual acquaintance – but the contents were of a different order entirely.

Mrs Darcy wrote to announce that she was also expecting a child and, like Charlotte, would soon approach a confinement. She and Mr Darcy had not bruited the news abroad for fear of another disappointment, but the doctors were optimistic, the child was kicking lustily, and there was every reason to hope for the best possible outcome.

Lizzy wrote: 'Just think, my dear Charlotte, our

children may one day be friends, so close in age as they will be. I certainly hope so. I regret not telling you of this before, especially after receiving *your* happy news, but I know you will understand the reasons for my reticence, and share in our joy and anxious hopes. I shall pray for you as you approach your delivery, and beg you to do the same for me.'

CHAPTER XXXVIII

SOMEWHERE DEEP IN LABOUR, HER body as burdened as a pack animal's, Charlotte faced that moment of believing she could not go on; that something was wrong, that she was facing imminent death, that the child struggling to exit her body would kill her, or she it; above all, that she was too tired to continue. She wanted it all to stop, the possession of her vast and heaving body, the pains that both convulsed and pinned her down with weighted claws, the rusty smell of blood and vinegar. She wanted to escape, to flee, to be a narrow-waisted girl again, walking in the fresh air, not to be trapped on this bed, the linen sodden with sweat and other fluids.

But, she remembered, she had felt this pitch of terror and exhaustion during every other one of her labours, even though (according to Mrs Talbot) the births of her girls had been easy. And then the moment passed as another contraction clamped down and around and through and in and on her, and she became once again a groaning beast on an arduous journey that had to be completed.

It was hours later, with a weak dawn filtering through the curtains, that she gave a final heave. Mrs Talbot, red-faced with exertion, tugged – there was a slither, a gush, and the first angry snuffles and squeaks could be heard as the midwife said, 'It's a lass. A bonny girl.'

Charlotte, exhausted, was amazed at the clarity and strength of the emotions that ran through her. Joy, but also relief. There was no decision to make: this child was hers. And if Anne de Bourgh stood by her promise, this little girl was safe. No one person could guarantee any child happiness, although she, Charlotte, would move mountains to make it so; but dignity and security lay in her new daughter's future.

Mrs Talbot put a practised hand on Charlotte's distended abdomen, then bent to peer between her thighs. 'Mrs Collins, we must go back to work. I do believe there is another infant coming.'

All was rush and flurry; the housekeeper was called to hold the first blotchy red and white bundle still squalling with indignation at being forced to breathe spring air, and it was not long before the second infant breached the barrier from inner to outer life. 'A boy,' said Mrs Talbot, and Charlotte gasped with more than joy.

The afterbirth was delivered, the fire stoked, the two women helping her shadowy figures against its mobile light as they worked to clean and comfort her newborn babies, sounds of water in ewer and basin – and here they were at last, swaddled, in her arms, on her breast.

The little girl, the elder, was given to her first; as tightly furled as a bud, with a sprinkling of nutmeg freckles across her button nose. 'Pandora,' said Charlotte, touching the nose with a finger, 'you shall be called

Pandora,' and her daughter opened eyes a lighter shade of blue than was usual in a newborn. 'Her eyes will probably stay that colour,' said Mrs Talbot as she handed her charge the second infant.

Both babies looked like wrapped parcels at this stage, but like any fond new parent, Charlotte traced their minute features with fascination, seeing beauty and hunting for resemblances in features as yet clay. Her son was quieter than his squeaking sister, a starfish hand reaching for his mother's breast. His eyes were the deep blue of kittens, his squashed features topped by a quiff of dark hair. Charlotte peered; it was hard to tell, and perhaps it was wishful thinking, but his nose seemed to beak slightly from his face. None of the names she and Mr Collins had chosen for a boy quite fitted this exquisite creature; perhaps Anne de Bourgh might like to suggest one. Or she would reread the Old Testament, and choose the name of one of its heroes or prophets.

For now, it was enough that both infants were safely arrived; they were here, whole and healthy, a largesse she could never have anticipated. It might not have any basis in science, but a deep conviction took hold of her: that both her husband and her lover had become fathers that day. She would love, protect and cherish their offspring; it would be a way of honouring one man – loving him at a distance – and making reparations to the other. The last remnants of guilt and anxiety fell away from her; lulled by exhaustion and deep satisfaction, she cradled both babies more closely, turned her head on the pillow, and fell asleep.

1839

EPILOGUE

IN THE GRAVEYARD, CHARLOTTE SANK down on a raised bank, after first spreading her shawl to protect against chill and damp. Plagued as she was by rheumatism, today she was grateful that Sarah was undertaking the loving labour of tending that small piece of earth where Tom's bones rested.

While nibbling sheep and the sexton together kept the turf around the grave neat, it was time for prepare for the following spring. Charlotte watched as her daughter took a digger and knife out of the pocket of her apron, and worked her way around the small rectangle, nipping back any unruly grass blades and pulling out weeds. Then she dug a dozen holes in the earth, and reached into a basket for the papery bulbs that would in time explode into colour and scent. Each was tucked in, their tips just cresting the soil.

Next, Sarah made a trip to the trough in the corner of the field alongside, using a beaker to scoop water. Lithe as she was, it was still clearly a tricky business negotiating the stile while carrying the container, and it took her several journeys and some spilling, but at last each bulb swam in a little pool of mud with creamy scum on top.

Charlotte smiled in approbation, and closed her eyes to say a prayer not only for her son, but all the other children buried in this tranquil spot, within sight of the spire of the church where her late husband had once presided in the pulpit and before the altar.

When she opened her eyes again, it was to see Sarah sinking down, setting her feet wide apart, and spreading her skirt and shift around her before she urinated into the soft soil. Charlotte called out in reprimand, but her daughter was unperturbed: 'You know our own water is good for plants, Mama. I am merely nourishing these bulbs.' She gave her hips a brisk shake as she rose to her feet. 'Ha! Another reason I am glad I have not succumbed to this modern fad of drawers.'

Although Sarah also had her knife and a polishing cloth in her apron pocket, and offered to clean the headstone, Charlotte, rising stiffly to her feet, decided to leave the Tom's stone, decorated by orange and sea-green rosettes of lichen, untouched. The two women each took it in turn to run their finger over the unoriginal but no less sincere words carved into the stone:

In memory of Thomas William Collins: 5th February 1815–7th November 1818. Gone to the angels. Beloved son of Revd & Mrs William Collins.

'I sometimes feel badly that I remember so little of my brother,' said Sarah. 'But *you* loved him so much, Mama, and that love was as much part of our childhood as food on the table and books on the shelves.

It was like being haunted by a ghost, but such a beloved one; indeed, a friend.'

'Yes,' Charlotte agreed, leaning on her daughter's strong arm as they turned to begin the short walk home. 'I promised myself, and him, he would never be forgotten. He would – will – always be my son. Some forms of love never die. That is their burden and their blessing.'

They strolled at a gentle pace, and in every direction, the view was as pleasing as it was familiar. They stopped twice – once to admire the profile of the house and the towering chestnut trees on either side, the second time to watch a distant hawk circling over barley stubble, bracing against thermals invisible to them except in the taut span of its wings.

Approaching via the west entrance, they saw two sparring figures and heard faint cries: Laura and her husband were fencing on the greensward. It was typical of Laura to insist on fencing lessons, and then to fall in love with her master. When the dazed and dazzled man had dared to reflect the glory of her affection back to her, she had married him forthwith. They seemed never to stop laughing, and for that Charlotte was more than grateful, remembering the mirth that marked her continuing friendship with Mrs Darcy. Mutual amusement was an excellent basis for lasting intimacy.

The twins were watching from the stone terrace, or at least one of them was; Pandora, as always, had a book in her hand, and was in that tranquil trance into which she invariably fell when reading. Jonathan, down from his college at Oxford, was cheering on the duelling couple, offering encouragement without partisanship to both parties.

Charlotte waved at the cheerful group, smiling yet again at how apt the fanciful names she had insisted on for her youngest children had proved to be. Lady Catherine had scolded in vain, especially at Charlotte's obdurate insistence on Jonathan's name when a plain old-fashioned English 'John' would have sufficed. Today, her son was as beloved and admired by all who knew him as his Old Testament counterpart, while Pandora had signified hope from the very first day she had lain in her mother's arms.

Sarah escorted her to the corner of the terrace that acted as a sun-trap, and which still held the warmth of the day. Here there hung in the air the faint but familiar tang of tobacco, and a figure awaited them, attired in a pair of men's breeches, along with a man's shirt and hunting jacket: Anne de Bourgh.

'Ah, here you are! I was beginning to wonder if I would have to ride out alone,' she said, one thin arm extended beyond the embrasure, a cheroot curling smoke lodged between two fingers. She was as skinny and knotted as ever, but with a face now tanned and lined from winters spent travelling abroad.

Although she had ascended to the title Lady Anne when Lady Catherine died (of an apoplexy, nearly ten years ago), all the Collins offspring referred to her ladyship as their aunt, choosing sentiment over accuracy. It gave Charlotte great joy and some amusement to witness how Anne, who had never wanted children of her own, was considered a third parent, and treated as such, by her brood.

Jonathan, upon achieving double figures in age, had moved to Rosings to enjoy a more formal programme of education than his parents, by then settled at Longbourn, could offer. The problem was that he and Pandora were inseparable; and the deep unhappiness both children evinced at the idea of being parted was so palpable that Lady Anne had offered the same facilities and opportunities to both. As Jonathan was her purported heir, he began to refer to his benefactress as his aunt; a term of address his twin sister promptly adopted, the elder girls soon following.

Meanwhile, Charlotte, no matter how engrossed in the domestic opportunities that running Longbourn afforded, and while taking great pleasure in rejoining the society of her youth, found that she could never be parted from any of her children for long. The result was that she, as well as her two elder daughters, regularly visited Rosings for such long periods as to render it effectively their second home, and Lady Anne the honorary guardian of all four siblings. The continuing presence of four lively young people and their friends transformed the atmosphere of Rosings. While becoming a little less grand, it also became truly comfortable, possibly for the first time in its history.

Sarah had soon become enamoured of Lady Anne's pastime of riding; the pair of them would gallop for miles up the gently sloping hills, crossing acres dear to them both, speed and wind tearing at their hair. Moreover, she emulated her honorary aunt's habit of wearing men's clothing on these and other occasions.

This decision cost Charlotte some consternation, but she held her peace. There was no doubt that the outfits Anne and Sarah wore for riding were practical indeed; they greatly facilitated their comfort and their ability to control their mounts, and thus the pleasure they took in the exercise. The scandal caused when they had first started going about on horseback in men's clothing had galvanised the neighbourhood for months, but as it slowly became clear that the pair of them were impervious to public opinion, and therefore could not be punished for their eccentricity, the grumbling had died down to a resigned mutter.

Charlotte gave thanks yet again for the latitude offered by independent means: that her daughters were sufficiently secure in terms of home and income not to have to live in fear of the strictures of society and its wagging tongues – that their reputations as unconventional, bookish, and daring could do them so little harm.

Now, having found and placed a cushion behind Charlotte's back, Sarah left them to change into her masculine costume, which was the work of a minute. As she never left anyone in doubt, she deplored the fashionable stays and corsetry into which so many of her peers laced themselves, which (apart from interfering with the ability to breathe deeply) rendered them dependent on maids to dress and undress. She soon padded back in stockinged feet and sat with her mother and aunt for a minute as she tugged on her boots.

'Where shall you ride this afternoon?' Charlotte asked.

'If my aunt is agreeable, I thought we might try jumping the log fences out of the woods. And then make our way back home via the old pilgrims' way along the spine of the Weald.'

'I hope you fly,' Charlotte smiled; an old family joke, stemming from her habit of stopping to shade her eyes and gaze upwards whenever she saw a bird hovering.

'We shall, Mama. We shall indeed,' her daughter promised.

Her companions departed in the direction of the stables, and Pandora, alert to the needs of others even when deep in dream or book, rose to see if she could be of any service to her mother.

'Simply bring your book here, my love. That is, if your sparring sister can spare you as a spectator. I shall sit and warm myself in the last of the sun while you read.'

As Pandora settled beside her, imparting an affectionate squeeze to her hand, Charlotte watched the willowy form of her second daughter darting and parrying, advancing towards her husband, then dancing out of his reach before returning. It was no bad analogy for courtship; and as starlings massed in the trees beyond and the light thickened to honey, she thought back to her own courtship – the day she became an affianced woman – and the cautious composure she had felt on that occasion. How little she had dared hope for! And how little she had understood of love. She had felt none for the man who would become her husband; and yet how much had unrolled at her feet, how many objects of affection, planned and unplanned, had been granted her.

Although seldom contemplated, her second, secret courtship could not be forgotten either, and indeed, it had remained a source of private joy as letters had crossed, not often, but regularly, between Kent and Austria. In writing to her husband, Herr Rosenstein always included her and never failed to encompass her in his warm wishes. This was not an unalloyed bliss – the missive containing news of his betrothal had cost her some pangs until she could scold herself into reason. Yet she still treasured the kindness of his letter of condolence after Mr Collins had failed to wake from a nap in the orchard grass one late-summer afternoon. By then, no thought of reunion crossed her mind; her path was both fixed and infinitely dear to her. Thinking back, she felt no regret either. His friendship, and their secret history, had vouchsafed rich and unexpected gifts, including a path into a future that would outlast her.

She would always grieve Tom, but that grief had become as ornamented and enwreathed as the headstone on his grave, an object of both veneration and beauty, softened by the lichens that clung to it, the gentle abrasion of rain and frost. Her first son was beyond help, beyond anything she could offer, beyond the reach of her love, which could now be demonstrated only by tending that piece of earth in which his mortal remains lay. But keeping faith with the dead was the last honour she was able to pay his short life, and the blessing it had been to her.

That night, after dinner, Jonathan would play the violin for them, with Pandora accompanying him on the piano, their instinctive twin awareness of one another leading them to make the same errors at the same moment, so that few in their audience were any the wiser. She would watch her son's ivory fingers – he possessed the most beautiful hands she had ever seen on a man – as they steered his bow and danced on the neck of his instrument. Pandora might play the sonata with variations Charlotte requested on special occasions, and never heard without happy tears springing to her eyes. Lady Anne would preside, wearing the harem trousers and embroidered silk coat she had brought back from one of her journeys to Persia. And they would close the evening by all turning to her, Charlotte: raising their glasses in a toast to both her, and their late father, of whom they always spoke with affection. And then, as had become their habit, they would drink to the home that welcomed them all: Rosings.

A NOTE ON THE TEXT

I have been fascinated by the character of Charlotte Lucas, and the choices she made, ever since first reading *Pride and Prejudice*. In my telling of her story, I have tried to remain faithful to the plot of the original, with a few significant differences: lovers of *Pride and Prejudice* will know that Charlotte Lucas did not accompany the Bennet family on their visit to Netherfield Park – the occasion on which Mrs Bennet so cruelly and publicly slights the 'plain' Lucas girls, Charlotte in particular. One of the questions that prompted the writing of my novel was: 'What if Charlotte had overheard that conversation?'

The character of Charlotte in the original must surely have been aware of Mrs Bennet's opinion, and indeed her own mother's, of her looks: how did this affect her, in a world where the only collateral a single woman without a large dowry had was her beauty? I could not resist this small deviation from the plot because it seemed to me that these issues were vital in driving Charlotte's subsequent decisions and actions, and I wanted to explore these more closely.

Those familiar with Jane Austen's writings will notice that along with the characters, events, and locations of her best-loved work, I have threaded phrases and words not only from *Pride and Prejudice*, but her other works and letters throughout my own novel. I hope that readers enjoy spotting these and identifying their sources. Even more audaciously, I have woven my own words through some of Austen's passages so as not to lift the latter wholesale. I hope that the result is entertaining rather than heretical, and that purists forgive me for embellishing such an august and beloved source.

I have taken liberties not only with the text; although Pemberley is a fictional place, Jane Austen most likely based it on Chatsworth in Derbyshire, and I have done the same, while importing into its grounds the hawk house from Chirk Castle in Wales, and installing a maze some 140 years before it was actually planted. When it came to Rosings, I abandoned historical veracity and based it very loosely on the mansion at Stourhead. These are among the perks of being a writer of fiction.

READING GROUP QUESTIONS

1. What do you think of the novel as a retelling of *Pride and Prejudice*? Is Charlotte Lucas how you imagine her from Austen's original?
2. Who was your favourite character? Whose re-interpretation from the original Austen did you most enjoy?
3. Has *Charlotte* changed your opinion of Mr Collins? Do you think Charlotte made the right decision in marrying him?
4. Throughout the novel, Charlotte is grieving for the loss of her son. In what ways does *Charlotte* explore grief and parenthood?
5. In what ways are Charlotte, Elizabeth, and Anne de Bourgh confined by the position of women in the early nineteenth century?
6. What brings Anne de Bourgh and Charlotte together? Why do they become friends?
7. Do you think Charlotte loves Mr Collins, as well as Jacob? How does the book explore different kinds of love?
8. Why do you think Charlotte is attracted to Jacob?
9. In what ways is *Charlotte* a feminist novel? In what ways was *Pride and Prejudice* one?
10. What do you think Jane Austen would have made of *Charlotte*?

FURTHER READING

There are hundreds, if not thousands, of Austen sequels, fan-fic renditions, plays, re-interpretations, films and television series to explore. Then there are the more academic works – entire libraries' worth. It would be impossible to give a comprehensive reading list, or to provide more than a glimpse of all the resources I relied on.

However, I found the following works particularly helpful, and would recommend them to anyone interested in finding out more about Jane Austen's world, and indeed the one in which Charlotte lived.

Several solid biographies of Austen are available, but Claire Tomalin's *Jane Austen: A Life* (1997) remains a gold standard for many. I also highly recommend Carol Shields's treatment, *Jane Austen* (2001), as a short but nuanced introductory biography. And although it is strictly speaking a novel, Fay Weldon's *Letters to Alice: On First Reading Jane Austen* (1984) makes for a delightful read, both for its subject and the treatment. Inspired by Austen's own letters to her niece, this book makes the case for reading Austen in contemporary times.

I believe the most impressive *Pride and Prejudice* sequel or 'view from below' so far is Jo Baker's *Longbourn* (2013), and I am indebted to this work for the way it helped me to think about my own novel. As a South African and a product of colonial history,

I am concerned with who gets to speak and who does not, even in fiction, and as a feminist, I am most interested in those truths 'told slant', to use the poet Emily Dickinson's words. I found that *Longbourn* challenged and stimulated me to think about the world of *Pride and Prejudice* in new and subversive ways.

Although I once lived in Britain, and have made pilgrimages to every possible Austen site, it was necessary to immerse myself in works on the English countryside, garden design, and history to gain a sense of the world in which Charlotte might have walked. I read numerous books on gardens and gardening, but found Katherine Swift's *The Morville Hours: The Story of a Garden* (2008) and *The Morville Year* (2012) invaluable for giving me a sense of the way the seasons unfold in an English rural setting. Likewise, Adam Nicolson's *Sissinghurst: An Unfinished Story* (2008) helped me to imagine rural Kent as Charlotte might have experienced it.

ACKNOWLEDGEMENTS

Never has writing a book been a less lonely experience. In writing the story of Charlotte Lucas, I've had the support of the proverbial cast of thousands. Writing these acknowledgements has been an opportunity to remember, with fondness and great gratitude, all those who helped me get here.

Having been a Jane Austen fan for over three decades, I am indebted to those lecturers who taught me her novels, and all the students and other groups to whom I've in turn taught Austen. I've given public lectures on Austen at home and abroad, so thanks to all those who attended and asked amusing and pertinent questions, especially the lively gang at the University of Alaska, Fairbanks. Jeanne Heywood, who taught *Pride and Prejudice* at the University of Cape Town, was the first to draw my attention to Charlotte Lucas's resourcefulness and courage, thus planting this seed. To those who helped me write my Honours thesis on 'Feminism in the Novels of Jane Austen' many moons ago: a few lines from it live on in these pages.

While I knew for years that I wanted to explore what happened to Charlotte after she entered a marriage that looked more like penance than romance, this novel was born on a soft night in Ireland at the prompting of my fellow authors and co-erotica writers, Sarah Lotz and Paige Nick. I was grieving at the time, and Sarah encouraged me to express myself in the form of a novel. I immediately knew I wanted to tell Charlotte Lucas's story, and as a knowledgeable Austen reader, Sarah jumped at the idea. We spent hours plotting, and the next day, Paige cloistered me in my room and made me write up all the notes (complete with red wine splashes) made the night before. Both subsequently badgered me for chapters, thrashed through plot wildernesses, accompanied me on research trips, loaned me their homes in which to write, and more. Sarah made me cups of tea and offered tissues as I wrote the most painful scenes. My first readers, they were always brutally (often hilariously) honest, and mercilessly insistent that I finish the book.

My day job involves editing the fiction of others, and the authors I've worked with over decades have all taught me not only how to write, but how to live with imaginary people in one's head. I wish there was space to list all of them. I am particularly indebted to Ben Williams and the rest of the BookSA/BooksLive tribe for ongoing encouragement and witty online company. I learned a great deal about writing historical fiction and the courage it takes to approach a great classic from working on Tom Eaton's exquisite 'Night's Candles', a retelling of Shakespeare's *Romeo and Juliet*. I owe Lauren Beukes for her understanding of those 'my gold shoes pinch' days. Thanks to Karina Szczurek Brink and Joanne Hichens (fellow members of the Two and a Half Widows' Club) for insights on writing as survival. Rachel Zadok, Nick Mulgrew, and Colleen Higgs provided vital cheerleading, as did Diane Awerbuck. Elinor Sisulu, with whom I bonded over

Austen (also a penchant for Colin Firth), began urging me to write this book fifteen years ago, and has been a stalwart source of encouragement and support.

Beta readers included the writers Fiona Snyckers (also my birth scene coach) and Petina Gappah, whose excitement was fuel to my writing fire, and psychologist Sally Swartz, who insisted that I stop hiding in the margins of other authors' books. I am very, very thankful.

I was greatly inspired by Jo Baker's *Longbourn*, and have hidden several Easter eggs from it within the pages of *Charlotte*. I am grateful to Jo for her permission to do so.

Space in which to write is priceless to authors. In this respect, I'm indebted not just to Paige and Sarah for providing that spell (pun intended) in Ireland, but to Eric Larsson, Jean Talbot, Katharine Larsson Laria and their families, who gave me free run of their beautiful ancestral home, Gay House, in a tiny village on Penobscot Bay in Maine, for six weeks. The productive peace of that time was invaluable, as was the warmth of that community. I went from the gloves and scarves of a New England fall to the bone-soaking heat of summer in the Little Karoo back home, where Billy Kennedy of Temenos Retreat Centre kindly offered me a refuge in which to finish an early draft.

Travelling in a hard-currency country is daunting for South Africans. Without the hospitality of Mara Singer in Oxford, Sue Mottram in Dorset, Sarah (again) in Shropshire, and Louisa Treger in London, it would have been nearly impossible to do location research. Louisa, whose journey as a historical novelist has preceded mine, has also provided essential practical advice, as has Bonnier stablemate Amy Heydenrych.

I'm grateful to the staff and volunteers at Chatsworth and numerous National Trust properties for answering my questions with such chatty expertise – especially the gentleman at Eyam Hall who was responsible for Charlotte's bacon safe.

Anne de Bourgh's travels around the French Riviera are largely thanks to Clifford Hall, who guided me round a variety of locations, including the Île de Saint-Honorat, on which I have roughly based the Île Sainte-Madeleine of my story (although with several outrageous liberties, such as replacing monks with nuns).

Paul Tizzard allowed me to spend several hours watching him tune and repair my century-old piano, and answered my many questions about Jacob's profession.

Regarding the above, any errors concerning geography, history, location, musical matters, and the intricacies of piano care are mine.

I finished this novel while recovering from major, life-saving surgery. Thanks to all who cared for me during that time, and also Dr Carol Thomas for giving me my life back. I can't believe you yourself are now gone.

South Africa was in the grip of a postal strike when contracts needed to move across oceans, and Nicky Smuts-Allsop came to the rescue, acting as my personal Pony Express. She also took me on various Austen walks and drives in the UK, and tolerantly posed in historical dress at the Bath Costume Museum – the most glamorous research assistant ever.

Now to praise the wonderful people who transformed *Charlotte* into a book. First, my very clever agent Oli Munson at A.M. Heath, who made the placing the manuscript look easy (also Florence Rees, who first championed my MS); and the enchanting Eleanor Dryden, who coached me from London via Skype (waving a mug with HANGOVER stencilled on it), and made the initial offer for the manuscript. Then came the rest of the Bonnier team, an entire platoon of fairy godparents. MD Kate Parkin believed in the book from the outset, Margaret Stead, my wise publisher, has been appropriately steadfast and steadying, Clare Kelly keeps a stream of fantastic publicity coming, and Katie Lumsden is unfailingly helpful with matters both great and small, as well as being another Austen Sister. Alexandra Alldren read the manuscript closely, and then produced this most beautiful and apposite cover, as well as the exquisite endpapers. Stephen Dumughn is the maestro of marketing – also responsible for the beauty of the advance proof copies. Arjumand Siddiqui, Elise Burns, Stuart Finglass, Vincent Kelleher, Ruth Logan, and Stella Giatrakou make up the rest of Team Charlotte, and I look forward to our adventures together. Copyeditor Rhian McKay took great care over these pages, and I remain impressed that she picked up my misspelling of 'violoncello'. Neilwe Mashigo of Jonathan Ball, who handles distribution in South Africa, is always swift with action and reassurance.

They say an index of emotional maturity is the ability to be happy for the successes of others. In which case, my friends must be the most balanced people in the world. The best thing so far about publishing *Charlotte* has been sharing news of her progress and witnessing their joy. This is especially true of my parents, Rodney and Dinah Moffett, and my sister and niece, Kathy and Lauren Wootton.

Finally, I want to circle back to Paige and Sarah, aka Mrs P and Mrs S, aka the Porn Elves. Without you, *Charlotte* would not exist, and I might not either. This is as much your book as mine.